A
SUGARLAND CREEK
NOVEL

BROOKE
MONTGOMERY

Sugarland Creek series
Reading Order

Come With Me (Prequel)
Here With Me (#1)
Stay With Me (#2)
Fall With Me (#3)
Only With Me (#4)
Sin With Me (#5)

Each book can be read as a stand-alone and ends in a happily ever after. However, for the best reading experience, read in order.

'Cause I'm selfish
    Restless like a river, can't help it
    I'm taking what you give me but
    I still want more
    'Cause I'm selfish
    Yeah I'm selfish, I'm selfish for you

Have you seen yourself in a full-length mirror
    Spinning around lately
    I'd lie, cheat, and steal
    Feel the sweet scent overtake me
    But the Lord sent an angel to save me
    So he can't blame me
    When my hands get a mind of their own
    Girl, if they get ahold of you, I ain't never letting go

-Selfish, **Jordan Davis**

Playlist

Listen to the full *Fall With Me* playlist on Spotify

Belong Together | Mark Ambor
Holy Smokes | Bailey Zimmerman
What If | Ryan Kinder
Heartbreaker - Acoustic | Warren Zeiders
Rain | Sleep Token
Happiest Year | Jaymes Young
Selfish | Jordan Davis
imgonnagetyouback | Taylor Swift
Risk | Gracie Abrams
Your Heart of Mine | Jon Pardi
Holding Me Down | Picturesque
A Lot More Free | Max McNown
Wind Up Missin' You | Tucker Wetmore

Welcome to

SUGARLAND CREEK

RANCH AND EQUINE RETREAT

SUGARLAND CREEK, TN

The town of Sugarland Creek is home to over two thousand residents and is surrounded by the beautiful Appalachian Mountains. We're only fifteen minutes from the downtown area, where you can shop at local boutiques, grab a latte, catch a movie, or simply enjoy the views.

We're an all-inclusive ranch. While we provide rustic lodging, each cabin is handicapped-accessible with ramps and smooth walking trails. If you need assistance with traveling between activities, we'll provide you with a staff member to pick you up in one of our handicapped-accessible vehicles at any time. Please request at the front desk or dial '0' on your room phone. We're here to help in any way we can.

To make your stay here the best experience, meet the family and learn about everything we have to offer at the retreat to ensure you have the vacation of a lifetime!

Meet the Hollis family:

Garrett & Dena Hollis

Mr. and Mrs. Hollis have been married for over thirty years and have five children. The Sugarland Creek Ranch has been home to over three Hollis generations. When the family officially took over twenty years ago, they added on the retreat to share their love of horses and the outdoors with the public.

Wilder and Waylon
Twin boys, the oldest

Landen
The middle child

Tripp
Youngest of the boys

Noah
The only girl and baby of the family

Whether you're here to relax and enjoy the views or you're ready to get your hands dirty, we have a variety of activities on the ranch for you to enjoy:

Horseback trail riding & tours
(10:00 a.m. and 4:00 p.m.)
Hiking, mountain biking, & fishing
(Maps available at The Lodge)
Family Game Nights
(Sundays and Wednesdays)
Karaoke & Square Dancing
(Friday and Saturday nights)
Kids Game Room
(Open 24/7)
Swimming
(Pool open 9:00 a.m. to 9:00 p.m. each day)
Bonfires with s'mores
(Fridays)
…and much more depending on the season!

The Lodge building is staffed 24 hours a day. It's home to our reception & guest services, The Sugarland Restaurant & Saloon, and activities sign-up.

Find all of our current information at sugarlandcreekranch.com.

We pride ourselves on serving authentic Southern food, so please let us know if you have any dietary restrictions or needs to better serve you. We offer brunch from 8:00 a.m. to 1:00 p.m. The restaurant is open for dinner from 5:00 p.m. to 9:00 p.m. If you wish to dine or find other activities off the ranch, we're less than an hour from Gatlinburg and are happy to provide you with suggestions.

Thank you so much for visiting us.
We hope you have the best time!

-The Hollis Family & Team Sugarland

See map on the next page!

A	The Lodge/ Guest Services	D	Pool House & Swimming Area
B	Ranch Hand Quarters	E	Trail Horse Barn & Pasture
C	Guest Cabins	F	Riding Horse Corral

SUGARLAND CREEK

RANCH AND EQUINE RETREAT

SUGARLAND CREEK, TN

Content Warnings

This book contains the following that may trigger some people, so please read with caution:

Traumatic death shown on page in prologue (option to skip)
Mention of suicide, not shown on page
Mentions of being drugged that result in injury (on page)
Discussions around prison and injustices
Mentions of family member with mental health issues
Amnesia resulting in accident

Fall With Me is a stand-alone novel in the Sugarland Creek series and recommended for ages 18+ for mature content. The following triggers are mentioned or shown on page in the prologue: traumatic death (shown: drowning) and suicide (mention). If either of these make you uncomfortable, please skip to chapter one. You don't need to read the prologue to understand the rest of the story as it'll be talked about briefly in other parts of the book.

Prologue
LANDEN

"Yeehaw, motherfuckers!" Tucker shouts as he sprints off a fifty-foot cliff.

It's his fourth time in fifteen minutes, but still, we watch as he does a double backflip in the air before plunging into the waterfall creek below.

"Has he always been this reckless?" my cousin Warren asks.

"I can't believe his body ain't gettin' sore from slammin' into the water so many times," Warren's girlfriend, Maisie, says.

Tucker swims toward the rocky shore. He throws a fist up into the air and shouts something inaudible.

"Since the day we met, he's been certifiably insane." Smirking, I think back to the dozens of memories Tucker Sánchez and I have made since we became best friends in third grade when he moved to Sugarland Creek, Tennessee.

Experiencing our first middle school dance where we both asked out the same girl and raced our dirt bikes through a rainstorm to determine who'd get to be her date.

I beat his ass.

1

Driving our tractors through corn fields and playing chicken until the other person swerved into the ditch.

The fucker never swerved.

Sneaking out in the middle of the night to tip cows and steal pigs just because we were bored little shitheads.

And got numerous trespassing violations.

After graduation in a couple months, he'll go off to college in California to study medicine while I stay here in Tennessee to work on my family's ranch and equine retreat. It's sad to think this is our final spring break before we go our separate ways and won't see each other for weeks at a time.

Even so, I'll be glad to be done with high school.

But mostly, I'm ready to get away from my ex-girlfriend, Angela, who's thankfully moving to Florida to study only God knows what. Considering she skips classes at least four times a week, she's failing most of them. Either way, I'm happy she'll be far away from me.

Even though she's the one who broke my heart last year and claimed *I* was incapable of loving someone and then left me for an older dude, she continues to cling to me any chance she gets.

Including now.

For someone so "emotionally dead inside" as she claims I am, she's still eager for my attention.

Moments ago, she called me *baby* and tried grabbing my hand to get me to jump off the cliff with her.

Even if the water were filled with gold coins, I wouldn't go in with her.

I didn't even want her on this trip, but Talia's her best friend and Talia's dating Tucker.

The other couple with us are Rhett and Addie. Rhett moved here four years ago and joined the baseball team with Tucker and me. Addie's friends with Talia, but not Angela. She tolerates her as much as I do.

So naturally, with three other couples here, Angela wanted to play house with me this week.

Not happening.

"I'm gonna miss this place," Rhett says as he holds Addie's hand. We came here last year, too, but this will be our final time as a group.

My aunt and uncle let us rent out one of the luxury cabins on their ranch resort and we've had a blast partying, hiking, swimming, and horseback riding each day we've been here.

"Y'all should visit during your school breaks," Warren tells them, wrapping his arm around Maisie as if he's hinting the same thing to her.

My cousin's the same age as me but lives two hours away in Willow Branch Mountain. He's also staying and working full-time for his parents, which has caused tension between him and Maisie since she's moving to New York City to pursue a career in publishing. He swears they'll make it work, though, so for his sake, I hope they do.

"This place would be the perfect romantic honeymoon," Addie says, giving Rhett a knowing look.

Considering they've been practically attached to the hip for the past three years, I wouldn't be shocked if they got engaged right after graduation.

"According to the thousands of reviews online, that's what most couples come for. Or a romantic getaway without their kids," Warren confirms.

For as long as I can remember, my parents would bring me and my four siblings up here every summer for a week of camping. Or rather "glamping" as it's promoted. There's no off-grid, tent-style suffering out here. It's all glamourous

3

accommodations with your choice of a nature immersive dome, two-story cabin, or their infamous modern-day treehouse. They get better Wi-Fi here than I do at home.

It's a special place to visit and there's no wonder why they're always fully booked. While my family's retreat is very kid-friendly, their resort focuses more on relaxation and helping couples reconnect with each other through outdoor and indoor activities.

While we've been here, we've taken full advantage of the fancy onsite restaurant and in-room massages. Yesterday, the guys and I went fishing while the girls relaxed in the hot tub and watched a Netflix movie on the large projector screen.

It's been the best spring break ever.

And I'm sad that tomorrow's our last day.

"How many times have you and Maisie snuck into one of the cabins for a *romantic weekend*?" I tease.

He smirks while Maisie's cheeks burn pink. I already know he booked under fake names for their prom night and her birthday weekend last year. I'm only surprised his parents never found out.

"Can't believe Aunt Lindsey hasn't caught on." She's my dad's sister and one of my mom's best friends.

"That's because I'm good at being sneaky." Warren grins. "I also add in a *no disturbance* note."

Shaking my head, I laugh.

"Who's next to jump?" Tuckers asks, wiping his face with a towel when he reappears.

"Talia!" Angela blurts. "She's the only one who's chickenin' out…"

Glancing at Talia, her face heats from the unwanted attention. It's obvious she doesn't want to, but she's on the shy side, which has always made me wonder how she's even friends

4

with Angela, who's loud, obnoxious, and never shuts the
hell up.

I used to like that about her. The way she'd party just as
hard as I did and never complained about doing random wild
shit on the weekends.

Now, hearing her voice is like a chainsaw cutting through
metal.

I'd rather swallow a teaspoon of cinnamon and hot sauce
than listen to her.

"C'mon, Talia. You don't wanna be the only one who
doesn't jump, do you?" Angela taunts.

"You don't have to, Talia," I say, patting her shoulder and
giving her a reassuring smile. "Don't do anything you're not
comfortable doing."

Angela glares at me, but I ignore her.

I took a lifeguard training program when I was sixteen and
have worked at the retreat's pool during summer breaks.
Although this is much more extreme than jumping into a ten-
foot-deep pool, I can tell she's uncomfortable about the idea.

"It's *fun*, Talia! The adrenaline rush will be worth whatever
fear of heights you have," Angela adds, but Talia's face goes
pale as if she's about to throw up. Her not liking heights makes
sense as to why she hasn't come close to the edge to watch like
everyone else.

I stand next to Warren and Rhett, not wanting to be near
Angela because the urge to push her off the ledge gets stronger
each time she opens her mouth.

"Baby, it's not that bad, I promise. But if you don't wanna,
we can go do something else," Tucker tells Talia.

"What a loser," Angela mutters to Addie, but when Addie
doesn't reciprocate the same thoughts, Angela laughs it off.

The sound makes my skin crawl.

She continues whispering to Talia as we contemplate what activity to do next.

"We could go ziplining. Or go for a hike to the other waterfall that's twice as tall," Warren suggests.

"It's cool to look at during the sunset. The lights reflect against the water," Maisie adds.

"Aww, that sounds so romantic…" Addie coos as she walks over.

"Talia's afraid of heights, so we should think of something else," I suggest.

"We could go four-wheelin' through the trails and play flashlight tag in the dark." Warren grins like he's up to something. "It can be a little dangerous, but my siblings and I play it all the time."

"And how many end up gettin' hurt?" I snort, knowing my cousins are just as unruly as me and my siblings.

"No one's ever ended up in the hospital if that's whatcha mean. Just some minor cuts and bruises from gettin' smacked with tree branches."

I laugh at how similar our families are even though we don't get to spend lots of time with each other.

"Angela, wait!" Talia screams and we turn our heads at the same time to witness Angela shoving Talia closer.

"Just take a look, you big baby." Angela stops just before Talia can fall over. "The only way you're gonna get over your fear is by facin' it. You don't wanna be scared of heights forever, do ya?"

"Leave her alone," I shout at Angela.

"Mind your business," she sneers. "Talia wants to be included. She just needs a little encouragement to do it."

Talia stays quiet as she leans over slightly, but her body is tense as she hangs onto Angela's hand with a death grip.

"See, it's not that high," Angela says.

"I-I dunno…I'm not a great swimmer." Talia's voice shakes as she steps back.

"We'll jump in together so I can make sure you get back to shore," Angela offers.

"I'll jump with you, baby," Tucker eases. "But only if you want to."

Talia chews on her lip as she contemplates her answer but then nods.

"Yay! So the three of us will go together!" Angela removes her sandals. "On my count!"

The rest of us watch as the three of them stand on the ledge holding hands.

"One, two, three…GO!" Angela shouts, except she and Talia don't jump. Angela pretended to by bending her knees and leaning over, but her feet never left the ground.

Tucker makes a splash, but Talia's screams grab my attention seconds later. Her limbs flail as she flies through the air. She's not in the right position for a safe dive. Her body should be rigid like a plank so she can easily glide through the surface instead of slamming against the water.

"What the fuck did you do?" I snap at Angela at the same time Addie asks, "I thought you were going in with her?"

"She needed the motivation, but I didn't wanna take away from her experience, so I stayed up here," Angela says as if that's a legitimate defense.

"You *pushed* her," Addie says.

Angela shakes her head. "She jumped in after Tucker." *Bullshit.*

Talia wouldn't scream like that if she had jumped of her own free will. The way she flew in the air meant she wasn't expecting it, either.

"Uh, guys, where is she?" Warren looks down and when I spot Tucker, he's treading water and frantically calling her name.

The swooshing of the waterfall crashing into the creek creates ripples through the water. My eyes scan all over, looking for any evidence of Talia swimming up to the surface, but there's only Tucker.

"Talia!" Addie shouts from the top of the cliff as I rush down the trail and toward the shore as fast as I can without my shoes.

My heart pounds as I step over rocks and dirt. Warren and Rhett keep up behind me, and when the three of us jump into the water, I dive as deep as I can swim. When I don't see her, I come back up for air and then go back down again. The guys are all looking, too, and the fact that none of us find her after twenty minutes sends me into a panic attack.

Where the hell could she be?

I'm not sure how deep the water is or where the stream goes underneath the waterfall, but as I dive farther down, I see large rocks and boulders. When I return to the surface, Addie's still on the phone with 911 and Warren tells me he's texted his parents.

"What the fuck did you do?"

My gaze snaps to Tucker, who's screaming in Angela's face.

"Nothing!" She waves her hand in the air dismissively. "Why're you blamin' me?"

"She didn't wanna jump in the first place." He hovers above her, shoving a finger in her face. "You were supposed to go in with her, but I saw you shove her over!"

"I did too," Maisie confirms with her hands on her hips.

"Fuck you, guys! She wanted me to! She didn't wanna look like a coward in front of y'all and asked me to help her get the courage, so I did what she asked!" Angela defends, standing taller but nowhere near Tucker's six-foot frame.

"That's bullshit." I walk closer. "You gave her no warnin' and that's why she was screamin' for her life."

"What're y'all even talkin' about? She asked me to do it!" Angela stands her ground, but no one's buying it.

Tucker goes back in to help Rhett and even though my body's sore and tired, I follow. We frantically search as best as we can, calling out her name and swimming around the entire length of the area until a rescue team arrives. We're told to stand back and wait as they dive into the water. Uncle Grady explains that the water goes down deep enough and can be hard to get to without proper gear. Aunt Lindsey paces while we wait for a miracle.

I call my mom and dad to tell them what's going on. They grab my siblings and start the two-hour drive up here.

"We should call her parents," Addie says in a daze as if she doesn't want to take her eyes off the water.

"I already gave their number to the sheriff," Tucker says. He's been shaking nonstop even though he's covered in a large, heated blanket. I don't blame him, though. My nerves are on fire.

The sound of a helicopter grabs our attention and we look up. The sun's no longer beaming on us, and soon, we're going to be surrounded by darkness. The divers have flashlight attachments on their wetsuits, but still, I don't know how far it allows them to see.

After an hour of searching, one of the divers pops up and waves to a team member who's waiting on shore.

"What's goin' on?" Addie asks.

"I dunno…they're whisperin' about something, though," I say, keeping my voice low.

The one guy who stood ashore returns and speaks to another guy, who looks in charge. After a moment, he speaks into a radio, confirming they found a drowning victim.

My heart drops to the bottom of my stomach as I let his words sink in.

Deep down, I knew this wouldn't be a good outcome, but hearing the words makes it more real than I was ready for.

She's been down there too long.

But maybe, just maybe, they could somehow get her heart beating and she'd be okay.

"Wh-what did he just say?" Tucker's jaw trembles.

Goose bumps cover my skin as the commotion in the water grabs my attention.

Two of the divers are holding Talia's *lifeless* body.

The other guy on shore brings out a flat gurney and once they get her on it, they carry her out.

One of the EMTs who arrived with them checks her airway and then begins CPR.

"How long has she been under?" the EMT asks in between.

"Took us thirty minutes just to get out here and an hour to find her," one of the divers responds.

Not to mention the twenty minutes we looked before the 911 operator could confirm they'd send help out here.

Tucker drops to his knees as the realization hits him.

Talia's dead.

They can't bring her back.

Rhett and I sit next to him as his whole body trembles.

"Deep breaths," I try to comfort him.

Knowing there's nothing I can do to take away his pain has my mind spiraling. Or maybe it's a panic attack. My heart's racing so hard, I swear it's going to jump right out of my chest at this rate.

Either way, our lives are never going to be the same.

Talia was confirmed dead nearly two hours after Angela pushed her off the cliff.

Her funeral was nine days later where hundreds of people showed up to pay the family their respects and to say goodbye to one of the nicest girls I knew.

Talia would've turned eighteen two days after her parents said goodbye to her for the last time.

The following day, Angela was arrested.

After we gave our statements and it was confirmed that Talia's cause of death was drowning, the sheriff got the judge to put out a warrant for Angela and to make her stand trial for homicide.

When she finally got her day in court, the six of us testified on what we observed that day and acted as character witnesses for both Angela and Talia. I made sure it was known how Angela was as a girlfriend and how she treated her "friends." My testimony proved that her pushing Talia wasn't out of character, especially considering we told her to leave Talia alone and she didn't.

Her attorney tried to paint us as irresponsible young kids and unreliable witnesses, but the jury believed us and the evidence over Angela's story that Talia asked her to do it. Hearing how she feared heights and wasn't a good swimmer, they didn't believe she'd ask to be pushed off.

I was willing to do whatever it took to get justice not only for Talia and her family but for my best friend. Tucker lost everything that day, too.

He'd hoped to get married and build a future with her after med school. Then they'd have some kids and grow roots wherever his career took him. He wanted nothing more than to have Talia by his side and together they'd be happy forever.

But Tucker didn't get any of that. He was so grief-stricken and filled with guilt for not standing up to Angela and getting Talia out of that situation. He couldn't focus in his college classes and flunked out before the end of his freshmen year.

One year after Angela was charged with voluntary manslaughter and fifteen years in prison, our lives were rocked once again when Tucker took his own life and a part of mine when he did.

I should've seen the signs. Looking back, I knew he was struggling and had hoped with time he'd get better. I encouraged him to see a grief counselor and he promised he would.

The week leading up to his death, he was the happiest I'd ever heard him. We talked every day and made plans to make a trip up to Willow Branch Mountain again. He had some of Talia's ashes and wanted to spread them there. I was relieved and couldn't wait to see my best friend again.

Except the next time I did was when he was in a casket.

Two people died because of Angela's reckless actions, and although Talia's family also won punitive damages in a wrongful death civil suit, Angela didn't get nearly as long as she deserved. She should rot for the rest of her sad, lonely life.

When she's eligible for parole in eleven years, I'll do everything in my power to keep her behind bars for as long as possible.

Chapter One

ELLIE

SEVEN YEARS LATER

Stay focused.

Eyes on the prize, Ellie.

And that prize is winning first place.

I inhale the humid summer air mixed with dirt and leather. The smell combination is one I'm used to and brings a warmth of memories to the surface each time.

There's nothing better than being at a rodeo. It feels like home.

The crowd cheers for Marcia Grayson, who just ran the barrels at probably the fastest speed I've ever seen her race, but when her time is announced, I smile to myself.

It's good enough for first place but not enough to beat me.

I started barrel racing when I was thirteen. It's all I've focused on for the past six years.

Between attending clinics and consistently training, I've established a good technique for what works for us. Although

I'm not always on my A game, I'm competitive and arrogant enough to believe I'll win regardless.

It's nearly dark out, so the arena is beaming with bright stadium lights. Although the sun's gone down, sweat drips down my back as the nerves take over. This rodeo is at a county fair an hour outside of my hometown, and although it's a non-pro event, I'm still just as driven to win. Any prize money I win goes toward Ranger's lifetime earnings and with it being close to home, it wasn't a big deal to make the trip. Since the riders are a mix of non-pro and pro barrel racers, I get to run against men and women I don't usually compete against.

The race time ranges depend on how big the arena is and how fast the riders are. Tonight, they've been between sixteen and seventeen seconds. Well, not including the couple of riders who knocked down barrels and got five-second penalties added on.

The time to beat is Marcia's at sixteen point one one two seconds.

As I sit on Ranger, he whines and stomps in place, waiting for our turn. He's as eager as I am to get in there.

If I didn't know any better, I'd say Ranger's more competitive than me.

But my voice is enough to calm him.

"Hang tight, buddy." I lean down from the saddle and rub his neck, then speak softly near his ear, "We got this. Just like we always do."

He's the gelding quarter horse I've had since I was sixteen and runs all my races with me. We've spent hundreds of hours practicing together, and I trust him with my life.

Now at nineteen, I may not have a social or dating life, but I have Ranger.

I love dressing up in all pink for these events, and even

though he's a male, he's decorated the same. It gives our duo some personality flair. Sparkly pink cowboy hat, pink cowboy boots under my jeans, and a bright pink collared button-up shirt that matches his pink saddle pad, breast collar, leg wraps, and bridle set. He's my boy who wears pink with pride.

"Good luck," Easton says when I exit the waiting pen.

"We don't need it, but thanks!" I wave as I guide Ranger toward the alleyway where the music and cheering grow louder.

Ranger's flowing with adrenaline and when he hears the emcee speak, he does little sideways tippy taps as we wait for the gate to open. I always hype him up before we run down to get him ready and to double-check my balance.

"You ready for this, Ranger?" I ask, and his ears tilt toward me as he waits for my command. "Let's show 'em whatcha got."

The moment I give him a quick kick, he runs full speed down the alleyway. Ranger's gaze is locked on the first barrel the moment he sees it.

"Like a glue stick!" I remind him, then smile proudly at how good he does staying in the pocket to avoid knocking over the barrel and manages to twist around it without losing too much speed. "Thatta boy."

My words come out between short-labored breaths, but he hears every word.

When my body shifts in the saddle, my boot slips out of the stirrup, and the side of my foot nudges the second barrel on the turn. My tight grip on the saddle horn releases, quickly grabbing the edge of the barrel and keeping it upright as I keep a firm hold on the reins.

"Whew, that was close," I say before Ranger takes off like a rocket to the third one and completes the cloverleaf pattern.

"Yes, *hustle home*!" I lean forward, hovering closer to his mane and keeping my hold on the reins as he sprints back to the alleyway.

I refuse to use a whip on him mostly because I don't need to. We have a deep connection, so he knows what to do just from my body language and the tone of my voice. He reads my cues well enough and knows what I need him to do without a crop.

He's my soul horse, and I'd be lost if anything ever happened to him.

The crowd shouts so loud that we spin around to look at the screen.

My heart races as I read the time and my name next to the number one spot.

"The Rodeo Princess does it again, folks!" the emcee announces. "Ellie Donovan takes the lead with fifteen point nine five two!"

They gave me that nickname after winning every race I entered my first year competing at the pro rodeo events, which is also how I was able to upgrade my permit to a cardholder in less than a year.

I wrap my arms around Ranger's neck. "Such a good boy."

I'm lucky that we bond as well as we do. Most riders go through a handful of horses before they find their perfect barrel-racing horse.

My parents make their way toward me, jogging and flailing their arms in the air like they always do when they're overly excited.

I'm an only child, so I get *all* their attention.

Sometimes *too much*.

But I'm grateful for their support. If it weren't for my mom pushing me to do an extracurricular activity after what happened to my cousin, who was like an older sister to me, I wouldn't have joined a local 4-H Club and enrolled in their horse training program.

And who knows where I'd be if I hadn't.

I started showing depressive episodes when I was thirteen. Mom wanted to keep my attention off the news and for me to put my energy and focus into something productive. Truthfully, it worked. I became addicted to the sport.

Hell, I'm still addicted to it.

A few years after I started and was outshining everyone in the juniors division, my parents gifted me Ranger for my sixteenth birthday. Most of my friends got cars or trucks for theirs, but I got him, which was even better. I'd been training on my 4-H leader's horses, but I was ready to level up.

It was a game changer.

Ranger saved me. And I like to think we saved him, too. His previous owner neglected him and he got put up for auction. From the first time we met, he trusted me for some reason.

It's like he knew I needed him as much as he needed me.

We invested time and money into getting him the proper care and training he needed and now he's never been better.

"You did it, sweetheart!" Mom shouts.

Maybe. Easton still has to race.

He's only been training for the past three years, but he's good.

Just not as good as me.

We first met at a 4-H Club outing years ago and have been friends who talk about horses ever since.

I ride Ranger toward the waiting pen so Easton can take his turn. Holding out my hand, he gives me a high five as we pass each other.

"Damn, you popped the clutch on that entrance," Easton

calls out, referring to how fast Ranger sped through the alleyway. "And good save out there with the tipsy barrel."

"Thanks! Good luck, E!" I shout as the distance between us grows wider.

When my parents reach us, they shower Ranger with love and tell him how amazing he did.

"Noah couldn't take her eyes off y'all! She loved it and was cheerin' along with us," Mom gushes.

The corner of my lips curves up. "Really? That's awesome!"

I was so amped up that I forgot Noah Hollis was in the crowd watching me.

My dream trainer.

The top one in the state and she came to watch *me*.

I've been working with a former barrel racer at my grandparents' farm where I board Ranger, and she's been wonderful in getting me to where I am now. However, if I want to get my name out there more and challenge myself to faster race times, I need a professional trainer who can help push us there. Noah's known as a horse whisperer and if she agrees to take me on, I can board Ranger at her ranch and utilize their training facility.

What makes her even more unique is the fact she's only twenty-one years old.

Most trainers are *twice* her age and still not as talented as her. She's wise beyond her years, with great resources and knowledge to help me make this a successful full-time career.

The more races I win, the more opportunities there are to get money and prizes—which vary between belt buckles, horse breast collars, saddles, tack, or other equipment. Each event has its own incentives, but each win gets me closer to qualifying for larger events, such as regional championships, national finals, or even invite-only rodeos. But making it to the national or world finals and winning first place at least once during my career is my ultimate dream.

"One final rider of the evenin'…"

The emcee's voice grabs our attention toward the arena, and we watch as Easton and his American Paint Horse, Scotty, gun it around the first barrel.

"He's fast…" Dad admires.

The other riders, including Marcia, are all watching, too.

She doesn't look too happy about the potential of being pushed into third place.

"Here he comes…" Mom holds her breath as we wait for him to cross home and get his final time.

"Fifteen point nine six nine! That puts Easton Hawthorne in second place!"

"Yes!" Dad shouts. "You did it, kid!"

We don't have time to celebrate before I'm directed back into the arena for a victory lap. Not every event does this, but when they do, I put on my best smile and wave to the crowd as music echoes above me. I might be new to pro rodeo, but I hear my little fan base screaming for me. Since I'm local to the state, more people recognize me from TV interviews and articles they've written about me when I won Rookie of the Year.

Tonight's prizes go to the top three, so I walk Ranger over to the event's sponsor committee for an oversized check for two thousand dollars and a champion belt buckle with the event's name, year, and logo. The one I'm wearing tonight is from the last rodeo I won. After each new one, I wear it to the next. It's been my good luck charm.

The high after winning a race sets in and after I congratulate Marcia and Easton on placing, take photos, and speak with one of the local newspaper journalists, I walk

Ranger back to my trailer where my parents and Noah are waiting for me.

"You did amazing!" She beams. Her long blond hair in a high ponytail bounces with each step she takes toward me.

With my arms still full, I give my check and buckle over to my mom, then Dad grabs Ranger's reins so I can free my hands.

"Thank you! I'm so glad you could come." I lean forward and give her a side hug.

We've talked on the phone previously, and considering we're from the same small town, I've known her name ever since I started riding horses, so it feels like we're already close friends.

"Are you kiddin'? I was more than excited to see you in action. You didn't disappoint."

Getting her approval fills me with pride, but I know there must be things she saw I could work on.

"So what'd you think?" I ask eagerly.

"I think you and Ranger make a solid team. There's always room for improvement, though. We can work on tightening your frame so your stirrup doesn't go rogue." She winks.

"Yeah, that was unexpected," I admit.

She shrugs casually. "It happens. You handled it well, though. You kept him tight in the pocket, but there's always a chance you might not be so quick to bump the barrel back into place. That's something we can work on so y'all don't risk that going forward."

I nod. "Did you notice anything else?"

"Mostly minor things that can easily be worked on and fixed. I think your reins are too long and you'd do better with shorter ones. Practice ridin' more straight and square so your body stays in an upright position. Although Ranger seems to have good muscle memory, he also follows your lead and it could result in knocking down a barrel if you lean too far. You don't wanna risk that five-second penalty. Common for almost every rider is forgetting to breathe properly while you're runnin' the barrels. We can do some exercises for that."

"You sound like you know what you're doin'." Mom smiles, shifting her eyes to me in excitement. She supports my desire to train harder.

"Do you race?" Dad asks Noah.

"No, but I've been a professional trainer for many years. I got certified when I was eighteen, but growing up on a ranch meant I was surrounded by horses since before I could walk. I've spent several years hyperfocusing on horses and pretty much every equine sport."

"Noah has a keen eye on fixin' issues and knows how to help me evolve my skills," I explain to my parents.

I'm not a beginner racer by any means, but I need someone like her to help push me so I'm ready to compete at those higher-level competitions.

"I have two other pro clients and they're on their way to qualify for finals this year," Noah adds.

"Wow, that's incredible!" Mom wraps her arm around my shoulders and squeezes me into her side.

She's almost more excited than I am.

"I'd work on your athleticism, too. You must be in shape just as much as Ranger, so I'd put together a workout schedule for you as well."

"Oh…great."

Noah smirks. "Nothin' you can't handle, I promise."

"How often would you train?" Dad asks.

"That's completely up to y'all. If you wanna board Ranger, daily exercise is included for the horses and then you can add on additional trainin' in our facility. The two girls who are on tour right now board their horses when they're not travelin' and then we work together when they're here."

"I'd love that," I say.

"And you'll get to utilize our vet and farrier services, so you won't have to worry about keepin' up with that on top of everything."

"Sounds perfect. Almost too good to be true," Mom states.

"My family and I love horses and want to make it as easy as possible to care for 'em. I'm somewhat of a workaholic, so I never get tired of it."

"When do you have time for a social life?" Mom quips.

"Well…" Noah chuckles. "I've been single for a year and my best friend, Magnolia, comes and hangs out with me a lot. But besides that, I see my family every day and we have a special supper every Sunday."

Everyone local and even outside of the area knows the Hollises. They're well-known for owning the Sugarland Creek Ranch and Equine Retreat. There are five siblings in total and they each do various jobs on the ranch. Noah's the youngest, but I'd argue the most talented and hardest working.

"Sounds like me. I talk to a few girls from my 4-H Club, but otherwise, I've been super focused on racin'," I say.

"When can Ellie start?" Mom asks.

"A week too soon?" Noah smirks. "I have a boarder leavin' in six days and then we'll get it ready for Ranger."

My face splits into the widest grin I've ever had. "That'd be perfect."

Chapter Two
LANDEN

"Why're you naked?" Tripp asks once I'm settled into the passenger's seat of his truck.

"Yeah, it ain't your birthday," Wilder taunts from the back seat.

Of course he'd bring him to witness my humiliation. I sent my younger brother a 911 emergency text to come pick me up in town. Since the family ranch is a good fifteen minutes from Sugarland Creek, I hid in the stairwell of an apartment building and cupped my junk while I waited for him.

Once I'm buckled in, I throw my middle finger over my shoulder at my older brother.

Yep, I'm the middle child of five. Technically speaking, Wilder and Waylon are twins, so they're both the oldest. Tripp's two years younger than me and our sister, Noah, is two years younger than him.

At least she's not here to bask in the glory of my embarrassment.

Tripp chuckles as he drives us onto the street.

"Did you bring me some clothes?" I ask.

25

"We grabbed basketball shorts and a T-shirt because I didn't know what classified as *spare clothes*," Tripp explains.

I shrug. *Good enough for me.*

Wilder tosses them to me and then leans over the back of the bench seat with his arms folded as if he doesn't want to miss the show.

I slide the shorts on first, which are too tight and not concealing a damn thing, but since I have no room to complain, I keep my mouth shut. Next, I grab the white shirt and bark out a laugh when I see the words *Two-Seater* with two black arrows. One pointing up toward my face and the other pointing down toward my dick.

"Where the hell did ya find this?" I ask, putting it on.

"In your closet," Wilder says.

Hmm. Don't remember this shirt.

Not surprised, though, because my friends and I often borrow each other's clothes when we need fresh ones after a night out. I probably crashed at a friend's house and then stole it the next morning.

"So…are ya gonna tell us what happened to your clothes?" Tripp asks.

Glancing over at his shit-eating grin, I know he won't drop it until I do.

"I met some chick last night at the Twisted Bull. She took me to her apartment, and when I woke up this mornin', she was gone. Along with my clothes and boots."

The Twisted Bull is the most popular bar in town. It has a full dance floor and features a mechanical bull where drunken idiots try to stay on it for eight seconds. My brothers and I have done it numerous times, all while mostly shitfaced.

"Guess she was hopin' it'd force you to stay." Wilder laughs.

"Yeah, maybe she was gettin' y'all some coffee or something," Tripp adds.

"I waited twenty minutes for y'all to get here and didn't see her car pull in, so very doubtful. I think she just wanted to be a terror."

"Maybe it's payback for not satisfyin' her." Wilder smacks my shoulder. "Need your older brother to give ya some tips? I've got a wicked tongue trick." He sticks his out, then flicks it up and down as he flashes his piercing. "Or did you get whiskey dick?"

Glaring back at Wilder, I'm tempted to yank his barbell right out.

"Absolutely the fuck not. We had a great time."

"What's her name?" Tripp asks.

"Um…Tessa." I swallow hard. "Or maybe….*Jessa*?"

"I bet he called her by the wrong name and she got even by stealin' his clothes," Wilder muses.

"That's why I don't say their names. That's an amateur move. You call 'em baby, sweetheart, darlin'. Anything but their names."

Tripp snorts. "Classy."

"What? It was consensual. She liked it—no, *loved* it. Pretty sure her neighbors were poundin' on her walls because she was so loud."

"Ah, see…when they're that loud, they're fakin' it," Wilder says.

"How would you know?" I ask.

"Because when a woman is in the middle of an intense orgasm, she's too out of breath to scream. If they're screamin' that much, they're tryna get it over with so they can hide in the bathroom and get themselves off instead." He flashes his infamous know-it-all smile. "Or in your case, plottin' revenge."

27

"It was before that, thank you very much. When my head was between her thighs and she was shakin' all around me. She was definitely *not* fakin' it."

Tripp chuckles. "According to a recent study, up to eighty percent of women admit to fakin' it with their partner."

"What the fuck?" I narrow my eyes. "You're readin' sex articles now?"

"Noah and Magnolia were talkin' about it, and I overheard," he admits.

I smile to myself because the poor bastard is obsessed with our sister's best friend. He just won't admit it.

"Whatever. Even if she faked it—which I'm not sayin' she did—that's no excuse to steal my goddamn clothes," I say. "Oh, did you bring me some boots?"

"Yeah, your work ones," Wilder says, pulling them up from the back seat floor.

"Thanks. Noah asked me to help her at the stables this mornin' since you two jerk-offs ain't workin' today." I slide on my boots and realize how ridiculous I look wearing them with basketball shorts.

"And I'm gonna enjoy every minute of it," Wilder gloats. "Tripp and I are gonna fuck shit up at the festival tonight."

Tripp furrows his brows, and I laugh to myself. I've never seen Tripp fuck anything up. He's too careful and guarded to do that.

"I'll be done by six, so don't leave without me," I tell them. "Is Waylon going?"

"I think he has a date tonight," Wilder replies. "But who knows, he'll probably chicken out like last time and cancel it last minute."

Waylon tends to do that. He goes out of his way to ask out a girl and then gets too anxious to follow through with it.

28

Not sure why. He's good-looking and knows how to have fun.

He just gets too into his head.

"Well, either way, we're gonna have a blast." I smirk.

"Don't you ever learn your lesson?" Tripp taunts, glancing at me with a frown. "Maybe don't go home with a chick every weekend and you wouldn't risk losin' your clothes."

"I don't…" I argue. "Sometimes they come home with me."

Tripp rolls his eyes and Wilder laughs.

I smack Tripp's shoulder. "Oh c'mon. You can have fun and have a beer or two. Wilder said y'all are gonna fuck shit up."

"Not if I gotta drive you drunken idiots home," he counters.

Tripp's our DD ninety-nine percent of the time, but he's a good sport about it.

When we arrive at our family house on the ranch, the three of us jump out of Tripp's truck and instead of getting in my own, I opt for my dirt bike.

It's way more fun.

"See y'all later!" I shout over the engine before I slowly release the clutch and rev it into first.

By the time I get to the boarding stables, Noah's outside with Trey and Ruby—two of our ranch hands who work with her.

"Landen! Turn that off!" Noah shouts as I approach.

"What? You wanted me here!" I park and turn off the bike.

"You know that spooks the horses." She scowls, folding her arms, and then lowers her glare to my outfit. "What the hell are you wearin'?"

I glance down and laugh. "Don't ask. What do you need me for anyhow? You got your two lackeys here."

"Hey!" Trey and Ruby both scowl.

Noah stands in front of me. "Ellie's a new barrel racing

client of mine and Ranger is her quarter horse. I want your thoughts on how they do, so I figured you should meet 'em."

Go figure she'd con me here so I can't say no to her face.

"It's prime breedin' season," I remind her. "I'm not gonna have a ton of extra time for that."

After high school, I became the breeding operations manager and summer is my busiest time. Even if it were off-season, I stay busy taking care of the stallions and booking mares for the following year.

"She'll be here when she's not travelin'. She wants to be good enough to qualify for finals and needs all the help we can give her. C'mon, we made a good sister-brother team last year." She gives me her best puppy dog eyes, and dammit, she knows it works on me. Especially when it comes to something I'm already passionate about.

I'm not as good of a trainer as Noah—hell, no one in the state is—but I have a good eye for recognizing issues and giving ideas on how to improve. Horses respond well to her, which means she's always booked solid. I'm more of an observer who watches and makes suggestions so she doesn't have to spend as much time researching and instead have more time working the horse.

"So you're sayin' *you* need *me*?" I taunt.

"Don't be arrogant." She gives me a little shove. "She's really good, but the competition from the more experienced riders is gonna blow her away, so it's all hands on deck to help her advance."

I roll my eyes when she pierces me with a pleading gaze. Leave it to my little sister to add to my already full workload.

"Fine," I grind out between my teeth. "But only when it works for *my* schedule."

"Deal!" She smiles victoriously.

"And you owe me," I add.

She frowns. "Like what?"

I shrug. "Whatever I want whenever I think of something."

"Yeah, yeah. We'll see."

"You meet Ayden's girlfriend when she was here?" Ruby asks while we wait.

"No." *Didn't even know he had one.* "Who is she?"

"Her name's Laney. They were high school sweethearts ten years ago and she just randomly showed up and told him he had a nine-year-old daughter," she informs me.

My jaw drops because that's the last thing I expected.

Ayden's the boarding stables manager and only three years older than me. I couldn't imagine having a child right now or finding out I had one I didn't even know existed.

Honestly, that's probably my worst nightmare.

"That's wild. How's he handlin' it?"

"As good as he can, I guess. He's plannin' to take a trip to Texas in a few weeks to meet the daughter."

"So is the ex-girlfriend hot?" I waggle my brows and Trey snorts.

"I wasn't here last weekend to meet her in person, but I saw photos, and yeah, she's beautiful," Ruby says. "Way out of your league, though."

I scoff, but the conversation dies when a Ford Super Duty towing a horse trailer comes down the gravel driveway toward the barn. I was so wrapped up in Noah asking me for help that I forgot to even ask who this Ellie chick is.

"Here she is. Be *professional*, Landen," Noah says.

My brows pinch together. "What's that mean?"

She clears her throat, giving me a side-eye. "Cover up your shirt!"

I don't know how she expects me to do that without

crossing my arms and looking like a beefed-up tool bag. But there's no time to figure it out before three people exit and Noah greets them with hugs and smiles.

At first glance, I notice how petite Ellie's frame is and her cutoff shorts reveal long, lean legs. It doesn't surprise me that she's fast on a horse and probably flies around the barrels. I know it's not all about size, but it sure doesn't hurt your speed to be on the smaller side.

Her wild, wavy blond hair reaches below her shoulders, but it looks like she's threaded her fingers through it a few times.

As my gaze lowers down to her pink cowboy boots, my heart and stomach do this weird flutter flip—something that's only happened once before ages ago—and although it's a foreign feeling, I'm pretty sure she's the reason for it.

Though I don't know why.

Ruby and Trey stand next to me while we wait for Noah to introduce us.

"She's a cute little thing," Ruby murmurs.

"I wonder why she's lookin' at Landen like she wants to murder him." Trey chuckles.

"Yeah…what'd you do?" Ruby nudges me with her elbow.

"I've never met her before," I argue and then remember to fold my arms over my chest to cover the text on my shirt the best I can. I'm going to kill Wilder for picking this one out of all the others I have in my closet.

Pretty certain he did it on purpose.

And maybe I should kill Noah for not giving me a heads-up so I knew to go home and change first.

"You sure? She looks like a woman scorned." Ruby chuckles.

My arms drop when I give her a little shove because she loves to give me shit.

"Let me introduce y'all to my ranch hands and brother," Noah says, finally bringing them up here to meet us.

Ellie's parents walk behind her and as soon as their eyes land on my shirt, their smiles fall.

Fuck. My arms go back to covering the text. I should've turned it inside out but got distracted the moment I laid eyes on Ellie.

"This is Ruby and Trey. They clean the stalls, feed and water the boarders, and also help tack up the horses for me. You'll probably see a lot of 'em when you're here."

As they exchange pleasantries with Ellie and her parents, I study her for any recognition that we've met before, but nothing comes to mind. She doesn't even look old enough to get into a bar and if we met at a rodeo or anywhere else for that matter, I'd remember those bright blue eyes. But still, she stares at me like I've insulted her or somehow did her wrong.

"This is one of my older brothers, Landen. He's gonna help with your trainin'," Noah tells Ellie.

I hold out my hand to tell her how it's nice to meet her, but she ignores it. Instead, her brows rise to her hairline as a wave of panic flashes across her beautiful face.

And then her gaze snaps to Noah. "I thought I was only workin' with you."

"Primarily, yes. But with only three months until the season ends, we can use any extra eyes to help with your trainin' and gettin' your name out there before next year. He's good at pointin' out problem areas and has been around barrel racin' for years. It won't be every session, just when I need a second opinion."

Ellie's eyes finally meet mine and they're cold as ice. "Oh."

Her mom touches her shoulder and squeezes it. "If it's for

33

the sake of you and Ranger, more help and experience is a good thing."

Although Ellie looks tense and ready to argue, she releases a shallow breath at her mom's words.

"Should be fine, then." Ellie's gaze lowers down my T-shirt before I remember to cross my arms again.

Well, that was beyond fucking weird.

She doesn't even know me and already has a vendetta against me.

But what the hell for?

When I look at her father, he's giving me that stern look you'd give to some punk kid taking out your daughter for the first time. Not someone who's helping her.

"Let's go inside the barn for a tour, and I'll show y'all Ranger's new home." Noah waves them toward the large doors, and I'm left standing in confusion.

"Shit…they do not like you." Ruby chuckles.

"So it wasn't just me who noticed?" I deadpan.

She giggles, giving my shirt another glance. "I bet the parents didn't appreciate your choice of clothes but not sure why Ellie was givin' you the stink face."

"How uptight do ya gotta be for a shirt to insult you that much? I mean, c'mon…" I pull the hem and stretch it out, reading it again upside down. "It's not even mine, but it's hilarious at the very least. Woulda made for a good icebreaker if she weren't attemptin' to blow up my head with her devil eyes."

Ruby full-on belly laughs. "Now that I woulda paid to watch."

"Maybe they've heard about your *reputation* and don't wanna be associated with you," Trey suggests.

"What reputation?" I ask, insulted. "That I'm a hard

worker, that I've been helpin' on my family's ranch since I was five years old, or how I work sixty-hour weeks? Yeah, goddamn. What a rep to frown upon." I roll my eyes because now I'm just annoyed at the accusations that I did something to piss her off when I've never even met her before two minutes ago.

"Probably the one where you're a playboy and they don't want you anywhere near their precious barrel racer." Ruby pokes me in the side. "Whatever it is, I wouldn't go out of your way to annoy her. It's Noah's reputation on the line, too."

I scoff because Noah's a saint in everyone's eyes and has nothing to worry about. She could bring a man home twice her age and no one would blink twice about it.

"Does she have an older sister you slept with and later ghosted?" Trey asks.

"I don't think so…" I shrug, but honestly, that's the only thing that'd make sense.

"Wait, I think she's an only child. Pretty sure that's what Noah told me when I asked if she had a hot older brother," Ruby says.

Well, shit, there goes that theory.

"Didn't you and Nash just celebrate your six-month anniversary up in Willow Branch Mountain last weekend?" I ask since I'm the one who gave her that suggestion in the first place. I haven't been there in a hot minute, but I know it's still a hot attraction for couples.

"We did, but it doesn't mean I'm tied down. A girl can still window shop," she defends.

I snort. "And *I'm* the one with the playboy reputation?"

Ten minutes pass before Noah returns with Ellie and asks me to help unload Ranger while she goes over the paperwork with Ellie's parents.

I follow Ellie to the back of her trailer, admiring every inch of her body, but when she quickly turns around, my gaze is still on her ass.

"If you could keep your pryin' eyes off me and act professional, I'd appreciate it. I'm not payin' two grand a month to be gawked at. Especially by you."

The corners of my lips twitch with the urge to laugh because this is the first time a woman has ever asked me *not* to look at her.

"Who says I'm gawkin' at you?" I widen my stance, straightening my spine and holding her glare with my own.

"Because I have eyes and can see with them that you were checkin' out my ass."

"It's a nice ass." I shrug because I can't even deny it, but goddamn, she's pressed as if I touched it or something.

"Regardless, I'm not here as your eye candy and would appreciate you not sexualizing me."

I take a couple steps back as if she's physically slapped me. "Whoa, whoa, whoa. I'm doing no such thing. I just glanced at your ass and complimented it. Doesn't mean I was thinkin' about you in that way."

"Oh, so you glance at everyone's asses, then?" She crosses her arms and pops out her hip. "The T-shirt has a nice touch of sexual implications, too."

"It's a *joke*. And it's not even mine. But either way, not like it's forcin' you or anyone to *literally* sit on my face."

Not that women haven't, but I've never had to *force* them.

Trey must overhear our awkward conversation because he comes over at the perfect time to save *my* ass.

"He checks mine out all the time," Trey says. "Have you seen it?"

Trey does a little twirl and shows off his tight Wranglers showcasing his own ass.

This whole thing just got fucking weirder.

Ellie's nose scrunches and her brows pinch together in annoyance. She's not amused in the least.

"Ignore them." Ruby marches over, shoving herself between Trey and me. "Something you learn hangin' out here regularly is these cowboys are…well, they're a little unhinged. They work twelve-hour shifts, are usually hungover, and have no filter or common sense most days. The only way to survive being around them is learnin' to ignore their stupidity."

Not sure if I should be offended or give her a high five. Either way, Ellie's not buying into it.

"I'd rather just be left alone to train and work," she says. "I'm not here to fool around."

"Totally understandable." Ruby smiles at her, but when she glances at me over her shoulder, she gives me her narrowed-eye stare down. "I'll help you get Ranger into his stall."

Trey and I step back to allow Ruby and Ellie to get him out. He has a gorgeous chocolate brown coat with white down its nose.

"Damn, she does *not* like you," Trey muses as we follow the girls into the stables. "You offended her before even sayin' a word."

"That's a new record for me."

Once Ranger's in his stall and Ellie meets back up with her parents in Noah's office, I lean against the door and let him sniff me. He'll see a lot of me, so it's best he gets used to me now before I work with them.

"He likes you at least." Ruby stands next to me and then leans in closer, lowering her voice. "She's the most uptight city girl I've ever met, so you better keep your distance."

"I'd hardly call her a city girl."

"She might be a barrel racer, but she's never lived on a ranch," she clarifies.

"Neither have you," I remind her.

"I've worked here since the summer after high school, so that counts for something."

I chuckle because Ruby's the same age as Noah and only graduated a few years ago.

"Red alert…" Trey murmurs as he walks past us. Behind him are Noah, Ellie, and her parents, and they're walking right toward me.

"So I went over everything for Ellie and Ranger. Their official trainin' will begin on Monday with a session every day through Friday, except when they're traveling. I'll work him in the corral for a while each morning and when Ellie arrives, we'll take him to the trainin' center and set up the barrels."

"When do ya want me to come watch?" I ask, forcing my gaze *not* to drift toward Ellie.

"Just a couple times a week for now."

I nod. "Alright."

"We look forward to seein' her progress," Ellie's mom says.

"She's in good hands," I promise her, and since she's the only one who hasn't glared at me, I smile for extra reassurance.

Noah walks the three of them outside toward their truck, and I'm left wondering what the hell I just got myself into.

I continue petting Ranger, appreciating he's not giving me a hard time, at least not yet. Maybe he can put a good word in for me with his owner.

Noah returns a few minutes later and smacks me upside the head.

"What the hell?" I rub where she hit.

"Whatever you're thinkin', don't. Ellie's off-limits."

"Who said I —"

"She's focused on her career and too driven to succeed to be sidetracked. She's not lookin' for a fling to distract her from that goal. Also, she's six years younger than you, barely outta high school. So keep it in your pants."

"I'll have you know, it's very much in my pants."

"Good, keep it that way." Then she glances down at my shirt again. "Go change. You look ridiculous."

She marches off before I can ask why she's giving me the third degree, but if I know my sister as well as I think I do, she assumes I'm after every pretty woman I come across.

Joke's on her, though, because Ellie's made it crystal clear she'd rather run me over with her horse than have me anywhere near her.

But I just can't figure out why.

Chapter Three

ELLIE

"I feel like we got off on the wrong foot and for the sake of professionalism and helpin' you train, let's start over."

My back goes ramrod straight at the deep, recognizable voice behind me.

I hoped I wouldn't see him today and even hid in the grooming stall with Ranger. But this proves that luck hasn't always been on my side.

Reluctantly, I turn around and am faced with his stupidly handsome face and smug expression. It's no secret he's attractive, in an obvious charming kind of way, but my body and heart feel nothing for him except anger.

As soon as he catches me lowering my gaze down his muscular body, the corner of his lips curve into a satisfied grin. Then he proceeds to hold out his hand and without waiting for me to take it, continues, "Hi, I'm Landen Hollis. It's a pleasure to meet you."

I deny his pleasantries and curl my arms behind my back. "You're at least dressed normally today."

He glances down at his scoffed-up work boots, dirty jeans,

and gray T-shirt with the family's ranch logo on it. "You caught me on a rough mornin' the other day. Wasn't my best first impression, I'll give ya that."

I didn't need to meet Landen in person to know I didn't like him.

I've spent the past seven years of my life loathing his very existence.

And secretly wishing karma would come for him sooner rather than later.

"Like I said before, I'm here to train. We don't need to be friendly about it."

He tilts his head like a confused puppy and the thought of that image nearly has me bubbling with laughter. But then he'd think I like him and his ego is already suffocating me, so I bite the inside of my cheek to stop myself.

He narrows his eyes. "Why can't we be friends?"

"I don't see the point."

"Acquaintances?" he asks, arching a brow.

"Why?"

The wrinkle between his brows grows deeper as if he can't fathom why any woman would argue about being in his presence. "Because we're gonna see a lot of each other. I'm not just workin' with Ranger's technique, I'll be critiquing yours, too. I'm usually on friendly terms with the rider I'm trainin' and prefer to get to know them a little bit beforehand. It helps us form a level of trust."

"Well, if that's what you need to do your job correctly, then I suppose you're not that great at it in the first place."

He jerks back as if I smacked him across the face. "You are ." He shakes his head as if to erase the words he wants to say aloud. "Gonna be a challenge, ain't ya?"

"Not everything in your life can be easy, can it?" With a

conniving smirk, I spin back around and continue brushing Ranger.

Before walking away, I swear he curses under his breath, and I smile to myself.

Good. Now maybe he'll leave me the hell alone.

He doesn't.

But working with a professional trainer like Noah has been my dream for the past two years. It took almost that long to get off her waitlist, so I'm not letting her brother be the reason I don't get what I want. If putting up with him is what it takes to advance my career, then I'll deal with it for the short term.

But I didn't realize he'd be so involved and frustrating.

Or stupidly attractive.

But his looks don't matter when the urge to be as far away from him as possible is stronger than anything else.

Another day of doing training exercises means another day of Landen trying to crack jokes or get me to laugh at them.

It's not going to work.

After two weeks of coming here, avoiding Landen the best I can, today I'm stuck with only him.

And though he doesn't know where my dislike for him stems from, nor does he remember who I am from years ago, him constantly pointing out every little thing I do is only encouraging me to hate him more.

"Stop droppin' your shoulder when you turn," he tells me. "Your hips are too angled."

"They are not!" I reply, holding the reins firm in my grip so I'm not tempted to jump off Ranger and use my fists on him instead. He's been on my ass for the past hour while Noah's been dealing with an unexpected issue.

He stands tall and confident, looking smug as always. "You shifted too early, which caused Ranger to shoulder. Shift your pelvis slightly so you're almost sittin' on your back pockets and it'll help you stop that habit."

"My pelvis is angled fine. I have narrow hips," I tell him.

The corner of his lips tilts up slightly, and I know there's an inappropriate comment swirling in his mind just begging to come out.

He shrugs unapologetically as if he doesn't believe me. "Not from my view. Your left shoulder drops on the second barrel."

"It's my weaker one," I admit. "I dislocated it when I fell hard off Ranger about six months ago. Bruised up like a peach."

"Did you do physical therapy for it?"

"A few times, but it doesn't hurt. It just pops back out sometimes."

He furrows his brows, and I know I'm about to get another lecture from him.

"Get down and come here," he demands, and I hate how his deep, raspy voice puts me in a trance to follow his orders without a second thought.

Another reason to loathe him.

I tie Ranger's reins to one of the posts and walk toward him.

The training center is massive, which gives us plenty of

room for drills and practice, but as soon as I stand in front of him, the space closes in on us.

"Can I touch your arm?" he asks.

I sigh. "If you must."

He smirks, then motions for me to spin around. As soon as I do, he grabs my elbow and stretches out my arm. "Does that hurt?" he asks while digging his fingers into my shoulder blade.

"No more than usual when the son of Satan is near me."

He chuckles, then hovers above my ear. "Ooh, baby, careful with that dirty talk. My heart just did that little flutter thing."

"Sounds like you have a murmur. Might wanna get that checked out before you collapse to your death."

"Wouldn't you like that, huh? Doubt they'd find anything, though. It only acts up when I'm 'round you."

I snort but not in a ha-ha kind of way. More in disbelief that he's not getting the hint that I cannot stand him. "Does that pickup line usually work?"

He's silent for a few beats before finally exhaling a long breath. "It wasn't a *line*, Little Devil."

That's the second time this week he's called me that, and I haven't dared to ask him why. I probably didn't help my case by calling him the son of Satan, but *I* was being serious. He calls me *Little Devil* like it's a cute pet name.

He raises my arm and then shifts it back and forth. "You should start doing daily stretches to help with this clicking. You need to strengthen it so you're not tempted to lower it."

"Noah already has me joggin' three miles every day. I'm sure it'll get stronger in time."

"I'll get you a shoulder brace to wear during practice runs and print out some exercises for you to do at home. The more you work on it now, the better it'll be for when you race."

Instead of arguing, I stay quiet. His offer is quite sweet, but it'll be a cold day in hell before I admit that out loud. He's only doing his job and as long as it helps me in the long run, I won't fight him on it.

He continues feeling around my back and arm, but the longer he stays silent, the more I forget how much I hate him.

"Are you almost done?" I finally ask.

He releases me, but then gives it a little squeeze. "Most women don't complain about me touchin' them. In fact"—he leans down until his breath whispers along my neck—"they beg me not to stop."

Turning around, I'm faced with his cocky smirk. "And I suspect those women regret pickin' convenience over personality."

He tries to hide his reaction by scrubbing a hand along his scruffy jawline as if he's contemplating how to handle me.

Good. The sooner he realizes I'm not here to entertain his ego, the better for both of us.

He licks his lips. "If you keep being mean to me, I'm gonna end up fallin' in love with you."

I wrinkle my nose at the unexpected comment. "Is that what you're into? Women degrading you?"

"So far, only when it comes from you. I'm startin' to think you feel it, too."

My nostrils flare at the unwanted flirting. *He's fucking delusional.*

"You're insufferable and the only thing I'll ever feel for you is *hatred*. If you think that's me flirtin' with you, you need to get your head checked. Maybe you have a leak. Would explain the lack of oxygen gettin' in there."

He smacks a hand over his heart. "Careful. The more you

45

say you don't like me, the harder I'm gonna fall." His lips curve into the cockiest smirk I've ever seen. "Wanna fall with me?"

Crossing my arms, I match his grin. "I'd rather *fall* out of a plane without a parachute."

"I see you two are still gettin' along nicely…" Noah singsongs as she makes her way over toward us. "Am I too late? Has the first punch been thrown?"

"She's the one using me as a verbal punchin' bag," Landen says, shifting his gaze from Noah to me. "But nothin' I can't handle."

"Great!" Noah smiles, her eyes beaming. "Then you won't mind me cuttin' in for the last ten minutes of practice and seeing how y'all did?"

"By all means." Landen waves out his hand, a knowing expression on his face. "Go ahead, Little Devil."

I wrinkle my nose at the annoying nickname but don't want to argue in front of Noah. My respect for her trumps my anger for her brother, so without a word, I grab Ranger and settle into the saddle.

Landen grabs his timer and while Ranger trots down the makeshift alleyway, I feel his eyes burning into me. I have no idea why he's so hell-bent on flirting with me, but it seems nothing I say will get him to realize that I'm not just playing hard to get.

I wouldn't think twice about running him over with my horse trailer if I knew I wouldn't get caught.

With his de-lulu brain, he'd probably think me trying to murder him was foreplay.

"Alright, Ranger. Let's show Noah what we've got." I click my tongue and then give him a little kick.

He sprints down and aims right for the first barrel. As soon as we round the second, I focus on my technique so he doesn't shoulder, and thankfully, he rounds it perfectly.

"Yes, *go go go!*" My legs bobble against him, but my boots manage to stay secure in the stirrups. We twist around the third barrel, slightly wider than I'd like but still in a good position to race home.

"Hustle, hustle!"

As soon as Landen calls time, I blow out a breath and pull on the reins to slow us down.

"Whew, such a good boy." I pat his neck.

When I turn us around toward Noah, she looks thrilled.

"Fifteen point nine five one," Landen announces. "Not bad. Lost two microseconds on that third barrel."

The way he says those words dampens my excitement.

"Yeah, we'll work on that," Noah says as I swing my leg off the saddle and jump down. "You rode nice and straight, though. Your breathing is gettin' better. I can tell your workouts are payin' off."

Workout is a pretty loose word for jogging and doing jumping jacks every morning, but I'm not admitting that.

"You should try singin'."

Landen's words grab Noah's and my attention. My brows furrow in confusion.

Once Ranger's tied up, I step closer. "Did you say *singing?*"

"It'll help you work on your breathwork while you run. You'll build up your stamina faster," he explains. "After a while, it'll feel effortless when you're racin'."

"You sure know a lot about stamina and breathwork..." I cross my arms, then raise a brow. "Or is it breath*play?*"

Landen winks, then licks his lips.

Gross.

"That's not a bad idea." Noah points at me, ignoring my comment to Landen. "Taylor Swift jogged for three and a half hours straight while singing to get ready for her tour. I bet it'd help with your nerves, too."

"And the calmer you are, the better Ranger will follow your lead and commands," Landen adds.

I blink in disbelief. "You want me to *sing* while jogging three miles?"

"Not like you have to be on key." Noah chuckles. "Go as long as you can and each day aim for a little longer."

"If it helps, I'll run alongside you." Landen smirks. "I'll sing backup."

No, thank you.

I narrow my eyes. "As temptin' as that is to have you stalk me on my runs, I'd much rather go solo."

"And if you need song ideas, her *Reputation* album will get you amped up." Noah smirks before grabbing her clipboard to record my race time. She's been keeping track of my progress and makes notes after each lesson.

When I glance at Landen, he's already grinning at me, and I mimic a faux one in return. "Good idea. I connect with her song 'Look What You Made Me Do' and could sing it on repeat."

Noah barks out a laugh. "Remind me to introduce you to my little cousin Mallory one of these days. She's eleven and obsessed with her music. She even named her horse Taylor Alison Swift and has all her lyrics memorized."

That makes me smile genuinely for the first time today. "She sounds like my kinda girl."

"Magnolia and I have slumber parties with Mallory one weekend a month and blast her music while we bake goodies and do facials. You'll have to join us sometime."

"That sounds fun," I say honestly, but it immediately brings me back to being Mallory's age and having scary movie night sleepovers with my older cousin. I haven't had one of those since she was taken away from me.

The happy memories with her are what helps me through the rough times when my mental health isn't at its best.

"Why am I never invited?" Landen's exaggerated gasp has me rolling my eyes.

"Because you're neither a woman nor a Taylor Swift fan," Noah informs him, then pats him on the shoulder. "I doubt it'd beat your nights out gettin' your clothes stolen by *unsatisfied* ladies."

Landen's jaw drops as if he hadn't expected his sister to call him out. She snickers as she walks away, leaving me alone with him *again*.

I stand in front of Landen and twist my arms behind my back. "Sulking. Your best look yet."

He leans down, imitating my stance. "Gloating...is not yours."

"Comical you think your opinion matters to me."

Landen's jaw clenches as he steps back. "Your attitude is gonna be a problem if you expect me to continue helpin' you."

"Correction, *you* have a problem with my attitude, and that is *your* problem, not mine. Also, I never asked for your help. Ranger and I would do just fine with Noah."

For the first time since he walked into the training session an hour ago and ruined my day, he lifts his backward baseball cap and scrubs his fingers through his thick brown hair.

I gulp at the intense way he keeps his gaze on me while he does it. Then he adjusts it back on his head and closes the gap between us, leaning down into my personal space.

"I'll see ya tomorrow mornin' at seven. Bring your runnin' shoes and have your singin' voice ready."

He walks off before I can tell him to his face he's lost his damn mind, but if Landen Hollis thinks he can continue barging into my life after my not-so-subtle hints of my hatred for him, I'm not going to make it easy for him to be around me.

In fact, he's going to wish we never met.

Chapter Four

LANDEN

PRESENT DAY
FOUR YEARS LATER

I wish I'd never met Ellie Donovan.

Lies.

Well, maybe not, depending on the day.

After years of knowing her, the woman is nothing but a complete mystery.

She's ruthless, unkind, and downright mean.

But only to me. She's halfway pleasant to everyone else.

And I haven't a single clue as to why.

Since the first day we got introduced, she's had it out for me although I was nothing but nice to her. Hell, I ran with her five days a week for three months. All while listening to her sing Taylor Swift songs and giving me the cold shoulder.

Not once during our runs did she speak to me or thank me for coming along in case she passed out or needed encouragement. She did make me hold her water bottle, though. And like the sap I am, handed it over every time she reached for it.

I was basically her butler running buddy. The only thing left would've been to bow at her feet and chant *Long Live the Queen*.

She qualified for the National Final Rodeo after her first full year and placed third after the ten-consecutive-day competition but didn't take home the win. Overall, I think it was a great experience for her after winning the Southeast regional championship. Once the next season started, she traveled on and off for ten months, but I went to a few with Noah to watch her race in the local pro rodeo circuit events.

She's now in her fourth year and training harder than ever to win first at this year's NFR. The past few years, she's consistently been in the top three but lost first place by mere microseconds. Since then, she's had more media press and sponsorship opportunities, which has only helped get her name out there more.

You can't walk through downtown without seeing an Ellie & Ranger poster or banner in the windows of several small businesses. Every little girl I see under the age of twelve wears a sparkly pink cowboy hat to support their favorite local barrel racer. So many damn reminders of her.

It's fucking torture.

I don't see her in person much, only in between competitions when she's here to train. Even when she's around, her dislike for me has never faded, which brings me to today.

Wishing I'd never met her.

Because even after all this time and her obvious hatred for me, my heart reacts the same every time I see her. And that pisses me the fuck off.

Even when she's somewhat nice, I'm instantly suspicious about it.

Last summer, I ran into her with one of her 4-H friends as they were walking out of Millie's Ice Cream Shoppe. I quickly stopped to say hi and the girl recognized me from the ranch, so after a few minutes of constant flirting, I asked her for her number.

Ellie smiled at Clara like she totally supported the idea, and she hadn't shot me any murderous glares, so I figured it was fine. We made plans for that following weekend, and since Ellie had a race, I ended up taking Clara to the rodeo with me.

We had a fun time and seemed to find things in common. But then, after Ellie's race, when we went to congratulate her on the win, she barely acknowledged her friend, or me—but that was normal—so it was easy to assume she didn't like that we came. Considering I was already on her shit list, I didn't want to get in between her and Clara, so I never asked her out on a second date.

The following weekend, I ended up drunk at the Twisted Bull and took some chick home. It wasn't my finest moment, and I felt like shit about it afterward. But then the next morning, still hungover, I walked out of my house to find a knife in my truck's tire. Every single one had been slashed.

I drove my dirt bike to the barn, and when Ellie saw the knife in my hand, her face split in two. Before I could even ask her about it, she *thanked* me for bringing it back to her. I was so shell-shocked that she openly admitted to doing it, I couldn't even form words to ask her what the hell her problem was or why she did it.

If it was for dating her friend or hooking up with someone else after not continuing to date her friend, I hadn't a fucking clue. She was confusing on a normal day.

53

But this really took the cake.

During Noah and Fisher's wedding, I asked her to dance, but she claimed to have broken her toe. I offered to bring her some ice and instead of using it, she left it on the table to melt. *Because there was no broken toe.*

I should get over her and escape the delusion that she'll someday feel the same or at the very least, give me a chance. It's clear there's a one-sided hatred situation going on between us. There's no reason I should be as infatuated with her as I am, and still, here I am—unable to get her out of my stupid head.

It also doesn't help that as I go through roping techniques with my new trainee, Antonio—a fifteen-year-old little shithead —who won't shut up about her. It's torturous enough seeing her around the ranch, but now I have to listen to him give me shit while he watches her practice.

"Goddamn, she snatched that."

"She's fire out there."

And then, whenever he catches me staring, he loves to put me in my place.

"Nah, you're too mid for her. You got no rizz."

"Stop simpin', bruh. You're too old for her."

I swear to God if he calls me *bruh* one more goddamn time...

Leave it to some punk teenager to humble me like I'm some creepy old man. I hate that at twenty-nine, I've turned into my dad, who can't understand the younger generation's slang.

In a lot of ways, he reminds me of Tucker's daring personality. It's probably why even though Antonio drives me up a wall sometimes, I can't help but want to push him to do his best. Tucker was smart and fearless, but it didn't come easy. He worked for everything he had.

"You think six years is that big of a deal?" I ask him, looking above his head to stare at Ellie, who's across the training center. "Because it's not."

When I look back at him, he's making a disgusted face. "Cringe."

"Wait till I tell you my sister's husband is twenty-two years older than her."

"Ew, gag. He could lowkey be her dad!"

I can't even conceal my laughter because if he only knew her husband is also her ex-boyfriend's dad. The whole thing is fucking hilarious to me. She dumped Jase and then three years later, made him her stepson. Oh, and a big brother.

"They just had a baby last year, too."

His jaw drops, and I laugh.

"I bet six years ain't lookin' so bad now, huh?"

He rolls his eyes and then continues practicing with the roping dummy. Although I manage the breeding operations, Noah *once again* talked me into signing up to help the local 4-H Club so they can participate in the fair's junior rodeo event the following weekend.

Ellie climbs on Ranger after setting up the barrels and runs a lap in front of us. Her blond hair is pulled back into braids underneath her cowboy hat. Although she usually leaves it down for the races, both looks are sexy as hell. She has this crazy curl to it when it's untamed. The polar opposite of her. Ellie wouldn't know how to let loose if her life depended on it.

"Hi, Ellie!" Antonio waves obnoxiously like the lovestruck teen boy he is.

"Hey, lookin' good over here." She slows down, flashing him one of her flirty smiles I've only ever seen a few times. Never at me, though. *Always for someone else.*

Antonio takes that as his cue to show off and whip his rope

in the air, nearly smacking me in the face in the process, and then throws it over the practice steer. He tightens up the slack and lets out a loud *yeehaw*.

Ellie's eyes brighten with pride. "So incredible! I can't wait to watch you win first place."

"No cap, you gonna come?" he asks with way too much enthusiasm.

"Of course!" She beams, adjusting her tank strap that fell down her shoulder. "I'm racin' there before I leave for the Franklin Rodeo. It's gonna be a fun time."

Antonio's smile widens. "Period."

"Well, good luck. I'm gonna do some drills with Ranger for a bit."

Antonio's so lovestruck, I swear I see drool on his chin.

She gives him a cute little finger wave before glancing at me. The high curve of her lips turns into a frown and her wide, bright eyes narrow into slits as soon as our gazes meet.

Just to further piss her off, I shout, "Nice seein' ya, Ellie!" Then I wink before she takes off to the other side of the building.

Antonio chuckles. "I don't think she's feelin' ya, bruh."

That's an understatement.

"Now who's giving cringe, *bruh*." I roll my eyes and then check the time. "You only have twenty minutes until you get picked up, so stay focused."

He shakes his head at me. "You're weak."

The fuck does that even mean?

As he continues practicing, I only manage to glance over at Ellie twice before Antonio's ride shows up. Watching her anytime she's here is an obsession I can't seem to kick. I probably look like a creep, standing and staring while she practices, but I'm mesmerized by her talent and how much she's excelled over the past few years. Although she hates it when I interrupt her lessons to give advice or tips, she usually applies them anyway and they end up helping her—which of course she hates because then that means I was right.

"Holy...motherfucking...shit."

My eyes scan over my phone screen as I reread the email attachment from Tucker's mom. We don't stay in contact much anymore, but we'll exchange hugs whenever we run into each other in town. I could tell seeing me only made her sadder because she used to call me her second son when Tucker was alive.

The letter she forwarded is from the attorney who helped Talia's family win their case in the wrongful death lawsuit. It states that Angela is scheduled for her parole hearing in a month and that due to her good behavior and getting a bachelor's degree in psychology, they may approve it. It sounds like she's going to play the *I'm a better person now* and the *I can help others based on my experience* cards.

I don't care if she shapeshifted into Jesus himself. She doesn't deserve to get out early. She never would if it were up to me.

Tucker's mom writes in the body of the email that Talia's family lawyer suggested that everyone who testified against Angela should write letters to the parole board on why she shouldn't be released early. Considering Tucker died after the trial, it only leaves five witnesses — me, Rhett, Addie, Warren, and Maisie. They deserve to know that she's technically responsible for two people's deaths and should stay behind bars to serve her full sentence.

I always knew there was a chance she could get parole, but I hadn't realized it'd already been eleven years.

Sometimes it still feels like yesterday when I dived into that cold water. I can still smell the fresh mountain air mixed with pine trees. For months after Talia's death, the crashing sounds of the waterfall haunted me in my dreams as I recalled every minute of that day. Losing Tucker made me spiral more than I wanted to admit. At the time, I couldn't see how much I was struggling. Nonstop partying, drinking to numb the pain, sleeping with women to *forget*.

It was a dangerous road I was on, but then I quickly realized I had to deal with the grief instead of pushing it to the side. When Tripp lost his best friend, Billy, during his senior year in high school, he became a shell of the person we knew and loved. I watched him put all his energy into work and instead of talking about it, he silently drowned in his guilt. It happened two years after we lost Talia, and I knew I had to manage my grief to help him get through his.

I didn't want him to go down the same wrong path I had.

After work, I take a shower and change into clean clothes, then form a group text with Warren, Rhett, and Addie. I talk to my cousin at least once a month, but I haven't spoken to Rhett and Addie in a couple years, though I see their life updates on social media. After they got married, they moved an hour south and now have three kids.

LANDEN

Did y'all get the email about Angela?

RHETT

We're reading it now.

ADDIE

Absolute bullshit! I'll be writing a letter and making sure they know everything about Angela and the type of person she is.

At Angela's criminal trial, we could only answer questions based on the incident and character witness testimonies when asked, but during the wrongful death lawsuit, we had the opportunity to speak out about our personal experiences with Talia and Angela.

Addie made a compelling testimony about Talia that had most people in tears. She spoke about her with such grace and kindness that even the jurors were fighting with their emotions. She expressed strong opinions about how Angela's actions weren't out of character based on the several years of knowing her, so I have no doubt she won't hold anything back on expressing her thoughts on keeping Angela behind bars.

LANDEN

Me too. Changed or not, she deserves to serve her full sentence.

My testimony focused on the emotional abuse that revolved around our past relationship, including how she wasn't even

59

invited on the trip but always manipulated people to get what she wanted. I mentioned how her lack of self-awareness hurt everyone around her. And now, I'll include the repercussions of her actions that led to Tucker's suicide.

He was so distraught that he could hardly speak at both trials. Looking back, I wish I'd been able to be there for him more. He shut down, and I thought I was doing the right thing by giving him space to grieve. It's been nine years since we lost him, but I can still hear his rowdy laughter in my head.

WARREN

Just read it. I'll do whatever I can to help!

Since Warren didn't know Angela nor Talia very well, just from the few times they hung out during our spring breaks, his testimony focused on what he witnessed and Angela's lack of remorse after the incident.

Warren and Maisie got married once she graduated from college in New York City, but when she got a job at a Big Five publisher, she moved back there. Warren didn't want to leave his hometown and she didn't want to sacrifice her career. He doesn't talk about her or everything that he went through, but I know it fucked him up. I'm not even sure he's dated since then because his only focus has been on his family's ranch and resort.

LANDEN

Maybe we should get together and write a joint statement for either outcome. You know as soon as news about it gets out, journalists will come looking for our comments.

RHETT

Not a bad idea. Plus, it's been too long since we've hung out.

ADDIE

Agreed!

WARREN

You know y'all are always welcome up here.

RHETT

We'd love to come! Let us check our schedules and we'll get back to ya.

WARREN

Sounds good!

LANDEN

I'll make time to come up whenever y'all are available.

After our text convo ends, I text our sibling group chat and update them.

WILDER

Want me to seduce the parole board members? It'd be a hardship, but I'd do it for the cause.

I roll my eyes and shake my head. Give it to Wilder to make it weird.

WAYLON

We better start saving up for his bail now.

WILDER

Huh, why?

TRIPP

Google is free, man.

NOAH

Do you even know who parole board members are made up of?

WILDER

Uh...hold on.

LANDEN

Anyway...while he utilizes the internet, I'm probably gonna make a trip up to Willow Branch Mountain in a month or two. If anyone wants to catch a ride with me, let me know so I can tell Warren to book us a cabin.

With Warren being the oldest of his siblings, he took over a lot of the management duties for the ranch and resort. My aunt and uncle still stay plenty busy with other tasks, but as their kids get older, they get more responsibilities and will eventually take over when the parents retire.

WILDER

Hell yeah! Count me in.

NOAH

Depends. This is my busiest time for traveling to rodeos with clients and training. I'll have to check with Fisher, too. But I'd love to go if I can.

TRIPP

Yeah, I'll have to ask Magnolia if she wants to get a sitter for Willow or take her with us.

NOAH

Take her with you so Poppy has a friend!

It's funny enough that Noah and Magnolia have been best friends since they were in elementary school, but then Magnolia started dating Tripp a year and a half ago. Shortly after, she found out she was pregnant with her ex's baby. Noah announced her pregnancy at the same time and they ended up giving birth on the same day. The babies are only ten months old, so I laugh at Noah trying to push Tripp to bring along an infant to a couple's resort.

Although Willow isn't Tripp's biological daughter, he loves her just the same. Magnolia tried to give Tripp an out to walk away, but he was determined to stay and be there for both of them. I'm glad they finally got together after all the years of back and forth. I've never seen Tripp as happy as when he became a dad and husband.

I hope to have that someday, too.

Ever since meeting Ellie four years ago, my dating life has been nearly nonexistent, except for a drunken time or two, so the chances of me getting married and having kids anytime soon aren't likely.

But I'm still not ready to give up.

TRIPP

You wanna take her overnight so I can get my wife alone for once?

NOAH

We'll see.

WILDER

Wait a damn minute…the parole board members are all old people from various white-collar jobs?

TRIPP

Congrats on figuring it out.

WILDER

Well good thing old ladies love me!

WAYLON

Love or tolerate?

NOAH

I'd pay big money to see you try.

LANDEN

Don't encourage him...he doesn't need any more incentives.

WILDER

About to go on a deep dive to find out who their granddaughters are...I'm sure I can work my magic somewhere.

TRIPP

That sounds like a threat...should we warn them first?

NOAH

How about no one commits a felony trying to alter their decision and we just let the justice system do its job?

LANDEN

Assuming they do this time...

Yeah, I guess after eleven years, I'm still bitter.

Angela deserved way more prison time. I'll never be satisfied knowing she's the reason Talia and Tucker are dead and she won't be rotting in a cell for the rest of her pathetic life.

Chapter Five

ELLIE

If there's one thing I thrive on, it's routine—waking up at six a.m., jogging on the trails by seven, and then heading to the stables to groom and work on Ranger's techniques before running drills and practice runs. By noon, Noah meets me at the training center to watch my progress and give any critiques. If it's a weekend race, I pack the day before and then get Ranger ready for travel.

I'm in bed by nine p.m. every night.

Wash, rinse, repeat.

No social life included to get where I am and where I want to go.

This is what I worked hard for and won't take any of it for granted.

My parents pay my way and most of my earnings go right back into it, minus the amount I put into a savings account.

Barrel racing is an expensive hobby. Even at the career level, you're still hardly breaking even when you consider the training and boarding costs, maintenance and upkeep of your horse, traveling expenses, and rodeo fees. I'm lucky to have a mom and dad who support me in doing what I love. Focusing on this helps keep me out of my depression cycles, and I enjoy doing it, so it's a win-win.

After almost four years of pro rodeo, I have things down to a T on what helps me prepare for each event. I'm strict with my schedule and workouts, and I stay on top of my training and Ranger's health, as well as my own. It takes a lot of time and energy to practice each day.

But if there's one thing—or rather, *person*—guaranteed to mess up my day, it's Landen Hollis.

During my first year of training with Noah, he'd show up a few times a week to watch me and whisper to Noah about what I was screwing up. Then she'd agree and tell me how to fix it using his suggestions.

The bastard's smug smirk after seeing it work is what drove me to hate him even more.

The next few years after that, he'd pop in and out while I trained. Sometimes he'd silently watch while I pretended his presence didn't affect me and other times he'd make himself known by giving unsolicited advice.

Today of all days, I find him in Ranger's stall, petting and murmuring to him after I actively ignored his presence yesterday in the training center when he was with Antonio.

"What're you doin' in here?" I snap, causing him to jump and whip around so quickly, his cowboy hat falls off.

He doesn't wear it often, usually only during hot, sunny days when he plans to be outside for hours and wants to prevent a sunburn.

I hate how much I like it on him.

Once he's picked it up, he looks at me. "Goddamn, you need a bell 'round your neck so you can't just sneak up on people."

"You're not supposed to be in his stall," I say, opening the door and wedging myself inside.

He steps toward me, caging us closer together. Well, fuck, this was a bad idea.

"You're aware I work here, right? Cleanin' and feedin' are all in my job description."

I snarl at his mocking tone. "Don't pull that shit with me. The stables ain't your responsibility."

He manages the breeding operations, across the ranch, which is the biggest perk of being at the stables. He rarely needs to be in here.

His arms twist behind his back as he tilts his head in a cocky gesture. "I'm so glad you know more about my duties than I do, but today, I'm takin' over for Ruby. She's got the flu."

Well, shit.

Thanks a lot, Ruby.

"You must not be doing a good job, then. She's usually done with Ranger's stall by now," I respond smugly, mocking his posture.

Landen steps back, giving me much-needed space to finally breathe, and then waves out his hand. "Let me give you the tour, Miss Donovan. There's fresh straw on the ground, his water bucket is full, he ate his breakfast of hay and grains, and I even lunged him in the corral afterward. I was just finishing up groomin' him for you."

I'm right on time, so I don't know how he managed to do all of that before eight a.m.

"I lunge him every mornin'," I counter. "And groom him afterward."

The corner of his lips tilts up slightly. "Now ya don't have to. He's ready for whatever you need to do today."

I grind my molars, annoyed he's taken an hour out of my schedule without even asking. Most would be grateful for it, but this is Ranger's and my quality time each day. Bonding is important before we go into work mode. It helps maintain our relationship and trust.

It's our routine.

"He's used to doing things at certain times. You've screwed everything up."

"He is or *you* are?" He arches a brow, pursing his lips. "I think the words you're lookin' for are *thank you*. So you're welcome, *Little Devil*. Now you have an extra hour to train or maybe go to The Lodge and have some breakfast."

The retreat's main building is where guests check in or sign up for activities. They offer a full buffet for all three meals that extends to staff members, too. I've been told I'm free to help myself to it, but I've never been a big breakfast eater. I'll have yogurt, toast, or drink a protein shake before I leave the house. Anything more than that, and I'll feel nauseous while I'm jogging or riding.

I pop my hip, cross my arms, and then glare at him. "Let me guess, you're going there to eat now?"

His smirk deepens as if he's not surprised I drew that conclusion. "I could. Wanna carpool on my dirt bike? You can sit in my lap."

Rolling my eyes at his lame attempt to get me to go, I push around him to get closer to Ranger.

"No. You're not supposed to drive that 'round the horses, anyway."

"As long as I don't rev the engine near the trainin' center, it's fine."

"Well, either way, my answer is no." I put my back to him as I grab a brush and begin at Ranger's neck.

His arm rubs against my shoulder before I hear the click of the stall lock and a few knuckle taps across the wood. "If you change your mind, I have an extra helmet."

"Hard pass to smashin' my brains across the pavement," I retort.

He bellows out a laugh. "Says the woman who literally risks her life each day being a barrel racer, but yeah, sure, better not risk ridin' on a dirt bike *with* a helmet. God forbid you actually take the stick outta your ass and have some fun."

My jaw drops, and I whip around toward him, but he's already walking away.

God, I hate him.

I arrive home at exactly a quarter after four. The fifteen-minute drive from the ranch gives me just enough time to process my day.

After my lessons with Noah, I gave Ranger a break while I ate lunch in my truck. Sometimes I'll take a walk and find a place to sit and eat, but today I wasn't up for it. Afterward, I took Ranger on a trail ride where I focused on balance and letting him guide me without holding the reins. To reduce the risk of injury or hoof issues, I only take him on one in particular that weaves around the retreat pond. With the heavy horse-riding traffic, the ground is mostly flat, which leaves the trail wide open. We'll usually run into Wilder and Waylon, who lead the trail rides for the retreat guests and stop to give quick hellos while their group passes.

Ranger and I ended the day with a final hour of technique practice and lunging before I groomed him one last time. He's due to see Fisher—Noah's husband and the ranch's farrier—to get new shoes and his hooves trimmed. It's a six-hour drive, so I'll bring the horse trailer with living quarters so we can stay overnight.

My parents take turns traveling with me on my weekend trips since my aunt Phoebe lives with us and can't be left alone for long periods at a time. My grandma comes over if they both have to leave the house for a few hours, but otherwise, either my parents or I are home with her.

Aunt Phoebe experienced a psychotic break a decade ago after going through back-to-back traumatic events and hasn't been able to safely live on her own. She struggled with her mental health before everything happened, but then after, she resorted to self-harming. When her mind escapes reality, she sees or hears things that aren't real and gets confused easily. She went into treatment after her husband left. Since she's my mom's sister, Mom wanted her home with us where we could shower her with love and make sure she continued getting care.

She still gets medical help and biweekly therapy sessions, but witnessing how much she's changed from the Aunt Phoebe I knew as a child is a constant reminder of what happened to our family.

It's not fair how one event or person can ruin lives and change ours forever.

"Hi, sweetie. How was your day?" Mom beams as soon as I walk through the door, the aromas of pepper and sausage hitting my nose.

She's at the stove, preparing dinner, right on time.

I shrug, removing my boots, and then set them on the mat. "Ranger was off his game today."

More like Landen screwed up our routine.

"Sorry to hear that. Horses can have bad days just like humans. I'm sure he'll be better tomorrow." She smiles at me over her shoulder as she continues stirring country gravy, a family favorite.

"I hope so. Are you or Dad comin' with me this weekend?" I ask, walking to the sink to wash my hands so I can set the table.

"I can't, sweetie. I'm sorry. Aunt Phoebe is havin' withdrawal symptoms since her doctor changed one of her prescriptions and it's makin' her go to the bathroom every hour. She won't want me to leave."

"Okay, no problem. I'm sure Dad will record every second of it for you, anyway." I grin at how supportive he's been throughout the years. He's always in the front row with his phone out and cheering with the crowd. My family owns the local feed mill store and Dad starts his day at five a.m. each day to be home in the evenings and have off on the weekends.

Once I've placed the plates, glasses, and silverware on the table, I walk into the living room where Dad and Aunt Phoebe are watching *Seinfeld*. It's her favorite sitcom and she watches two episodes every day between four and five p.m. After the final episode, the four of us will sit at the table and eat together.

"Hi, Daddy." I kiss his cheek and he smiles.

"Hi, sweetheart. How was your day?"

"It was alright. Yours?" I ask, not wanting to go into the details about mine.

"Great. My new employee asked 'boutcha today. He wants to know if he can get your number."

My nose scrunches in confusion. "How's he know what I look like?"

The corner of his mouth curves up. "I only have my office covered in your photos."

I shake my head in embarrassment because I know exactly what he's talking about. Pictures of me with Ranger, us racing, my professional headshots, and our family photos paint his walls.

"And lemme guess, you told him I'm single?"

"Well, ya are, ain't ya?"

"No, I'm in a long-term relationship with my career." I snicker, then move around him to hug Aunt Phoebe.

"Aren't you even gonna ask if he's a cutie?" she asks when my arms wrap around her.

I pull back, scowling. "Whose side are you on?"

"The one where you get a life outside of racin'."

Rolling my eyes, I stand between them and cross my arms. "Fine. Is he cute?"

I'm only asking to appease them because they constantly give me a hard time for being so focused on work.

"I'd say he's of the attractive sort. He's a little shorter than me, has that shaggy blond hair thing goin' on where he shakes it out of his eyes every three seconds, and is on the lean side, but he's strong. Gotta be to lift the hundred-pound bags of feed. Oh, and he's an Aries. Whatever that means."

"Great, so he's a teenage version of Justin Bieber whose Zodiac weakness is insecurity and he needs a haircut."

Aunt Phoebe belly laughs at the image I painted. "Could be your future husband?"

"Hard pass," I tell them and then walk back to the kitchen.

As Mom takes the biscuits out of the oven, I grab the sweet tea from the fridge and then fill my glass.

"You know, Gage is a nice young boy. You should give him a chance."

My brows furrow. "Who's Gage?"

She waves a hand toward my dad. "The astrology-lover pop star lookalike."

"Ugh. Not you too." I take a long gulp of my drink. "When do I have time to date anyway?"

Almost every part of my day is scheduled. That's how I learned to process everything when my life flipped upside down and staying consistent is how I hit my goals, so it's a win-win. Working hard, staying focused, winning races. That's my focus.

Men are a distraction. And from my experience with Landen each day, annoying too.

"You could make time, Ellie. You're gorgeous, talented, smart, and you'd have a lot to offer in a relationship if you put in some effort to find someone."

"You act like I'm forty-five not twenty-three. I still have time for all that."

"Forty-five ain't that far away."

"Mom!"

She laughs. "I'm just sayin'. You've been barrel racin' for a long time. It's okay to add in other hobbies and make friends. Otherwise, you're gonna end up old and alone."

"I have friends." I snag one of the biscuits and take a harsh bite, nearly burning my tongue. "And I can't have other *hobbies* if I wanna win first at nationals. I can't afford to slow down when I've been so close."

"You will, sweetie. But it wouldn't hurt for you to have a life outside of racin'." Mom pats my shoulder with a sincere smile. "And I'd like to meet these *friends* of yours."

"You've met Noah."

73

"Someone we ain't payin'." She gives me a challenging look. Holding up my hand, I count on my fingers. "Magnolia. Mallory. Fisher. Wilder. Waylon. Ayden. Tripp. Ruby."

Over the past four years, I've become friendly with most of the people who live and work on the ranch. Magnolia owns a mobile coffee business and whenever she's parked at the retreat, I always swing by for a latte and chat.

Fisher helped treat Ranger when a nail got stuck in his hoof a few years ago, but I still see him around, too.

Ayden and Ruby work in the stables, so I see them almost every day. Ayden's married with two kids. Ruby's been with her boyfriend for years but constantly reminds us they're not engaged. Trey moved to Georgia with his high school sweetheart over a year ago, but when he was here, I'd wave and say hello.

Mallory's fifteen and loves to talk my ear off about Taylor Swift and the latest boy she's crushing on. Usually ones with a J name, and I warn her to run far away from them.

And the other Hollis siblings, *excluding* Landen, I'm nice to them anytime I see them.

So if that's not having friends, then I don't know what is. We may not hang out and talk about pop culture or who's sleeping with who, but being social doesn't come easy to me. Small talk makes me uncomfortable, but I still attempt it so people don't think I'm being rude or ignoring them.

Mom tilts her head. "All from the ranch. And talkin' to 'em in passing doesn't count. You need to have actual conversations outside of work. Go to a bar like a normal twenty-something woman. Have some drinks and dance. Not every aspect of your life has to be structured."

Sighing, I drop my arm and blow out a frustrated breath. This isn't the first time she's lectured me about not having a social life, and I'm willing to bet it won't be the last, so I give in so she'll drop it.

"*Fine*. I'll make plans if it means you'll leave me alone about becoming an old horsewoman."

She laughs softly, and I take that as confirmation of a deal.

"*Seinfeld*'s over. Dinnertime." Aunt Phoebe comes in and sits in her spot across from mine. Before I take my seat, I help Mom bring the food to the table and then we all hold hands and say grace. It's Wednesday, which means it's breakfast for dinner—biscuits and gravy with a side of scrambled eggs.

We eat until five-thirty, Mom serves homemade Apple Pie à la Mode for dessert, and then by six, I'm loading the dishwasher and wiping down the counters. Tonight's laundry night, so I can pack tomorrow for this weekend's race, and then, like clockwork, I'll shower, get ready for bed, and read for an hour before I fall asleep by ten.

Routine. It's the only way I know how to function after my mental state tanked, and I lost the one person in my life who meant more to me than anything.

Chapter Six
LANDEN

As I watch one of our stallions attempt to mate with one of the many mares we board during breeding season, I find amusement in how watching them have sex is my job.

Ranchers from around the state bring us their horses, I make sure they get pregnant, and then once the season is over, we send them home to deliver their babies.

At the moment, Rocky's in the pasture with Maggie Mae, getting more action than I've had in the past two years.

When I'm not witnessing horses getting it on, I'm hooking up our stallions to a breeding mount, inserting their massive dicks into an artificial vagina, and collecting their sperm. It's another option for ranchers to impregnate their mares without bringing them to a stud farm. Afterward, we send the semen for evaluation and processing before it's shipped out.

So every day, I watch. I ensure the mares get pregnant to keep up our ninety-nine percent success rate.

Worst part? I signed up for this voluntarily.

My siblings love to give me shit for it, too. Wilder started sending me live webcam streams as a joke, but the joke was on him because who was I to say no to watching pretty girls? And because my brothers can't keep their mouths shut, word got out about it. Not only that, I asked Tripp *one* manscape question and Magnolia, having no boundaries with their phones, saw various angles of my dick.

That was the last time I reached out for help.

After my morning chores of mucking stalls and feeding, I walk over to the retreat to grab a coffee from Magnolia's Morning Mocha. She parks her mobile coffee trailer at the retreat twice a week and before she was Tripp's wife, we were close friends. I'd say we still are, but now she's busy juggling her business and family.

I love that for her and my brother, but it makes me feel more alone than ever.

When I arrive at her spot, I notice Ellie in line and stand behind her.

"You should try the Maple Me Crazy latte," I say, hovering above her ear.

She quickly whips around, steps back, and glares. "Why?"

"Try something new. You always get the same thing." I shove my hands in my pockets, flashing her a boyish grin even though she looks ready to knee me between the legs. She doesn't even give me credit for memorizing her coffee order. "Plus, it'd suit you better since you're always makin' *me* crazy."

She crosses her arms, standing fully in front of me now. "Was that another one of your lines? You'd think a playboy like yourself would have better ones, honestly. Your game must be off."

"If you must know, I don't have to give out *lines*. I'm also not what you claim I am. Haven't been out on a date in months."

At least over a year. But no need to look even more pathetic.

"Guess I'm right then."

"You're not."

"Prove it."

I scoff, lying through my teeth. "My game is fine."

"Says the guy who just admitted he hasn't had a date in months."

"When's the last time you've gone on one?" I counter, not wanting the answer. Though if I had to guess, it's been even longer than me. She's too obsessed with her career to give up time for anything else.

She twists a strand of her hair, wrapping it behind her ear over and over, one of her signs that she's frustrated. "None of your business."

"Even more of a reason you should go out with me." I pop a brow, hoping she'll take the bait. "We could both use the practice."

Instead of agreeing, she snorts and laughs. "It'll be an *icy, cold day* in hell before I sink that low. In fact, someone better sedate me if that day ever comes."

Smacking a hand over my heart, I act crushed. "You wound me, Little Devil."

Her glare deepens at the unwanted nickname, but I swear I see her eyes light up, too. Just like how I catch her checking me out when she doesn't think I'm paying attention.

"Aww. Poor baby."

I can't help smirking at her taunting tone. "*Baby*? Wait, are we fightin' or flirtin'?"

She pretends not to like me. To hate the attention I give her.

But the fire in her eyes anytime I'm near tells me otherwise.

She doesn't even dignify me with a response before she spins back around toward Magnolia.

"Ellie, hi!" She beams when Ellie approaches.

"Hey. Love your haircut."

I can't help but scoff and roll my eyes at their exchange. Of course Ellie's nice to her.

"Thank you! Willow wouldn't stop yankin' on it, so it was time for a change." Magnolia twirls a piece of her hair that's closer to her shoulders than before.

My niece is attached to her back in a baby carrier, peeking over Magnolia's shoulder. Instead of waiting in line, I help myself to the inside of the trailer and tickle her little feet.

"Are you helpin' your mama today?" I ask Willow. "How dare she wear you like a backpack."

She giggles as I blow raspberries on her cheek. I know my mom usually watches Willow when Magnolia works, but she must not have been available today.

"Landen Michael," Magnolia scolds, pushing me back. "You're too big to be in here with us."

"Or maybe your trailer's too small."

"Either way, I can't maneuver around you." She tries to hip-check me to grab a cup, but it's hardly a push. I step back anyway to give her room.

"You didn't mind when I was in here playin' your bodyguard and shot a man to save your life," I muse, crossing my arms, and yeah, I made a point of saying that loudly in front of Ellie.

Last spring, when she was five months pregnant, her ex and his dealer were after her. Since she couldn't avoid working, Tripp stayed with her during every shift up to the last thirty minutes so he could make his shift at The Lodge on time. For that half an hour, I stayed with her until she closed. But then the dealer found her location before the police could find him. The day he showed up, Magnolia was on her hands and knees looking for something underneath the counter, so he hadn't seen her when he approached the trailer. When he waved his gun at me, demanding I tell him her location, I pulled out my own gun tucked in the back of my jeans and shot him in the dick.

I hadn't meant to aim that low, but it was a happy accident. The guy got what he deserved and then went to prison for murdering Magnolia's ex.

Sugarland Creek labeled me the town hero—which I happily accepted—but Ellie hadn't seemed to care. *Nothing* impresses her.

Magnolia glowers at me. "How long are ya gonna keep bringin' that up?"

"Till the day I die, baby!" I drawl, stealing a glance at Ellie, who's looking down at her phone, and then she fucking *yawns*.

Goddammit.

"*Out!*" Magnolia shoves at me.

"I can't spend a few minutes with my niece?"

"Not when I'm workin'. You wanna see her, walk down twenty steps and come babysit."

She and Tripp live below me in the ranch hand quarter duplexes, but with our schedules, we only see each other in passing or at Sunday supper.

"Fine, I will tonight. Now make my drink." I smirk.

"Get in line and I *will...*" she says between gritted teeth, looking toward Ellie, who looks annoyed at me for interrupting. And now there are two more people behind her, waiting.

Well, that didn't go as planned.

She gives me her *you're an idiot* expression.

Before I walk out, I kiss Willow's cheek and then like a dog with its tail between its legs, I go to the back of the line.

Every Sunday night, my parents, siblings, and I get together for supper and scrapbooking. It's been a tradition for years and even though I'm not a huge fan of decorating a page filled with photos, I get sucked into staying anyway. I don't mind it, though, since Gramma Grace bakes the best desserts.

Now that two of my siblings are married with a baby, we sit at two tables to accommodate everyone, which means there's more shouting but also a lot more laughing. It's always a good time.

"Why're you sittin' so close to me?" Mallory scoffs, elbowing my arm.

"Why're *you* sitting so close to *me*?" I elbow her back and though I know it's childish, it's too easy to annoy a fifteen-year-old. "Better be nice if you want me to teach you to drive."

Noah shrieks from the other table. "You think outta all of us, she'd pick you to teach her?"

"Have you seen my pickup? It's badass!" I shout above other conversations.

Tripp helped me restore a 1970 Chevy C10 and we only finished it six months ago. I only drive it around town or on the backroads during sunlight to reduce any risk of getting into an accident or hitting a deer. I utilize my beat-up Ford or dirt bike to get around the ranch instead.

"You'd lemme drive it?" Mallory pipes up.

I give her a pointed look. "Only if you're nice to me."

She scowls. "All the time or just when we're drivin'?"

Noah chuckles, and I shoot her daggers from my seat.

"Why do chicks get a kick outta being rude to me? Do I have a sign on my forehead that says *I hate puppies* or somethin'?" At least that'd be a valid reason.

"Well, that just means they like ya," Gramma Grace says, passing out slices of her strawberry cheesecake.

"Nah, I don't think so. Ellie would stab me in the eyeball, twist the knife a dozen times, and then stab my other eye without a second thought."

"Thanks for the visual..." Mallory slides her dessert plate away from her.

"I'm sure there are plenty of single ladies who'd love to date you," Mom says.

Great, now we're going to discuss my dating life.

"My friend's mom is single," Mallory says.

I glower at her. "Just how old do ya think I am?"

She shrugs. "I dunno. Some men like older women."

"Cougar hunters! That's what they're called," Wilder explains. "Wouldn't mind findin' me a cougar."

"*Wilder*," Dad echoes his name, gives him a firm look, and then Wilder bows his head to focus on his cheesecake.

"Anyway...subject change. When are y'all havin' another baby, Fisher?"

His head pops up, clearly trying to stay out of the conversation.

"We just had one last year!" Noah exclaims. "You boys are up next."

"I wouldn't mind more grandchildren." Mom smiles as she holds Poppy, sneaking a dollop of cream cheese in her mouth.

"Just wait for the next cougar to be desperate enough for Wilder and he'll knock her up in no time," Waylon says.

"*Waylon,*" Dad mutters his name, and I swear to God, they're the reason he's going bald.

"Would you rather I date someone twenty years younger than me?" Wilder asks.

Again, Fisher looks up as if he's trying desperately to stay out of it.

"Ew, that'd be gross!" Mallory makes a face.

I snort. "And illegal."

Once everyone finishes eating, Mom and Noah bring out tubs filled with scrapbooks and supplies. I've been working on one of the family albums that Mom put me in charge of and thankfully, I'm almost done.

"Aww, look, Mallory when she was cute and sweet," I taunt, holding up one of the pages. It was our first professional family shoot after Mallory moved in with us.

Her parents died in a car accident when she was nine and then she was sent to us. She's been like a little annoying sister ever since. But I love her. I can't imagine what it'd be like to lose your parents at such a young age and then be taken from the only home you've ever known and thrown into another.

She's been a great addition to our family, though.

She scowls. "Are you sayin' I'm not anymore?"

"I'm sayin'...now you're a little less sweet." I smirk, nudging her with my elbow again.

"You try being a young woman in a patriarchal world, who is less valued than a man simply because I have a vagina and see how *sweet* you are. Next, you'll be tellin' me to smile more."

"Only if he wants a knee to his balls," Magnolia says.

He does not.

"Alexa, play 'The Man' by Taylor Swift," Noah says with a

laugh, and within seconds, the song echoes throughout the house.

"Of course," I mutter, shaking my head. It's bad enough I had to listen to Ellie sing it during our jogs, but now my entire family is humming along.

"Can't deny it's a bop, though." Wilder dances in his seat.

I throw a roll of washi tape toward him, and he laughs.

"It's usually me pissin' them off, so this is a nice change of pace," he taunts.

Noah snorts. "Don't worry, it's only Sunday. You still got all week to do that."

Chapter Seven

ELLIE

After successfully dominating in my division this weekend, I'm back at the stables to put Ranger in his stall for the evening. Dad and I stayed at the rodeo a little longer to watch the other events and indulge in their fried foods, but then we ran into his new employee, Gage. Dad invited him to hang out with us for the rest of the evening, which ended up being awkward and annoying. It was nice to spend some extra time with Dad, especially since I'll be traveling nonstop starting next weekend, and I'll be going alone for those since Dad works and Mom stays home with Aunt Phoebe.

"Such a good boy," I coo, sliding a brush across his back.

"Thank you."

My heart drops to the floor at the familiar voice behind me. Of course he'd be here.

When I turn to face him, I'm greeted with his infamous smug grin and tilted cowboy hat.

"Oh, wait, were you not talkin' to me?" He points to himself. "Damn. Thought you figured out my secret kink."

"Why do you make it a habit to bother me every chance you get? Have I not been clear that I don't like you or are you just a masochist who gets off on that? Do you need me to tattoo it on your forehead? Get a plane to write it in the sky, perhaps? Can you even read? Because I know you don't listen…"

"All I'm hearin' is how much effort you're willin' to put in to get my attention, Little Devil." He rocks back on his boots like the cocky asshole he is. "But you can have it whenever you want if you say *please*."

"Selective hearing…makes sense now." I roll my eyes and then turn back to Ranger, who actually deserves my focus.

"After four years, you still won't tell me what your problem with me is. Most people woulda by now, which is why I think you don't have a valid reason not to like me."

"I don't have to tell you a damn thing."

"But why not? Since the first day we met, you decided I was the bad guy, and I hadn't even done anything."

"My gut told me you were and it's never wrong. And, well, look how insufferable you've been since then. Guess it was right."

"Most women—"

My blood boils as I whip around with the brush in my hand, eager to throw it at him. "I'm not most women! I will not bow at your feet or pass out at your mere presence." As I raise my voice at him, my breath comes out in short pants. "No, this ain't me playin' hard to get. I have my reasons, but I do not have to share them with you." My jaw clenches before I add, "And *stop* calling me that."

He blinks blankly before slowly licking his lips as if he's fighting back his amusement. "I was gonna say before you rudely interrupted me…most women would love the chance to tell a man why they hate them so much, which is why it's so confusin' to me that you don't."

Swallowing hard, I lower my hand and straighten my spine. "I'm not interested in any conversation with you, even ones that involve crucifying you, and being forced to speak to you in any regard is pure torture for me!"

Wincing at my harsh words, he steps back slightly as if my verbal assault affected him physically. If that's the case, then good, I don't feel bad about it. And I won't apologize for speaking up about the boundaries he's often crossed.

It's bad enough Gage wouldn't leave me alone about getting my phone number. I don't need to come to my safe place and get hit on by another man who doesn't take no for an answer.

"Okay. You're right, and I apologize." He tips his hat. "I will never bother you again, Ellie."

He walks away, and I stare at his back, feeling only an ounce of guilt for being so harsh. I've told him off plenty of times over the years, but I've never mentioned that it was *torture*. It's not a lie, though. Just seeing him amps up my heart rate, makes my palms sweat, and fuels the rage inside that I've kept to myself.

I *could* tell him. Reveal what connects us and where my hatred stems from, but not only would it risk my relationship with Noah if she knew, I'd have to hear his side of the story.

And I'm not interested in that.

Since my mother insists I have a life outside of racing, I made plans to meet Noah and Magnolia at The Lodge for lunch today. We've been on friendly terms since the day I started coming here, but we've never really hung out or talked outside of work. And although it's not much, it's a start. Socializing is outside my comfort zone, so starting with this seemed the least likely way to induce an anxiety attack.

When I walk in, a dozen guests and all five Hollis siblings greet me.

Crap. I was hoping he wouldn't be here.

He doesn't look up at me, though, when Noah calls my name, but his brothers do.

"Hey, haven't seen you in here before," Wilder says.

I shrug, not liking the attention on me. "Figured I'd come to see what all the fuss is about."

"You came on a good day. It's broccoli cheese soup day!" Waylon smirks.

Noah stands and comes around to hug me. "You can eat whatever you want. Soup and salad bar over there, hot food in the middle, and all the pastries you can eat at the end."

"Sounds great, thanks."

Once I've grabbed a plate, Magnolia meets me at the salad bar. "Just between you and me, the Italian dressin' is the best you'll ever have. But don't tell the guys I told you or they'll take all of it."

I chuckle at this random piece of information. "Got it, thanks."

When I walk back to the tables with my beef tips and side salad, I sit between Noah and Magnolia and thank them for saving me a seat. Ruby's across from me, shoving a large forkful in her mouth.

"So are you excited about the Franklin Rodeo?" she asks,

still chewing. "I wish I could get off to come watch ya…" She shifts her glare toward Noah.

"Don't be lookin' at me. Ayden makes your schedule, not me."

"You could put a good word in for me so I could go for once. I'd love to watch Ellie smoke everyone."

Smiling at the nice comment, I take my first bite and am pleasantly surprised at how good it is.

Reluctantly, my gaze finds Landen, whose head is aimed down and only looking up when someone talks to him. I listen to his brothers chat while Noah, Magnolia, and Ruby discuss the upcoming local fair. That's my next race before I head to Franklin for a three-day rodeo event and then will drive west for a few weeks to compete in more.

"Fine, I'll see what I can do," Noah concedes. "But no promises."

"I'll take her shift," Landen speaks up, his eyes finding mine before moving to Noah's.

The entire Hollis family always goes to the Franklin Rodeo, so one of them staying behind would be a big deal.

"Yes!" Ruby cheers at the same time Noah says, "Nice try. You ain't gettin' out of volunteering at the Cantina lounge again."

"No, wait. I can do it. Servin' beer to hot cowboys? Count me in." Ruby smirks with a head nod.

"Have you ever bartended before?" Noah asks.

Ruby's shoulders fall. "Well, no. Does that matter, though?"

Noah gives her a sympathetic frown, nodding. "The ranch is a sponsor, so they expect the people we send to know what they're doing."

I hold back my amusement because I've heard the story of how Noah and Fisher met there three years ago—during the barrel racing event, no less—and she invited him to meet her there that night. Pretty sure they hooked up and when she figured out he was her ex-boyfriend's dad the next morning, she left and ghosted him. It wasn't until he arrived at the ranch a week later as the new farrier that they both realized their connections to each other.

Ruby sighs. "How hard can it be?"

"Why do you think we're always tryna get out of it?" Waylon snickers.

Ruby stretches her arm out, gesturing toward him. "See? I bet I'm a better bartender than him!"

Their back and forth causes me to laugh mid-chew, but when I swallow, a piece of meat gets stuck in my throat. I try clearing it and even take a sip of water, but it doesn't budge. I try not to panic as I stretch my neck and massage my esophagus. It moves slightly but not enough to go down.

"Are you okay?" Noah asks beside me.

Unable to speak, I shake my head and clutch my throat. I gag as the air is restricted from my lungs, and when I try to cough, nothing happens.

"Holy shit, she's choking!" Noah smacks my back as commotion swirls around me.

Landen's chair falls to the floor as he stands. Then he rushes around the table, pulls me to my feet, and wraps his arms around my waist.

I barely have time to process him giving me the Heimlich maneuver before the piece of meat flies out of my mouth, and I can finally suck in a deep breath.

"Oh my gosh, Ellie!" Magnolia stands next to me, rubbing a hand down my arm that's covered in goose bumps. To which I won't admit are from Landen touching me. "That was close."

When he steadies me, he pats my shoulder like he's testing my reaction to him touching me. "You good?"

"I think so." I nod, unable to look at him while my pounding heart struggles to slow down.

"You saved her life, Landen." Noah gushes, stepping closer to wrap her arm around me. "You're not allowed to die on me. You have the NFR to win!"

That causes me to release a soft laugh. "I'll try my best not to."

After the lunch that nearly ended my life, I went back to Ranger's stall to continue with our day. I didn't get the chance to speak to Landen privately afterward, so when he walks into the stables before I leave for the day, I call out his name and run up to him.

"I just wanted to say, um…what you did at lunch for me… was a nice thing."

Real smooth, Ellie.

He tilts his head like an amused Golden Retriever, shoves his hands in his front pockets, and then fucking smirks.

"I'm startin' to think you dunno how to say the words *thank you*. Because I think that's what you're tryin' to say in between those ramblings."

I huff out a breath, hating that he's right. Not about being able to say those words but not wanting to say them to *him*.

Instead of stepping into his trap of getting me to admit that, I square my shoulders and simply say, "Thank you."

His brows pinch together. "For what?"

He's going to make me say it. *Asshole.*

Sighing, I cross my arms and fight the urge to roll my eyes at his childish act. "For not lettin' me choke to death."

"Ahh, yes, that." His lips tilt up, showing off his boyish grin. "I mean, technically speakin', I couldn't just watch and do nothin'. It's against my oath."

My eyes narrow in confusion. "You have an oath?"

Besides the one to make my life a living hell.

"I'm a certified lifeguard and volunteer fireman. I've done all the EMS trainin'. I've vowed to help anyone in need at any time."

That'd explain why he was brave enough to run into his family's barn when it was engulfed into flames three summers ago. He even pulled out one of the guys who set it on fire in the first place.

"You battle water and fire, huh?"

"A double threat." He winks.

"So that's the only reason you helped me? Your…*oath*?"

He shrugs. "Figured a death at the retreat would be bad for business, too."

"Funny," I deadpan. We have a momentary stare-off before I add, "Just so we're clear, I still don't like you."

"Good." He stands firm. "I've decided I don't like you, either, *Little Devil*." Then one corner of his lips curls up slowly and deviously before he adds, "Fits you even better now."

Chapter Eight
LANDEN

Another night sitting at home doing laundry, watching *New Girl* reruns, and snacking on popcorn is sadly the highlight of my day.

Rocky was in a mood today, making my job extra stressful when I tried to put him on the breeding mount, and he nearly kicked me.

I'm already stacked with orders, which means I don't have time for studs to act up or try to castrate me.

Antonio came for his last training session before the fair this weekend and he wouldn't stop talking shit about how much Ellie ignored me while she was giving all her attention to him.

I knew she was doing it on purpose, but it didn't hurt any less.

We agreed we didn't like each other, and I vowed to never bother her again.

Doesn't mean my heart got the memo.

Watching her race never gets old. The way she and Ranger work so perfectly together is so rare and beautiful that it's impossible not to stare in awe. Doesn't help that she's flawless in everything she does, but she's stunning, too. She makes winning look effortless, but I know firsthand how much work she puts into it.

My cell rings, knocking me out of my thoughts, and when I see Warren's name, I pick it up without a proper greeting.

"Which planet is outta sorts right now makin' everyone extra crazy?" He's into that astrology shit, so he'll know.

"Um…Earth?"

I bark out a laugh, grabbing a beer from my fridge. "Touché."

"Should I even ask?"

"Just a rough day. So what's goin' on?" Taking a seat on the couch, I lie back and rest my feet on the coffee table.

"Maisie just showed up at my door."

I choke down the liquid I just swallowed and quickly sit up. "Excuse me?" I cough out. "*Maisie*? Your ex-wife, Maisie?"

"Yep…" He sounds distressed. "Except, she ain't my ex-wife. We're still married."

"I'm only on my first beer, so I know I ain't drunk and heard ya wrong. Y'all didn't get divorced?"

"She wanted to. I didn't."

"She coulda filed without you. There's laws or some shit that'd allow her to get one even if you don't sign," I respond.

"I know. And yet, she didn't."

I take another swig of my beer, relaxing against the couch again. "So why is she back? Did you tell her about Angela's parole hearing?"

"Not yet. She's engaged and needs me to sign so she can go marry another man. Doesn't want him to know she's been married all this time, so she needs me to sign and get it finalized quietly."

The hurt in his voice makes me want to drive the two hours north to hug him. But it wouldn't solve anything. Maisie is his first and only love.

"Fuck. I'm sorry, Warren. What'd you say?"

Blowing out a breath, he replies, "I said no and slammed the door on her."

I try not to laugh at the ease with which he says those words, but I can't stop myself. "I can only imagine how pissed off that made her."

"Shoulda heard her screamin' at me and poundin' on the wood. Really fired her up when I blared my music and turned off all the lights in the house. Pretty sure she woke up my chickens."

"Jesus Christ." I shake my head, chuckling. "But it's been like what, seven years? Why do you wanna make her stay married to you? She has her own life seven hundred miles away."

Last I knew, she opened her own literary agency in New York City.

He's silent for so long that I worry our connection dropped, but then he finally speaks. "Because she's the love of my life. The only woman I've loved or will love. How can I just let her go?"

I swallow hard because what I'm about to say isn't what he'll want to hear but what he needs to.

"Maybe it's time for you to move on. She's livin' her life. You should be, too."

He sighs. "I wish I knew how."

He changes the subject before I have the chance to respond.

"Talk soon, okay?" I say after we get through talking about

the drama revolving around Ellie. Might as well share my sad dating life so he doesn't feel alone.

"You got it. See ya."

Once we hang up, I stare at my screen for a few minutes before deciding to take my own advice about moving on and do what I said I'd never do—download a dating app.

What does your dream girl look like?

A prompt at the top of Cecilia's profile asks and before I'm allowed to message her, I have to answer the question.

But it's a loaded one because it's not what my dream girl looks like, it's who she is as a person, what her work ethic is, and how she treats her friends and family. It's more than her looks and although I need that attraction to be there, too, it's not the only thing that forms a connection for me.

In retrospect, I have no reason to like Ellie as much as I do. There are her looks that would appeal to any man, but it's watching her drive and relentlessness to succeed day in and day out that intrigues me. And if I'm being honest, her immediate distaste for me was a turn-on.

Maybe I am a masochist.

Not in the physical sense, but in the way she bluntly tells me off, and yet, I seek out any reason to be near her.

It's a sickness, honestly.

In my early twenties, most women I gave attention to jumped at the opportunity to hook up with me. It was strictly built on looks and how much alcohol we drank. Nothing real or beyond one night.

But now here I am, forcing myself to kick this bad habit of mine to find more than that and someone who doesn't hate my guts.

What a concept.

So I answer Cecilia's question as truthfully as I can without sounding like a sap, and moments later, she replies.

CECILIA
I bet your cowboy hat would look better on me.

I should've expected that from the profile picture I used of me wearing one.

LANDEN
Yeah? Guess there's only one way to find out.

For the next four hours in between laundry and cleaning my place, we text back and forth. She's funny and easily keeps up with my flirting. I laugh more than I have in months and it feels good to be connecting with someone who doesn't want me dead.

LANDEN
I have an early morning, so I gotta go to bed. But when can I take you out?

CECILIA
About damn time you asked.

LANDEN
Didn't wanna come off too pushy.

CECILIA

How about this weekend?

LANDEN

I'm going to the fair's rodeo event tomorrow night and Saturday, if something like that would interest you.

CECILIA

Fried food, overpriced beer, carnival rides, and a hot cowboy holding my hand? Oh no, how would I ever survive…

I chuckle at the sarcasm, wondering if all women are this easygoing on dating apps, or if I just got lucky on the first try. Either way, I'm putting myself out there and running with it. So far, I've learned she's a twenty-five-year-old hairdresser who lives in the next town over. She hasn't had a serious boyfriend in over a year but enjoys going out to the bar with friends and line dancing.

LANDEN

It'll be a hardship, but I'm sure you'll manage.

CECILIA

What time should I meet you there?

LANDEN

How's five-thirty?

CECILIA

I'll be the one in a white sundress with tan boots eating a footlong corn dog covered in mustard.

Smiling wide, I shake my head at the very specific image. She looks beautiful in her photos. Shoulder-length brown hair with matching chocolate eyes and an hourglass figure that looks sexy as hell in the blue dress she's wearing.

I can't wait to meet her in person.

LANDEN

You sure know a way to a man's heart with all that dirty talk.

CECILIA

Just wait until we meet in person.

After we say good night, I crawl into bed with the goofiest smile on my face and fall asleep feeling hopeful for the first time in years.

Chapter Nine
ELLIE

The local fair is one of my favorites to attend because even though it's on the small side, they go all out. Almost everyone from Sugarland Creek will be in attendance, which makes it even more fun to watch the other events in between mine.

"Hey, Ellie!" As I jump out of my truck and walk to the back of the trailer, someone shouting my name grabs my attention.

Harlow jogs toward me in her show-jumping clothes. She's one of Noah's clients that I see at least once a week at the ranch. We don't talk much, but she's always been nice when we do.

"Hi, Harlow. You look good."

She slides her palms down her navy show coat. "Thanks! I'm headin' to the fairgrounds now to get Piper ready but wanted to tell ya good luck tonight. Delilah and I will be cheerin' for ya."

"Appreciate that. Good luck with yours, too."

Although she's only been training for three years, she's

pretty good for only being nineteen. Her older sister is a trick rider and used to date Waylon, so he avoids her every time she's here. Delilah performs at the rodeo tonight before the barrel racing event begins, so I'll watch her from the waiting area, but it's a fun way to get the crowd amped up beforehand.

"Thanks! Piper's been a little moody lately, so I'm hopin' she cooperates." She quickly checks her watch. "But I better run. I'll see ya later."

"Sounds good." I watch as she rushes off across the lot. Since show jumping isn't a rodeo event, the fair hosts it at the fairgrounds in a large building.

Once I open the trailer door, I step in and grab Ranger's halter, then give him some scratches. "Hey, boy. Ready for another win?"

He rubs his nose against my face, and I laugh.

I snap on his lead rope and walk him out of the trailer, then tie him to the side of it.

"Gonna get you some water, buddy. Be right back." Grabbing the bucket, I head toward the hydrant and wait behind another racer.

Since the event begins in just over an hour, we'll head over to the waiting pen soon until it's our turn. Both my parents are here and brought Aunt Phoebe since it's so close to home. I'm excited for her to watch the show since it's been a couple years.

"Ellie, hey!" Delilah finds me as I approach the hydrant. She's dressed up in her trick-riding gear, which is super cute on her. Purple fringe and glitter suit her well.

"Hey. Just saw your sister a few minutes ago."

"Oh yeah, I'm on my way over there now to watch as much as I can before I haveta go to the arena. Our poor parents are gonna be racin' from her event to mine." She laughs.

"It's nice they can be here, though."

"It is! I just ran into Noah and Magnolia. They're pushin' the babies around in an adorable double-stroller. I can't believe they're gonna be a year old soon."

This kind of small talk makes me anxious, but I smile and nod along as expected. If Noah's at one of my races, she'll swing by before I go on and give me a little pep talk, which is always appreciated.

"Oh, maybe you'll know since they didn't. Do you know Landen's date's name? We saw 'em by the Ferris wheel, but none of us had ever seen her before and he's ignoring his text messages."

My head spins with the news, not because I have any thoughts about his dating life, but because she thinks I'd know anything personal about Landen. Besides what I learn against my will.

"No clue," I say honestly. Though I am surprised he brought a date tonight after he admitted he'd not had one in months. But I'm not too shocked since his playboy reputation was known to almost everyone in town when we'd first met.

She puts her hands on her hips and sighs. "Damn. Well, I'm sure Noah will get it outta him eventually. Waylon and Wilder were useless, but that's because Waylon runs in the other direction as soon as he sees me." She rolls her eyes, and I don't have it in me to ask about their past, but mostly because I don't care to know about it. Delilah's six years older than me and we live in very different worlds when it comes to relationships.

Perhaps if I had my own social life that included going on dates, I'd have more of an interest in that type of gossip, but right now, all I can focus on is this race and then the next one and one after that.

"Anyway, good luck tonight. I'll be rootin' for ya!"

"Thanks! You too."

I carry Ranger's water bucket back to my trailer and then grab all the tack and equipment to get him ready. I'm in my usual pink attire, but since tonight's extra special being at a local event, I brought some equine-safe glitter to rub on his coat and down his legs.

"Trust me, you'll like it," I try to convince him when he stomps.

When would Landen have time to meet anyone new? Breeding season is his busiest time of year, and usually, if the brothers go out, I hear all about it in passing from Ruby or one of the twins.

Shaking my head, I mentally slap myself. I don't want to be thinking about Landen and his date because what do I care?

Perhaps it's because I haven't heard about him going on any in close to two years. He even said it's been months, but it's probably been closer to years. With him working as much as he does, where would he have even met someone? And how long have they been talking or dating for him to be comfortable enough to bring her somewhere he knows his entire family would be?

No. I don't care. Don't want to know. Don't *need* to know.

The only thing that deserves my focus is winning this race.

When Ranger and I get into the waiting pen, Noah, Magnolia, and Tripp, who's wearing Willow in a baby carrier, greet me. It's comical to see a six-foot-something tall brooding cowboy in Wranglers and boots walking around with an infant on his chest.

I can't even blame Magnolia for crushing on him as long as she did.

The Hollis genes are top-tier.

Noah smiles at Ranger and pets him. "You're lookin' extra cute." Then she looks up at me. "How ya feelin' tonight?"

"Great. Ready to run." I adjust my cowboy hat, making sure it's secure.

"I see Marcia Grayson is here and some other new girls. You know them?" She directs her attention to Sarah and Samantha.

"Yeah, they're the Smith twins. They're from Alabama, but they've been comin' to more races up here."

Noah frowns. "They any good?"

I shrug because while they're not bad, they're just not as good as me. "I guess tonight we'll see."

She laughs. "In that case, I know you don't need it, but good luck."

"Thanks." I smack her palm when she raises it.

"She'll be screamin' for ya, don't worry," Magnolia teases.

"We're makin' a sign for the Franklin Rodeo next weekend," Noah adds. "But we'll be extra loud tonight."

I sigh. "Great."

Magnolia chuckles.

"I know you don't like the attention, but you're good in the spotlight. Everyone loves you and is rootin' for ya. We have a whole section of my family cheering," Noah says.

I smile at that. My parents know Aunt Phoebe gets triggered by seeing the Hollises, so they'll sit across the arena on the other side where it's less crowded. It's why she doesn't like coming out too often, but sometimes Mom talks her into it so she gets out of the house.

"Well, I'll be sure not to let y'all down."

The two girls Noah trained and helped go pro before me are also here, and she stops by them quickly to say hello. They travel all over the country, so she doesn't train them anymore, but I know she's stayed in contact with them.

My heart races as I watch Noah walk away, finally giving me time to have a mental breakdown in private. I don't usually get this nervous beforehand, especially in smaller races like this, but knowing so many people are here expecting me to win adds more pressure.

"You doin' okay?" Marcia asks when she rides up alongside me.

"Yeah, why?"

Her shoulder quickly lifts. "You look more pale than usual."

I don't know if she's being genuine and truthful or if she's trying to get into my head, but either way, I brush it off and smile through my annoyance as usual. "Nope, I'm great. Excited to race."

"Awesome." Her gaze lowers to Ranger's saddle before she grins wide. "Good luck."

I know I should say something nice back like *you, too*, but I just don't have it in me to return the condescending comment. So instead, I take Ranger's reins and guide him to the front of the waiting pen since I'll be the third one to race.

The emcee announces the trick riders and music blares as they perform. Delilah's bright purple attire is easy to spot, and I genuinely smile watching her. Although I don't know anything personal about the Fanning sisters, I do know they work hard and are focused on their careers, too. Delilah travels just as much as I do, but Harlow is still getting her name out there. I'm not sure how often they see each other, but it's nice they have each other for support.

It's the one thing I can't buy or work harder at to achieve because the one person who loves and supports me unconditionally can't be here to watch or cheer me on. Though I am forever grateful I have Noah and her family and am glad when my family can show up, it still feels different. Like my heart is never quite full because there's always a piece of it missing.

As soon as the trick riders are done, I give Ranger his usual pep talk. We'll be up in just a few minutes. The music starts playing again and he does little tippy taps as his excitement builds. "We've got this, buddy."

The pressure is extra heavy tonight, but I try not to let it get to me as the first girl runs down the alleyway. The crowd cheers, the emcee announces her time, and then seconds later, the next girl starts.

"We're up, Ranger. Let's do this." I give him a little kick to up his excitement as we exit the waiting pen.

"Three-time Southeast regional champion and three-time National Finals Rodeo qualifier, Ellie Donovan! Let's hear it for a Sugarland Creek local and her twelve-year-old quarter horse, Ranger!"

He charges into the arena as soon as the music blares and perfectly rounds the first barrel.

"Good job! *Go, go, go!*" I hold out the reins as he sprints to the second and then grab the horn while he twists around it.

"One more, buddy."

My eyes do a quick scan of the crowd when I hear Noah and Magnolia screaming for us. Landen and a brunette stand right behind them.

Just as I pull the reins to the side, my shoulder drops and

Ranger goes too deep into the pocket, cutting the turn too soon. I slide my foot out of the stirrup just in time to raise my leg up and over the barrel so I don't knock it down. The stirrup just brushes it but not enough to tip it.

Fuck, that was close.

"Hustle home, Ranger!" Clicking my tongue, I lean forward with the reins loose in my grip and listen to the crowd grow louder as we cross the finish line.

"That puts The Rodeo Princess in the lead with fifteen point eight nine two!"

Not the fastest I've run but not the slowest.

Once my foot's secure in the stirrup again, I lead us out so the next rider can enter.

"Damn, that was impressive," Sarah says as soon as I catch my breath. "Never saw anyone do that before."

"My trainer's had me practice for all kinds of situations."

And stupidly enough, it was Landen's idea when he was on my ass about my dislocated shoulder. Told Noah I should practice lifting my knee with and without the stirrup in the event Ranger shouldered too close. Of course she loved the idea and said it wouldn't hurt to be prepared for everything and anything.

"You cut the turn too soon or you wouldn't have had to do that," Samantha chimes in, riding up next to her sister.

My jaw clenches. "I'm aware."

The Smith twins are at least ten years older than me and think since I'm younger, I don't know what I'm doing.

But funny enough, when the emcee announces them, neither of them has the words *championship* or *finals qualifier* before their names.

Chapter Ten
LANDEN

S taying late at the rodeo and then getting up at seven for work the next day is killer, but if I want to muck stalls and feed the horses before Antonio's roping event, I have no choice.

I'm still half asleep an hour later when I stumble into The Lodge for breakfast and nearly bump into Ellie at the buffet line.

"Shit, sorry." I instinctively grab her elbow and then blink twice to clear the fog when her eyes meet mine. "Didn't expect to see you here."

Before the choking incident at lunch earlier this week, she'd never come in to eat.

"Didn't know I had to inform you when I needed food." Her gaze lowers to her plate sliding against the buffet table.

Guess she's a little moody after placing second last night.

"Oh, still snarky even after I saved your life? Alright, cool. I'd stay away from any meat, then. I don't help people who have a vendetta against me for no reason."

"I doubt you're the only person in here who knows how to

108

perform the Heimlich maneuver." She grabs three pieces of sausage links to prove her stubbornness.

"Choke and find out."

Her head whips up and her stare is murderous. *Good.*

Getting a rise out of her is my new hobby. Now that we're in a mutual dislike for each other, might as well push her buttons as much as she's pushed mine over the years.

Arching a brow, I challenge her to say something about my choking comment.

Before she can, the person behind me clears their throat, and I realize we're holding up the line. With the fair, the retreat is maxed out on guests.

Ellie gets the hint and moves along, keeping silent as we load our plates. Besides the meat on hers, the rest is filled with fruit. My gaze follows as she walks to a table with Waylon and Wilder.

Son of a bitch.

It's weird enough that she's eating here, but even more so that she's sitting with them.

But I'm not letting her ruin my day, especially after I had a great date with Cecilia. We laughed most of the evening and had a great time. We're planning to meet up at the fair again tonight for a couple hours and then we'll go to the Twisted Bull for drinks.

I walk over to their table and sit next to Waylon, ignoring the way she's burning a hole in my head. Wilder's talking about some twin girls they met at the rodeo and Ellie doesn't look happy about it.

Is she jealous?

"Well, if your goals were to find the bitchiest sisters in the South, you succeeded," Ellie says.

Waylon smirks. "Why do you think we took them to the house of mirrors and then bailed?"

"They're probably still in there tryna find us," Wilder muses.

"Wait, you ditched them?" Ellie asks, surprised.

I'm not. I'm only surprised she's surprised. *Has she met them?*

"As soon as they started talkin' shit about you, we got rid of 'em," Waylon says. "Figured they weren't happy you kicked their asses and didn't realize you were with us."

"With you?" Ellie lifts a brow.

"Yeah, you're an honorary Hollis. That means no one messes with you." Wilder grins.

"Except Landen." Waylon laughs, and I nudge him.

Ellie shoves a whole sausage link into her mouth while staring at me as if she's waiting to see if I'll confirm his statement or not.

"Nope. We're mutual enemies. She no longer gets my life-saving services. So you better *chew*," I mock with a smirk.

"Enemies to lovers, huh?" Noah asks behind Ellie, appearing out of nowhere. "My favorite romance book trope. Well, after monster smut. The tails do somethin' to me."

Wilder, Waylon, and I give her the same face of disgust.

"Have you come to rescue me?" Ellie asks, glancing over her shoulder.

Noah sits next to her. "Yep, sorry for runnin' late. Donut was giving me attitude this mornin' and Fisher wouldn't stop annoying me about gettin' off him."

That's Noah's show horse she practices all her training on. A few years ago, she fell off him during a trick-riding stunt and got badly injured. After she had Poppy, she promised Fisher she wouldn't do it anymore, but Delilah wanted help with advancing her skills before she went on a cross-country tour. So now Noah only practices when Fisher's there to spot her.

"So what's that have to do with you two meetin' here for breakfast?" I ask.

"We're havin' a client-trainer meetin', if ya must be nosy." Noah scoffs.

"Talkin' about that sick leg lift move she did last night?" Wilder asks.

"Yeah, you're welcome for teachin' her that," I deadpan. "And wait, why wasn't I invited to this meetin'? I'm her part-time trainer."

Instead of acknowledging what I said, Ellie directs her attention to Noah. "Since Ranger didn't get his hooves checked last week, I was hopin' Fisher could see him before I leave on Wednesday. Give him a couple days with new shoes before the race on Friday."

"Absolutely. Jase and he are going on a father-son fishing trip this weekend, but I'll put Ranger on Fisher's schedule first thing Monday morning. We're headin' out after chores on Wednesday, but I can meet you for a quick practice run on Thursday."

"I'll be there, too," I interject with my fork in the air. "So, just tell me when and where."

"My parents won't be comin' with me, so I'll be free anytime," Ellie tells Noah.

They don't even offer me a glance.

"You're drivin' alone?" she asks.

"I could drive her. Since I'm going there, too," I suggest, punching each word.

"Yeah, it'll be fine. I'll listen to an audiobook and chug some Red Bull." Ellie smiles at Noah when she laughs.

"*Hello*? Does anyone hear me…" I tilt my head toward Wilder and Waylon, who are watching in amusement.

"I think they're ignorin' ya," Wilder taunts with his mouth half full. "You can tell me about that hot brunette you were with last night instead if ya want."

I don't.

"Well, since no one's listenin', then I *won't* suggest Ellie should wear her shoulder brace to keep it from droppin' again. And I *won't* suggest that she should work on Ranger's third turn. I also *won't* mention he got a little spooked when the stirrup smacked against him and y'all lost a few microseconds. Coulda taken first. But since no one's listenin', I *won't* mention how to avoid it next time."

"I'll pack my shoulder brace too," Ellie tells Noah as she violently stabs a piece of her watermelon. "I was gonna anyway…but I know it'll keep me from droppin' it and turnin' the reins too soon."

"*Great* idea." Noah grins because she knows I just said the same damn thing.

"Are you ready, bud?" I pat Antonio's shoulder as he anxiously waits for his turn.

"Ellie said she'd watch me. She's not here. Is she comin'?" He looks toward the bleachers that are mostly filled with parents. It's still early afternoon and most people don't come until the evening events.

"If she said she would, then I'm sure she is." I try to reassure him without making any promises.

"I watched her last night with my mom. She's the GOAT! She deserved first place, though."

"Yeah, I saw," I deadpan, inhaling a sharp breath.

We continue waiting as a few other kids take their turns roping, and the closer we get to Antonio's, the more nervous he gets.

"She's not here!" he whisper-shouts.

Sighing, I take out my phone. "Hold on."

We've only texted a few times, but it's never been anything personal, only business.

LANDEN

> Antonio's wondering if you're coming to watch him. It's almost his turn.

When the jumping dots appear, I almost expect her to play dumb and say something stupid like *who is this*, but she surprises me when she responds.

ELLIE

> I'm two minutes away!

I show Antonio my screen and he smiles wide. "I knew she'd come."

Resisting the urge to roll my eyes, I stand with him and wait until she rushes into the waiting area.

"Ellie!" Antonio's whole face lights up.

"Hey! Sorry, the line to use the restroom took forever." She wraps him in a hug and it's like looking at a version of Ellie I don't recognize.

He hugs her back. "Stoked you're here!"

"Of course. I promised I would." She smiles so beautifully, I wonder what it'd take to get her to look at me that way.

Probably at my funeral. When she's looking down at me in my casket.

I give Antonio a quick pep talk before it's his turn.

"You've got this!" Ellie cheers loudly.

When Antonio enters the arena, I stand next to Ellie with my arms crossed as we watch him do exactly what I taught him.

"I don't get you," I murmur, softly brushing my shoulder against hers, and I swear she shivers.

She keeps her gaze on Antonio. "You don't need to."

"You just made that whole kid's life being here. You're his idol. But with me, you're cold and distant. Hell, you acted like I didn't exist all mornin'. And you give me no reason why."

I know I should drop it and let it be, but I can't. It's like an itch I need to scratch, to reveal what it is I did that made me the villain in her story.

She swallows hard as she avoids looking at me. "We all need someone to look up to, to rely on, and trust. I had that once, so I know what it's like when it's taken away. If having my support helps him build confidence in roping or any other equine sport he picks up, then I'm happy to give that to him."

What does she mean she had that once? Who did she lose?

Antonio rushes back after he gets his final score.

"Killed it!" I give him a high five.

"So proud of you!" Ellie gives him another hug.

"I think I'm gonna stick with it and maybe even learn to be a badass bull rider. Then in five years, I'll be good enough to go pro." He waggles his brows at her.

"And you'll still be too young for her," I remind him.

Ellie jabs her elbow into my stomach, and I grunt unexpectedly.

"That's a great goal to work toward." Ellie smiles warmly. "Noah's husband used to ride bulls. I bet he'd love to give you some tips or maybe lessons."

"Yeah? That'd be dope."

"I'll mention it the next time I see her and let ya know," Ellie says.

Antonio's mom comes over, and I step back to give them room.

"Thanks for the text. I lost track of time." Ellie finally turns in my direction and as she's about to walk past me, I grab her arm.

"Wait. Who'd you look up to?"

"What?" Her gaze focuses on where I'm touching her.

"You said you knew what it's like to have that taken away. Tell me who you lost," I plead softly.

Let me in.

I'm close to begging.

The corners of her eyes well with unshed tears, and I fight the urge to brush my thumb along her cheek just so I can touch her soft skin.

"Did they die?" I prompt.

She finally looks up at me, a mix of anger and sadness written across her face.

"No, she didn't die. But *I did* the day she was taken from me."

Chapter Eleven

ELLIE

Driving by myself wasn't too bad. Normally, it's a four-hour drive to Franklin, but with the extra weight of Ranger and the trailer, it took almost six. But it was enough time to get through half my audiobook and two twelve-ounce Red Bulls.

By the time I pull into Serenity Springs Ranch where I'm boarding Ranger, I'm ready to find a bathroom and some hot food that doesn't come from a gas station.

"Hey, ya made it!" Easton greets me with a hug, and I return the gesture. This is his uncle's ranch where he lets me and a few other pro rodeo members stay when we're in town.

"Sure did." Smiling at him, I notice how much muscle he's packed on since the last time I saw him. "You've bulked up."

He lifts his arm and flexes. "Been workin' out and trainin' for saddle bronc riding. Once I finish out the year pro ropin', I'm makin' the switch."

My eyes widen because this is the first time I've heard the news. "That's dangerous!" I poke my finger into his hard chest.

Easton's like a brother to me, so I worry about him. After

he retired from barrel racing a few years ago, he moved on to roping, and now I guess, saddle bronc riding.

"Aww…you concerned about me?"

Rolling my eyes, I cross my arms. "Nope. I'm not your mother. Go break your neck for all I care."

He chuckles. "Glad you haven't changed since the last time we talked."

Once he helps me unload Ranger, we get him settled into a stall. Then he introduces me to a few of his new horses and then leads me inside the large white farmhouse where his uncle greets me.

"If it ain't the Rodeo Princess herself," he taunts.

My cheeks heat at the attention. "You gonna watch me take the win this weekend?"

"You know I wouldn't miss it. Hope you're hungry," he says, setting the table.

I nod. "Starving."

After using the bathroom and cleaning up, I take a seat next to Easton and we dig into Uncle Pip's famous pot roast. They catch me up on all the local town drama and even crack a few jokes about how often Easton falls off the bucking horses.

"I'm still trainin'. Gimme a break."

"I can't wait to watch it in action," I tease.

During dessert, we talk about the upcoming rodeo and how excited we are about it. The rodeo technically starts tomorrow with free family night, but then starting Thursday, there'll be seven rodeo events each night through Saturday.

Since it's one of the larger ones in the state, the entire Hollis family comes and stays overnight in campers since they're one of the sponsors. Noah's trained a lot of the riders in other various pro events, so she stays and watches everyone.

"You sure you wanna sleep out here? There's a spare room," Easton says as he walks me outside.

"Yep, I'll be fine. All my stuff's already inside, and I like being close to Ranger."

"Okay, well, if you need anything, text me."

I open the trailer door and smile appreciatively at him over my shoulder. "Will do. Thanks, Easton. See ya in the mornin'."

After breakfast, I plan on making the thirty-minute trip to Nashville to see my older cousin. Anytime I travel west, I schedule a visit. We exchange letters each month, but it's not the same as seeing her in person.

Once I've showered and changed for bed, I call my parents to say good night. I'm sad they won't be here, but it comes with the territory. The only other person Mom trusts to stay with Aunt Phoebe is my grandma, and she isn't usually comfortable staying overnight.

Before I crawl under the covers, I flip through my binder filled with court docs, legal paperwork, and spreadsheets of expenses and earnings. I keep track of everything and document all the finances so I know exactly how much I have and how much has been spent.

Waiting in this cold room always makes me anxious.

Although I shouldn't be. Getting to physically see and talk to her fills me with the type of happiness I used to feel when we'd have sleepovers and talk about our futures. She'd always say she was going to marry a rich man so once I graduated high school, she'd take me on her private jet and we'd travel the world. Even at twelve, I knew it was just a pipe dream, but I loved the fantasy. As long as we were together, I didn't care what we did or where we went.

As I wait for my turn to go into the visitation area, I look around at everyone else waiting and wonder how many other families have been affected by wrongful convictions.

It's a tragedy, honestly. A justice failure.

"Ellie Donovan."

After my name's called, I stand and slide my sweaty palms down my jeans, then walk through the doors where I'm directed toward her table.

I wish I could hug her. Wrap my arms around her gaunt body and squeeze her.

She beams when our eyes meet. "Hey, cousin."

I sit across from her, smiling wide. "Hi, Angela."

Guards stand all around the room and as tempting as it is to reach across and touch her, I fold my hands in my lap.

"You look good," she says, the metal bound on her wrists clanging together.

"So do you."

She dramatically rolls her eyes because she knows after all these years here, she doesn't. "I'll look much better when I get parole."

Nodding, I agree. She's been here for eleven years.

Eleven years *too* long.

For something she didn't do.

"You will. There's no reason to deny you when you've been on your best behavior. I've been workin' on my support letter. I read it to your mom the other night and she gave me some good things to add in, so as soon as I finalize it, I'll send it in."

"Yeah? How is Mama doin'? She doesn't talk much when I call or ever write me back."

"Pretty well. My parents took her to the fair last weekend to watch me race. She got a little overstimulated by the crowd, so they had to take her home shortly after, but I was happy she could come. She misses you."

"And yet she can't come visit me."

I frown because I know it hurts her not to get any visitors besides me. With how much I travel, I don't make it out to see her as often as I'd like.

"It'd be too long of a drive for her," I say, but she already knows that.

Angela shrugs, waving it off as always. "Whatever, it's fine. Assuming I have any money once I'm out, I'll rent an apartment nearby so I can see her every day."

"You will. I've been adding money to your savings account every time I get a payout. If it's not enough to get your own place, you know my parents will make room for you."

My parents love Angela, but they don't go out of their way to visit her. When she calls to talk to Aunt Phoebe, they exchange pleasantries, but that's about it.

"Ellie, I can't. You're already payin' my lawyer fees. I'll never be able to reimburse you at this rate."

"You're my cousin and best friend. You deserve a fresh start after all this. Plus, I want to and wouldn't accept money from you anyway."

Every time I win a race, I put aside some of my earnings so she has some when she gets out. I know it'll be rough starting her life over at twenty-nine years old, so if I can help make the reentry into society a bit easier, then I'll do whatever it takes.

"You're gonna work yourself to death tryin' to take care of me. I'll find a job, hopefully." She shrugs again because it's going to be a challenge even with a college degree. She has a criminal record and no previous work history.

When Talia's family won the wrongful death lawsuit, my aunt and uncle had to sell their house, property, and pretty much everything they owned to pay for the damages.

"Luckily, I love what I do, so it's not that big of a deal," I reassure her.

Winning is always the goal because it's one step closer to finals, but the prize money is what keeps me going day after day. Once I pay Ranger's monthly boarding and training expenses and any of Angela's debts, I put whatever's left into her savings.

"Even if it means you have to deal with *him*?" She cringes at just having to think about Landen.

When I first got on Noah's waitlist, I debated not telling Angela in case she disagreed with it. But I couldn't keep a secret like that from her, so I told her and was relieved when she supported me all the way. She knew I wanted to make barrel racing my career and told me to do whatever it took to get to the top.

That's how I know Angela's not the person the media portrayed her to be.

"Comes with the territory of gettin' the best trainer and boarding facility in the state." I frown, not wanting to think about the person who's responsible for putting her away in the first place.

However, I do feel bad that Noah doesn't know. If it were widely known I'm related to Angela, it could risk my career now that it's taken off and my name is out there more within the rodeo community. The media didn't paint Angela in a good light throughout the trial and all the locals were convinced she was guilty even before the verdict. Since we don't have the same last name, and I'm six years younger than her, no one recognizes me from that timeframe. Luckily, since no one recognizes me in Nashville and I only come to visit every few months, I haven't worried about it.

If Noah knew I'm Angela's cousin, there's no way she would've agreed to train me. I'm sure she'd take Landen's side and not want anything to do with me, so as hard as it is to keep it from her, I have no choice but to stay silent in order to reach my goals.

When Landen and I met at the ranch four years ago, it was obvious he didn't remember me. I was only ten when Angela and him dated, and then only a couple years older when she was sentenced, so I wasn't surprised he hadn't. Which made it easier to be crystal clear that we'd never be friends.

Hell, I didn't even want to be anywhere near him.

Not after hearing him talk at Angela's trial and lying about the type of person she was. Then he lied to the court about what he witnessed and because it was five people's word against hers, the jury sided with the prosecution.

We lost everything that day and life hasn't been the same since then.

"He still regularly asks why you hate him?" Angela pops a brow.

"Pretty much, yeah. I think he has a new girlfriend, though. So maybe he'll stop botherin' me with it."

She sits up taller, her handcuffs clanging together as she does. "A *girlfriend*?"

My shoulder lifts because I'm not asking him for details. "He brought her to the fair last weekend."

Angela rolls her eyes. "Must be nice to go out and do normal things. God. I hate him so much."

Me too.

It wasn't just her life he ruined.

My parents had to take out a second mortgage to help pay for Aunt Phoebe's treatment when her husband left. On top of that, they were trying to be strong for me when the depressive episodes took over, but no matter what anyone said, I still couldn't understand how Angela went to prison for something she didn't do.

The justice system had failed her and all of us who loved her.

I cried more that first year than I had my entire life. It felt like I was mourning a person who wasn't dead, but she was gone from my life in a way I wasn't used to. We spent months writing to each other before I was allowed to visit. Not being able to hug her was a form of torture I hadn't anticipated.

But Angela distracted me the best way she could. She encouraged me to talk about 4-H and riding horses, and if I thought there were any cute boys at school. When we'd talk on the phone, she'd have me laughing within minutes because that's the type of person she is. She didn't want me to be sad.

"Do you think Landen knows you're eligible for parole?" I ask, wondering for myself too. He hasn't acted any different than usual, still his annoying, pesky self.

"Oh, I'm sure their nosy lawyer told everyone. My attorney already told me her family will try to persuade the parole board and write their own letters, but he said not to worry about it. They have no grounds on why I shouldn't get it."

"How's that even fair when you're innocent to begin with?" My molars grind as my frustration grows, but I try to remember to breathe so I don't get an anxiety attack.

Angela leans against the table, folding her arms. "Because they will forever believe I pushed her. But I know what I saw when none of them were looking, and she jumped, just like her boyfriend did a couple years later. They'll never accept that they made a suicide pact because then they'd have to admit they didn't get Talia help for her depression. They needed a villain and a fallback person to justify her death, and, well, here I am."

The bitterness in her voice makes me sad and angry. She's told me this story repeatedly, but it still hurts to hear each time. The local reporters painted her as this selfish, self-absorbed teenager who acted in a jealous rage. They called her vicious. Evil. A *murderer*.

But I knew they were wrong because that wasn't the person I considered a sister.

Angela was kind, sweet, and thoughtful. Always knew how to make me laugh.

She'd never harm anyone.

The year before she was sentenced, she skipped school just to come pick me up early and we spent the day together at the mall. We shopped, ate junk food, and snuck into an R-rated movie.

The person they described on TV wasn't the same one who'd held me as I cried myself to sleep after my gerbil died.

"I'll do whatever it takes to make sure they approve your parole," I promise.

"I know you will, Ellie. That's why you're my hero."

Tears well in my eyes, and I quickly brush them off my cheeks. "Anyway, have you seen or heard about Lexi lately? How's she doin'?"

"As far as I know, she's stayin' outta trouble since she got into that last fight. But it pushed her visitation rights back several months."

"That's too bad. Antonio would do well to see his sister."

"Did you get him into that roping program?"

"Yeah, I got to watch his first competition at the fair last weekend." I smile proudly.

"And Landen still thinks it was Noah's idea for him to volunteer?"

I sigh. "Yep."

I've stayed in contact with the local 4-H leaders and would stop in when I was in town, which is how I first met Antonio. When they mentioned needing more roping trainers, I brought it up to Noah so she'd recruit Landen. Even though I hate him, I did it for Antonio. He needed a role model after his only sister went to prison for stabbing her assaulter to death.

Again, the justice system failed another family.

It was her word against a dead man's.

"Have you considered what will happen if I get parole?" she asks. "Whether I live with you or not, there's no way the Hollises won't hear we're related now that they know you. Especially if my release is mentioned in the local papers."

I shake my head because there hasn't been time to think about anything beyond my next race and the next step in getting Angela out of here.

Shrugging, I say, "I'll figure it out as it happens. If they ask me and Ranger to leave, then we'll go back to Grandma's farm. I'll continue racin' and makin' money as usual."

"Maybe I could go with ya, then?" She smiles, hopeful.

"I'd love that. It'd be just like old times. You and me against the world."

"You got that right, kid." She winks.

We end up talking about other random stuff for the remaining half hour, and by the time I have to leave, my heart is full. There's always a sense of relief getting to see and talk to her in person.

"I love you. We'll talk very soon, okay?" she says.

I nod repeatedly, attempting to keep my emotions in check. "Love you, too."

Chapter Twelve
LANDEN

Mario's being a little shit this morning. He's one of our newer stallions and tends to rear when I lead him out to the pasture. Usually, I can redirect and settle him down, but he's being extra feisty.

Pretty sure I'll have a black eye tomorrow from his head lashing around and smacking into mine when I didn't get out of his way fast enough. But since I'm leaving for the Franklin Rodeo in a few hours, he'll be one of the other ranch hands' problems. At least until I get back.

"Save that energy for the mares, bud." I unclick the lead rope once he's securely inside and then lock the gate behind me.

"Rough day?" Tripp rides up on Denver, one of our family horses, and smirks after I flip him my middle finger.

"Just another stud actin' up as usual. What're you doin'?"

"Dad asked me to move the goats to the east retreat pasture before we all head out, so I'm lookin' for 'em."

"You lost the goats?" I muse, crossing my arms and leaning against the fence.

"No. They're…somewhere."

I chuckle, pushing to my feet. "Good luck with that. I once found a few up in the hay loft."

"*Shit*," he mutters.

As I walk to the barn to grab the next mare for Mario, my phone vibrates with a text.

CECILIA

What's a girl gotta do for a good night kiss around here?

I smile as soon as I read her text. After our back-to-back fair dates last weekend, I still hadn't kissed her, and then we had an ice cream date last night. Since I worked late, I couldn't hang out long, but when we went our separate ways, I hugged her goodbye and kissed her cheek.

We haven't made any new plans since I'm leaving for the Franklin Rodeo this afternoon, but we've been texting every day since we met.

LANDEN

You ever heard of a Southern gentleman? I'm trying to be respectful and take things slow.

Although I love how blunt and forward she is, I'd rather not jump right into bed before getting to know each other better.

Something I've never considered before, but if I'm truly attempting to *move on*, then I want to be sure there's a real connection between us.

CECILIA

Afraid a little tongue will turn you into a sex addict?

If only she knew it's been *a long* time since I've been with someone.

LANDEN

> Pretty sure you're the one who won't be able to keep your hands off me.

CECILIA

> Come to my place for breakfast and find out.

There's no reason I couldn't. Yeah, we're leaving at noon, but that's never stopped me from getting laid before.

But there's this nagging feeling in the pit of my stomach that tells me I'll regret it if we move too fast.

LANDEN

> Wish I could, but I have to finish eight hours of work in three.

CECILIA

> You sure I can't change your mind, cowboy?
> Maybe a little visual incentive…

A moment later, she sends a mirror selfie of her only wearing a black see-through lacy teddy with a red bow between her breasts.

God help me.

Lifting my cap, I scrub a hand through my hair and contemplate my next move.

LANDEN

> Fuck. You play dirty. Can I take a rain check for the minute I'm back in town?

The next photo she sends is her turned around, looking

over her shoulder in the mirror, and showing off the matching thong and stockings.

CECILIA

Not sure I can wait that long...

I should be tripping over my boots to get into my truck and speeding to her place. The old me wouldn't have to think twice about it. Chicks sending me nudes or enticing me to sleep with them used to be the norm, and I'd welcome it.

But now, I'm way too old to be acting like a careless, horny frat boy. It's one thing to put myself out there again, but I'm not looking to go back to my old self where I had unattached sex for the sake of feeling something.

LANDEN

I'm sorry. I gotta get back to work. I'll text you later.

Yeah, I'm sure that's going to deflate her ego or piss her off, but it'd be irresponsible for me to bail when I haven't even finished packing.

I started two nights ago but then ended up on the phone with Warren again to go over our letters to the parole board. He's still dealing with Maisie randomly showing up and needed a distraction.

Although it was a little emotional to talk about Tucker and Talia, I'm glad I didn't have to be alone while figuring out how to put into words that Angela deserves to continue staring at prison walls until her entire sentence has been served.

I'm relieved I got it written and sent out.

Now we just hope for the best outcome possible.

"Hey, Dad," I call out when I see him on the four-wheeler outside the stud farm barn. "Whatcha doing?"

"Hey, son. Just ridin' around to make sure everything's ready before we go."

"Yep, I got the stalls mucked and the horses fed. Then I wrote out a list for the ranch hands. Everything's stocked and good for the next few days."

"Great. Lookin' forward to takin' a few days off?"

I shrug, smirking. "Yeah, I'm not mad about it."

He chuckles. "Ellie on her way there now?"

"Left yesterday."

"Oh, okay. Well, I got somethin' for you and your siblings. Don't tell your mom." He pulls out an envelope from his front pocket and hands it over.

Inside are tickets to the VIP Corral. It includes all-inclusive food and beverages for the duration of the rodeo.

"What're these for?" I ask suspiciously. He's never done this in all the years we've gone.

He shrugs modestly. "I know how hard you and your siblings work, especially training Ellie to get her this far, so I figured y'all deserve the best spot in the arena to support her."

Wrapping my arms around him, I thank him for all of us. They're gonna love it.

Plus, it'll give us a front-row seat to watch Ellie up close.

The drive to Franklin consists of four heavy-duty trucks each towing campers. For three nights, I'll be bunking with Wilder and Waylon. *God help me.*

But I'm looking forward to the break from daily manual labor, hanging out with my siblings again like old times, and hopefully watching Ellie win Friday and Saturday.

Once we're set up on our lot, I check on Tripp and Magnolia's camper, and then Noah and Fisher's to see if they need anything while I run into town for bottled water and some beer. The shit they serve at the event is overpriced, so we keep extra at our campsite when we're not inside.

"Actually, yeah. Can you grab a pack of wipes? I thought I grabbed extra, but I must've forgotten," Noah asks.

"Like...Lysol wipes?" I ask, opening a note in my phone to write this down.

"Like...for your niece's butt."

Fisher's gaze meets mine when he realizes I'm still confused. "Baby wipes," he confirms.

I nod, typing it out. "Got it. Any particular kind or flavor?"

"Oh my God." Noah's tone tells me that was a dumb question.

"I'll just get the first ones I find," I confirm.

"Hey, you goin' on a grocery run?" Magnolia asks, climbing into the trailer.

"Depends. Whaddya need?"

"Use small words," Noah warns.

"Sorry for not havin' a baby and knowin' about that stuff," I deadpan.

"Oh God, what'd you do?" Tripp chimes in.

"Nothing. Now what do y'all need?" I wave my phone around so she knows I'm impatiently waiting.

"Condoms, extra-large. Lube. Water-based. The strawberry kind."

The ease of how fast she lists them off has me second-guessing if she's messing with me or not.

"Had me there for a minute, but I knew you were lyin' with the extra-large."

Tripp throws me a dirty look, and I chuckle.

"I'm serious! His parents are keepin' Willow overnight, and I didn't come prepared."

"I mean…would knockin' you up be the worst thing?" Tripp smirks.

Magnolia's eyes widen as she shoves him. "She's not even one year old."

Tripp shrugs, then points at me. "Then you better add it to your list."

"No way, man. I draw the line with flavored lube."

"Don't knock it till ya try it," Magnolia teases, licking her lips. "Mixed with the man's natural scent it's—"

"I'm gonna take Poppy and see how your parents are comin' along…" Fisher grabs her from Noah's arms and then excuses himself.

As soon as the door shuts, Magnolia and I burst out laughing.

"You two are embarrassin'." Noah scowls.

"You'd think he'd be used to it by now being in the family for the past three years," I say.

"I'm *in* this family, and I don't wanna hear about my brother's sex life." Noah shuffles her suitcase around, trying to find room for all the baby shit they brought along. "Plus, y'all are his son's age. It probably weirds him out."

I lean against the fridge. "You mean more weird than you sleepin' with his son before y'all met?"

"Alright, get out. All of y'all. I need to set up Poppy's pack 'n play." Noah points toward the door.

Tripp holds Willow as they exit, and I follow behind.

"Okay, for real. Do you need anything from the store before I go?"

"Beer and water?" Tripp asks.

"Already on it."

He tips his hat. "Then we're good."

Going to the grocery store was a bad idea. It was like the wild, wild west.

And because I wanted to be the cooler brother, I grabbed a box of condoms anyway. But no lube. They can deal with it.

When I return to the campsite, everyone's gone, go figure. They probably went to find food or knowing the twins, some unsuspecting women to pick up.

I drop off Tripp's condoms and Noah's baby wipes before putting the beer and water in my trailer. But when I open the door, a half-naked Cecilia greets me.

"Holy fuck." I stumble down the steps, nearly falling on my ass. "Jesus."

"Surprise…" She stands, wearing the same lingerie she had on in the pictures she sent earlier.

I set the water and beer down, trying to collect myself and calm the heart attack she just gave me.

"Uhh, yeah. Wh-what're you doing here? How? When?"

"When I couldn't get you to come over, I decided I'd come to you. So I left about an hour after you texted that you were on the road, and when I got here, I just looked for your truck."

I brush a hand through my hair, trying to decide what to do. I'm sharing a two-bed camper with my brothers. This isn't exactly an ideal situation to be in right now.

"Is it okay that I'm here? I don't wanna keep you from your family or—"

"No, it's fine." I step closer. "You just shocked the shit outta me, is all."

"So I can stay?" she asks sweetly.

I smile in return. "Yes, of course you can stay."

Chapter Thirteen
ELLIE

After visiting Angela yesterday, I returned to Uncle Pip's ranch and then Noah met me for some practice runs. Later that evening, I carpooled with Easton to family night and watched the kids' events—mutton bustin' was my favorite. Afterward, he introduced me to some of the guys on his roping team and then I was in bed by ten.

This morning, after I check on Ranger and muck his stall, I meet Easton in the house for some coffee.

"Hey, how'd ya sleep out there?" he asks, handing me a mug.

"Good. I forget how quiet it can be out in the country."

"Were ya scared?" he taunts.

I grab the carafe and fill my mug halfway.

"No, but I forgot my white noise machine, so I just listened to rain sounds on my phone."

"That's weird."

"How so?" I grab the cream off the table and add it to my coffee, then stir it in.

"You'd think it'd make you have to pee all night."

"Actually, you weirdo, it's relaxing. Do you just sleep in silence like a psychopath?" I bring my mug to my lips and blow on it before taking a sip.

"I listen to a podcast, usually."

"Hearin' people talk would keep my brain awake. I listen to audiobooks and it helps with my focus during long drives."

He lifts a shoulder casually. "Guess I'm used to it. I listen for about twenty minutes before I'm out."

"Hmm, maybe I'll try it on my drive home." I take a seat at the table and scroll on my phone for one that might interest me.

"So what're you doin' today before you gotta bring Ranger to the rodeo?"

"One of the local 4-H clubs reached out and asked me to be a guest speaker at a future meeting to talk about my experience as a pro rodeo barrel racer. So I'm meetin' with a couple of the leaders."

Normally, I wouldn't want to add to my already busy travel schedule, but coming back this way in a month or so gives me another opportunity to visit Angela.

"Ooh, aren't you so famous," he taunts. "Is it a paid event?"

"Of course not. I owe so much of my success to gettin' involved with my 4-H club, so I love being able to pay it forward any opportunity I get."

"Speakin' of you being so awesome and shit, will you take a selfie with me for my social media pages? The competition will get jealous and know I'm way cooler than them."

I sigh but nod anyway.

One of the downfalls of being in the rodeo spotlight is having to keep up with my social media. After each race, I edit my profile bio with Ranger's updated lifetime earnings and post a picture of us from that event. In the caption, I write a quick thank you to the event sponsors, mention what place we took and then whatever prizes we won.

"You know when you talk like that, it really proves how much younger you are than me."

"What? You're only one year older!"

"I was talkin' about maturity." I smirk, then stand so he can take his stupid picture.

After I chat with the leaders about possible talking points for my presentation, they invite me to go with them for lunch. With dozens of food trucks in town for the rodeo, a handful of them parked down Main Street since the event doesn't open until this evening. It gives the owners extra business and the locals who aren't attending the rodeo a chance to enjoy the food, too.

But it's so much more than a vendor fair. There's a music stage with a band playing and all the small businesses have their doors open with tables of merchandise along the sidewalk. It's still decorated from their parade last weekend with a Franklin Rodeo banner tied between two poles and mini flags on every post.

"I had no idea they did this," I say to Brynn and Gabby. "I guess I never ventured downtown when I came here before."

"It's somethin' the mayor only started last year. She wanted to drive more people to the local businesses so they didn't feel

the financial hit with everyone at the rodeo for four nights,"
Brynn explains.

"Love that idea."

And now I want to go into every shop and stop at each food
truck for the full experience.

I check the clock on my phone, deciding how long I can
stay before I have to get back to bring my trailer to the rodeo.
I'll have to do press thirty minutes before the race starts, but I
should still have enough time to stay here for a bit.

I shouldn't have had that churro dog, but it looked too good
to pass up.

And the fried Oreos.

And the pulled pork nachos.

And I really shouldn't have swallowed them down with a
large, fresh squeezed lemonade.

My stomach is battling for its life as I stand next to Ranger
in one of the waiting pens. After sweating through my
interviews, I found some water and chugged it, but it doesn't
seem to be helping.

I've been looking forward to this race for weeks, and now
I'm going to get out there and throw up all over the barrels.

It doesn't help that the arena is packed, and I'm already
overstimulated.

"You alright, Ellie?" Sarah asks, coming over with her
horse. Or maybe it's Samantha.

"Yeah, I'm great." I force myself to smile so she doesn't know I'm lying. She doesn't need to know I stress ate all afternoon after Noah texted and mentioned Landen's new girlfriend randomly showed up at their campsite last night.

Well, she didn't say it exactly like that, but it was implied her arrival was unexpected.

I shouldn't care. *I don't*, but it makes me anxious enough as it is when Landen's around. I don't need some chick he's hooking up with to watch me, too.

"Are you sure? You look sick," she says but then quickly adds, "No offense!"

"I'm one hundred percent perfect." *And somewhat offended.*

The other twin walks up carrying a bag and thermos in her hand and then offers it to me. "I drink this when I'm nervous before races. It'll settle your stomach and nerves."

"What is it?" I eye her suspiciously, curious as to why they'd want to help me when I'm their biggest competition, but she looks genuine, as does her sister.

"It's licorice root tea. It's good for digestive distress," she explains.

I cautiously take it from her. "It's not gonna give me diarrhea or anything, is it?"

"No, of course not. It has a lot of great health benefits. We drink it every day and look at us!" the other one says.

Okay, well, not sure that's a selling point, but if it'll keep me from upchucking in front of a thousand people, I'll try it.

After the first cautious sip, I decide it's not as bad as it sounds and drink more.

"Do you take a daily probiotic?"

"Um…no."

Is that something I should be taking? I thought I had another five to ten years before I had to worry about pumping my body with extra vitamins. But considering they're in their thirties, maybe that's why they know more about it than I do.

"Hold on…" She kneels, digging into her backpack before she reveals a Ziploc bag with a few pills. "Take these."

I eye them suspiciously. "For what?"

"They're for digestive health," she explains.

The other twin adds, "They also boost immunity."

"And regulate your bowels."

I scratch my cheek, contemplating turning around and walking away.

"And not that you need it for this, but it's known to support mental health," one of them continues.

Blinking a few times at the way she says those words, I decide to hold out my hand for the pills to get them to stop talking.

Once I've swallowed them down with the licorice root tea, I thank them for their help and excuse myself to find a bathroom.

I ask one of the other girls if she'll watch Ranger and once she agrees, I head out to the closest restroom.

When I look in the mirror, my face is paler than usual, but not *on my deathbed* sick. I smack my cheeks a little, not wanting to smudge my makeup, but hoping that brings out a little color.

By the time I return to the waiting pen to grab Ranger, they inform us there's been a delay due to the previous event running over and them still needing to drag the arena to level out the ground before the junior division can start.

Though I'm excited to race, I appreciate the time for my stomach to settle, especially since I'm the second runner.

NOAH

You holding up okay?

Brooke Montgomery

When I read her text, I give it a thumbs-up reaction.

ELLIE

Just fine.

No need to worry her or give her a reason to come out here. My stomach and head are battling for which one's going to take me out first, but as long as they wait until after the race, I won't complain too much.

NOAH

Okay, well just let me know! Landen and I are in the VIP Corral ready to cheer you on...and wait till you see my sign!

I shouldn't ask.
It doesn't matter.
But I can't help myself.

ELLIE

Is his girlfriend with y'all, too?

I want to slap myself.

NOAH

No, I guess she had to leave early to make the trip back for work tomorrow.

ELLIE

Oh, how disappointing she'll miss the rodeo.

NOAH

Yeah, pretty sure she didn't come for the rodeo.

I didn't need her winking emoji for me to know what she was implying.

After fifteen minutes, the junior division starts. Between the music coming on and off and the crowd cheering, a wave of nausea hits me.

Instead of focusing on it, I give my attention to Ranger so he doesn't get anxious. He tends to know when I feel off and I need him on his A game tonight.

Once the final rider races, they declare a winner, and then it's finally time.

I jump back on Ranger, give him his usual pep talk to rile him up to get pumped up, and then wait for the first girl to go.

"Good luck!" one of the Smith twins says as I ride past her.

I'm too focused on leading Ranger toward the gate to respond.

"You ready for this, buddy? We got this." I lean down and pat his neck.

He stomps and rears when the music grows louder.

"Almost, hold on…" I pull the reins back, trying to keep him settled until it's time.

As soon as the first girl returns, I lead him into the alleyway.

"Wait." I listen for the emcee to announce my name and then… "Let's go!"

I click my tongue, give him a little kick, and then he shoots off like a cannon into the arena.

Chapter Fourteen

LANDEN

The event being delayed would normally be a drag, but since we're in the VIP Corral, that just means we have extra time to enjoy the free perks.

"Okay, just texted Ellie. She's hangin' in there," Noah says, returning to her seat from grabbing more food.

"I dunno how she does this week after week. I'm a nervous wreck for her," Wilder says, snatching something off Noah's plate.

"Where the hell did you come from?" I ask, not even realizing he was here.

"It's the adrenaline," Fisher chimes in. "You get addicted to that feelin' quite easily. The crowd cheerin' you on, the smell of the arena, the high of winning. Ellie's in her prime, too. I'd be surprised if she still gets nervous or just feeds off the excitement."

Or Ellie's really good at pretending she doesn't and puts on a front.

"She's definitely more of the junkie kind," Noah confirms.

Wilder tries snagging another fry, and Noah smacks his hand. "What're you two doin' anyway?" she asks him.

144

"Waylon and I are makin' rounds, scopin' out the options for later."

Noah balks and makes a face. "Gross. You two *promised* to work the lounge tonight."

"We will!" He rolls his eyes, then grabs my beer.

"You can get your own, ya know?" I nod toward the VIP area.

"I know." He grins smugly but walks away.

"That reminds me, Landen…" Noah looks at me with devious eyes. "You and Cecilia must be gettin' serious already if she drove four hours here and back just to see you for one night."

Fisher narrows his eyes. "That's quick. Didn't y'all just meet last weekend?"

"Didn't you sleep with my sister the first night y'all met?" I scan my eyes around the arena. "In this exact place?"

Noah belly laughs when Fisher's face turns red. "In fact, it is the three-year anniversary of our one-night stand. I told him we should recreate our first time. Wanna babysit Poppy for the night?"

When she waggles her brows, I mimic a gag reaction.

"Hard pass. And my relationship is none of your business."

"I'm not judging, trust me. I like her. She's pretty and seems nice. But I'm not sure why she's interested in you, though."

"Ouch!" I shove her shoulder, causing her to bump into Fisher. "Just for that, I'm *not* babysitting so y'all can't get laid. Actually, I'll crank my music to keep her up longer."

Noah shoots me a death glare. "You wouldn't dare. I know where you live."

"Pfft. I know where you live, too."

Our parents stop by with Mallory for a quick check-in. She

pouts about not being allowed in the VIP area, but since she's a minor, she can't stay.

"In a few years, kiddo." I grin. "And then you'll be drivin' us here."

"Not me if you're the one teachin' her," Noah teases.

"I'm gonna be a fabulous driver, thank you," Mallory argues. "I've already memorized the student driver handbook for next semester."

"If you can drive a four-wheeler and tractor like a pro, I have no doubt you'll be fine with a truck," I say.

"Thank you." She nods firmly.

"Kiss ass," Noah mutters to me.

The emcee finally announces that after dragging the arena and setting out the barrels, the event is ready to start with the junior division.

"I'm gonna grab a fresh beer and more snacks. Want anything?"

"See if you can find Magnolia and then scold her for being late," Noah says.

Chuckling, I give her a mock salute. "I'll get right on that."

While I hang out in the VIP area, I grab my phone and text Cecilia to check she made it back safely.

CECILIA

Yeah, I'm home.

LANDEN

Glad to hear it. Can we talk when I get back?

CECILIA

Sure.

She's pissed, and I understand why, but she'd be even more angry with me if I hadn't told her the truth sooner.

By the time I return to the VIP section, I notice the barrels are more spaced out now.

"Is her division next?" I ask, standing behind Noah and Magnolia—who finally showed up. They're right in front of the railing now with their ridiculous sign that reads Ride that horse like you stole him!

"Yep, she'll be the second runner," Noah says. "Get ready to scream your guts out."

"Your brother will be rearranging my guts later, so I can't do that," Magnolia quips.

"Gross." Noah laughs.

"You're tellin' me. I live above them." I groan.

Magnolia pats his arm. "Oh, you poor baby."

When the emcee announces Ellie's name with her horse Ranger and mentions all her accolades in the pro rodeo, the crowd goes wild.

"Yes, Ellie!" Noah screams. "Go, go, go!"

Ellie smoothly rounds the first barrel and then quickly races to the next.

She looks beautiful as always in her pink cowboy hat and boots. Wavy, long blond hair flies around her neck as she twists around the second.

When Ranger rushes to the third, I get a better glimpse of her face. I notice her eyes are dazed and her cheeks are more flushed than usual. That could be from having to wait outside longer in this heat, but then I realize something's off about her posture.

She should be sitting back with her arms stretched, but instead, she's hunched as if she doesn't have the strength to hold herself up.

As soon as Ranger makes the final turn, Ellie falls off him and smacks her head on the barrel before tumbling to the ground and then rolls until she ends up face-down in the dirt. I clutch Noah's shoulder as an audible gasp echoes throughout the arena.

"Oh my God!" Noah sprints toward the exit to get down there, and I quickly follow.

My mind spins with a million questions about why she fell off in the first place. Based on how Ranger was turning, she shouldn't have. Even on her worst training days, Ellie's never fallen off like that.

The medical team rushes out while Noah and I run toward Ellie. We stay far back enough to give them room, but I keep my eyes on Ellie as one of the wranglers grabs Ranger and keeps him calm.

Noah quickly explains we're Ellie's trainers, and then they ask if she has any prior medical conditions or allergies.

"No, none," Noah responds.

I can hardly breathe as I watch them check for a pulse and then place an oxygen mask over her face. Memories of Talia's lifeless body resurface and the anxiety of what-ifs and worst-case scenarios sits on my chest. The last time I felt a panic attack come on this quickly was when I attended Tucker's funeral. I still couldn't believe he was gone when we'd just talked the night before he died.

A couple of the event's sponsors rush over, trying to conceal Ellie's body from the crowd.

"The ambulance is out front. Is she gonna be okay?" one of them asks.

One of the benefits of a larger pro rodeo event is they have their medical support team and ambulances on standby, so there's no waiting to get her to a hospital.

"By the look of her pupils, shallow breathing, and

hypotension, I wouldn't be surprised if she had a seizure. Won't know for certain until we get her to the hospital."

My heart stops and it's at this moment I know why I can't kiss another woman.

Because it only beats for Ellie.

I think it has since the moment I met her.

"A *seizure*? Holy shit," Noah blurts out.

Moments later, they put Ellie on a stretcher and carefully move her out of the arena. Before I follow, I grab Ellie's pink cowboy hat that flew off because I know she'll want it when she's conscious.

Once I'm outside with Noah, we watch as they put her into the back of the ambulance and drive away.

"She's gonna be okay," Noah mutters, clinging to my arm as if she needs to say the words aloud for them to be true.

But I've never been more scared in my life.

Hospital waiting rooms are the bane of my existence.

It's cold, too damn quiet that it's eerie, and the receptionist never knows when the doctor will come out to talk to you.

Noah and I have been pacing for two hours. Some of the others nearby have been giving me dirty looks, but I can't just sit and do nothing.

She called Ellie's parents and they're on their way now, but it makes me question why they weren't here in the first place.

Her dad normally travels with her, but she never said why they wouldn't be there this weekend.

Finally, after another hour, one of the doctors approaches us. He tells us she regained consciousness earlier, but they're keeping her overnight for observation since she showed signs of an epileptic episode and also has a concussion. Since we aren't immediate family, he can't answer any medical questions or tell us anything more without her present.

"Is she alert?" I ask.

"Somewhat. She was experiencing some discomfort, so we gave her some pain meds before the CT scan, which made her quite drowsy."

Noah frowns. "Can we see her?"

He nods and then leads us through the doors. Nervously, I scrub my sweaty palms down my jeans and then lift my baseball cap to run my fingers through the strands. As soon as I walk into her room, my heart shatters all over again.

The makeup she wore earlier has faded and too much blood has drained from her cheeks, making her look like a ghost. A large bandage covers one side of her head and she's connected to a blood pressure cuff that's currently squeezing her arm. Seconds later, the numbers appear on the monitor and it seems to have gone up some since the last time it took a reading.

A nurse who's adjusting her blankets greets us, and when our eyes meet, she offers a tender smile.

"I'll give y'all some privacy, but you can press the call button if she needs anything."

"Thank you," Noah says, standing beside Ellie and then taking her hand.

Once the nurse leaves, I stand on the opposite side and stare at Ellie. I've never seen her so peaceful before and it almost feels intrusive to see her this vulnerable.

Even if she hates me, I'll always think she's the most beautiful woman I've ever seen.

"What're you thinkin'?" Noah asks after ten minutes of silence.

I sigh, exhaling deeply. "Wonderin' what her first insult to me will be when she realizes I'm in here."

She chuckles softly. "Probably call you out for starin' at her like that…"

That makes me grin because I haven't exactly made my crush on her a secret. "At least then we'll know she's fine if she wakes up scoldin' me."

When they haven't kicked us out after thirty minutes, I grab a chair and sit next to her.

"I'm gonna step out and call Fisher," Noah says, and I nod.

I take the opportunity to slide closer and grab her hand. Noah was holding the other before, and I don't want her to feel alone.

Even if she'll wake up hating me for it.

My phone vibrates, and I dig it out of my pocket to find several texts. A few from Cecilia that I don't plan to respond to until later, my mom asking for an update, and Wilder in the sibling chat complaining about the lack of options at the lounge.

Like that's ever stopped him.

After I respond to my mom and hit send, Ellie's fingers twitch in my palm, and I snap my head up to find her looking at me.

"Oh shit." I jump in my seat. "Sorry, you scared me."

Her brows furrow as she studies me and then moves down to where we're touching.

"Noah's on the phone with Fisher, but she'll be back," I tell her, moving my hands to my lap.

She stays quiet as her eyes roam over my face as if she's seeing it for the first time.

"Sorry…I'm probably the last person you wanted to wake up to."

When she doesn't respond, I stand. "I'll go find Noah."

"Okay," she finally speaks, but her voice is hoarse.

When I step into the hallway, Noah's giving the doctor Ellie's parents' numbers.

"Hey, uh…she's awake."

Noah beams. "Oh good!"

The doctor follows us into Ellie's room, who's sitting up a bit higher now with a little more color in her cheeks.

He introduces himself as Dr. Murray and explains everything to her he told us earlier.

"I had a seizure?" she confirms when he finishes speaking.

"That's what the initial exam and bloodwork are showing. Do you have a history of those?" he asks.

"No…never," Ellie responds. "What happened exactly? How'd I get here?"

"You came in presenting hypotension, which is a sudden drop in blood pressure, but it's possible something else correlated with it to trigger an epileptic episode. It was an unfortunate event that it happened while you were on your horse, which caused you to fall and smack your head on the barrel and then gave you a concussion," Dr. Murray explains. "But the good news is the CT scan showed no signs of swelling or internal bleeding in your brain, and some of your bloodwork is still pending, but so far, nothing that makes me believe you have any kind of organ failure or infection."

"That's good, I guess," Ellie says, but then looks at Noah with panic in her eyes. "I don't remember any of that. It happened while I was in the middle of racing?"

Noah sheepishly nods.

"Is that normal?" Ellie asks the doctor.

"Most people don't remember their traumatic events," Dr. Murray says. "I'd say that's quite common."

Reminds me of when Tripp got one during high school while playing football. He didn't remember anything from that whole day.

"Wait, is Ranger okay?" Ellie asks Noah.

"He's fine. Fisher told me they got him back in your trailer unharmed."

She presses a hand to her chest, breathing out a sigh of relief. "Good. He must be so scared."

"So you have no memory of the race or before it?" Noah prompts. "Not even Magnolia, Landen, and me screamin' for you? I made the coolest sign."

"No...it's blank. I don't even remember going to the rodeo. The last thing I remember is arriving at Uncle's ranch. Wait, no, Easton's uncle's ranch. Anything after that, I've got nothin'." Ellie rubs her temple, then tilts her head in confusion. "I thought you were married to Fisher. Who's Landen?"

Noah's eyes widen as she looks at the doctor and then points to me. "Landen. My *brother*."

"Ohh..." Ellie studies me, and a whirlwind of thoughts enters my mind. "I figured he was one of those hospital volunteers who keep patients company or whatever. I did think it was weird how he was just stickin' around, but I figured hey, he's cute, so why question it?"

Noah chokes out a laugh, blinking rapidly. "You don't remember him *at all*?" When Ellie shakes her head, Noah adds, "You've known him for four years. He's helped train you."

"There's a sense of familiarity, but I don't remember *knowing*

153

him." Ellie glances from me to the doctor, panic written on her face. "Is that normal for me to forget people?"

Great…she hates me so much, her unconscious mind completely erased me from her memories.

Talk about a gut punch.

"With a concussion in addition to an epileptic episode, I'd expect you to experience some memory loss or brain fog," he says.

"For how long?" Ellie asks.

One of his shoulders lifts as he purses his lips. "Typically, a few days. But in some cases, it can take weeks or months. Sometimes it never comes back. With your injury, it's hard to say. Everyone recovers at their own pace. The key will be resting and not overdoing it."

She'll probably just randomly remember and then hate me even more.

"But I'm not dying, right? I know you said there are all these possibilities of what caused this and you're still waitin' on some of my test results, but overall, I won't die, probably?"

The doctor's mouth curves into an amused grin. "No, not on my watch anyway."

Ellie exhales sharply. "That's halfway reassuring."

Dr. Murray checks the time. "I'll be back to discharge you tomorrow afternoon, assuming you don't experience any worsening side effects like more vomiting or having another seizure—so don't do that if you wanna go home." He smirks. "The nurse will go over your recovery, restrictions, and scheduling your follow-up before you go."

"Sounds great. Thank you." Ellie grins.

Once he leaves, Noah sits on the bed next to her. "What'd I tell you about not being allowed to die on me?"

"At least not tonight." Ellie snorts. "Did I fall gracefully at least? Oh wait, who won?"

"Uh, no. It was terrifying. I never want to witness that again. And honestly, I dunno. We left right away and none of my family stayed."

Ellie leans back against the pillow as if she's fighting to keep her eyes open. "I swear to God, if Marcia Grayson won, I'll never hear the end of her gloatin'."

Noah snickers. "Unfortunately, she may win now that you're gonna be out the rest of the season."

"What? Why?" The panic in Ellie's voice makes me sad for her because I know how much she loves racing.

"Recovering from a concussion can take weeks, sometimes months. Plus, you have a huge bump on your skull." Noah points to her bandage. "It'd be irresponsible to let you compete in this condition."

The corners of Ellie's eyes fill with tears, and I wish more than anything that I could scoop her up in my arms and comfort her.

"Are my parents coming?" Ellie asks.

"Yeah, they should be here in a couple hours. They were tryna get ahold of someone to come sit with your aunt."

Her brows furrow, but I'm not sure which part confused her. I'm quickly realizing I don't know much about Ellie at all. Like where she lives or who her aunt is.

"I should get back to the campsite to check on Poppy and let you get some rest," Noah says, but I'm tempted to argue because I don't want to leave her.

"Okay." Ellie meets my stare. "Would you be able to stay? At least until my parents get here?"

I'm so taken off guard that my brain freezes for a solid ten seconds.

"Oh, um…yeah. I could do that."

Noah narrows her eyes at me, secretly telling me this is a bad idea, but I don't care. Spending quality alone time with Ellie? I can't pass this up. Plus, if I told her no I'd hurt her feelings.

"I can grab an Uber back," I tell her.

Ellie smiles wide, and it feels wrong to enjoy it because in normal circumstances, she'd never smile at me like that. But I can't help the way my stomach does that stupid flutter thing at seeing her reaction to me.

"I'm just gonna use the restroom quickly and then I'll walk you out," I tell Noah before closing the bathroom door behind me.

There's no way I'm letting her go through a dark parking lot alone at midnight.

My head spins at the unexpected situation I'm in and although I should feel guilty about stealing this time with Ellie, I can't. If she has no memory of hating me, maybe she'll realize she likes me more now than when she hated me before.

After drying my hands, I reach for the door handle but then hear Noah say my name and pause.

"Why'd you ask Landen to stay?" she asks.

Kind of a rude question, but I want the answer, too.

"Um…because he's hot?"

"My *brother*?"

"Yeah."

"Landen?"

I roll my eyes at Noah's insistence to keep asking her.

"Yes! Do you think he likes me?"

If my heart wasn't already racing at how insane this situation is, it'd be rocketing to the fucking moon right now.

"I-I'm sorry. I know you have a concussion and you don't

remember him, but…what in the actual hell are you talkin' about?"

I hold back laughter at Noah freaking the fuck out. Not that I blame her.

"What do you mean? Oh shit, is he married? I didn't see a ring."

Definitely *not* married.

"No." Noah laughs again. "But you don't exactly like Landen. Hell, I'd argue that you hate him."

I pinch the bridge of my nose and contemplate barging out there to shove Noah out of the room just to shut her up. But I don't because I want to hear what else Ellie has to say about me.

"Why would I hate him? He seems very sweet. Plus, he's too hot to hate."

"Actually, I dunno why because you never told me, but trust me. You can't stand him."

"So why is he here if I hated him so much?"

Question of the century. *Because I'm stupidly obsessed with you.*

"Well, Landen helped you train. Technically, he helped me help you train. And he was very worried about you, so he drove us here as soon as the ambulance took off from the rodeo."

"Did he know I hated him?"

"Yeah, we pretty much all do."

"So wait. You're sayin' he helped me train and came to watch me race even knowing I hated him?"

Noah pauses, then finally responds, "Yes."

"That doesn't sound right. What guy would do that for someone who doesn't like them? I couldn't have really hated him, then?"

"Trust me, you did."

Goddammit, Noah. Put in a good word for me or something.

"Landen continued to be nice and supportive because he liked you. He tried for years to get you to like him back. But I guess he finally realized you never would and has a girlfriend now."

Fuck my life. She really just threw out any ounce of hope I just had out the window.

"Oh…" Ellie's voice sounds disappointed, and now I'm worried I've been in here too long. "Do you think it's serious?"

Noah bursts out laughing. "Now I know they gave you the good pain meds if you're pushin' this hard for Landen."

And that's my cue to get out of here.

"Ready to go?" I ask Noah, trying to avert my gaze from Ellie as if I didn't hear everything she said about me.

"Yep." Noah leans over and carefully hugs Ellie. "I'll check on you tomorrow first thing. Text or call if you need anything."

"Will do."

"I'll be right back," I reassure Ellie before we walk out the door.

When we get to the nurse's station, Dr. Murray rounds the corner and stops us. "I didn't want to mention this in front of Ellie, but seeing as you're her friends and will be around her, I need to caution you on not telling her too much about the things she doesn't remember. It's better to let it come back naturally or it'll just confuse her mind even more. She won't know what's a real memory and what she just remembers being told."

I glare at Miss Big Mouth. *A little too late for that.*

"What if she never remembers?" I ask. "Do we share with her at some point?"

Dr. Murray crosses his arms, nodding. "Yeah, I'd say if in a couple months she needs help filling in holes of what she does remember, that'll be fine. Most likely then, it's a lost memory anyway and won't come back. But in most circumstances, the brain fog leaves within a few weeks. She probably won't remember the day of the accident and possibly the day before, but everything else should come back to her as her brain heals. It's why she shouldn't do any vigorous activity."

Not sure if that should put me at ease or on edge. Either way, I wish I knew how long I had for this second chance at showing her who I really am.

Noah and I thank him, and then I walk her out to the truck.

"You sure stayin' with her is a good idea?" she asks.

"Would you rather she be in there alone?"

"Her parents should be comin' soon."

"She asked me to. If I said no, I woulda hurt her feelings."

She sighs. "Just please, don't give her false hope."

"About what?" I play dumb.

Her shoulders tense before she relaxes them. "She has a crush on you."

"Oh!" I pretend to be shocked. "And why is that a bad thing?"

"Uh…because you have a girlfriend. And I know the moment her memory resurfaces, she'll be livid to find out you two were alone together."

"Her forgettin' me and realizin' she likes me just proves that she never genuinely hated me in the first place."

"Maybe…but you don't know that for sure. It could just be a side effect of her concussion and she'll remember in a couple days how much she hates you."

"Well, aren't we the glass is half empty type," I deadpan.

"Landen, I'm serious. Don't string her along. Plus, you're not a cheater."

"Cecilia is not my girlfriend, so you can stop worryin' about that."

She rolls her eyes. "Title or not, you're with someone. She was literally with you last night."

Yeah, but she doesn't know I rejected her. It's why she left so soon.

"I will always treat Ellie with respect. That'll never change," I say, hoping to ease her concerns.

She pokes me in the chest. "You better, Landen Michael. I don't wanna hear tomorrow that you have a black eye because she punched you when she remembers."

"Good night, drive safe…" I goad, opening the door for her.

She huffs but then gets into the driver's seat, and I shut it behind her. I watch as she starts the engine and then I wave as she takes off.

Now, back to my alternate reality where Ellie doesn't hate my guts.

I can only hope she forgives me when she remembers she does.

Chapter Fifteen
ELLIE

Although my head is throbbing, I remove my blood pressure cuff and crawl out of bed as soon as Landen and Noah leave and go to the bathroom. When I look in the mirror, I gasp with horror.

"Oh my God…"

My hair looks like it got stuck in a windmill and all my makeup rubbed off, making me look like a banged-up ghost who got electrocuted.

You'd think I'd be tan from working outside all day, but I wear a lot of sunscreen to avoid getting burnt and to prevent skin cancer.

It's bad enough I don't remember Landen or anything about our history. I don't also need him seeing me like this.

It'd be my luck that I'd wake up to the sexiest man I've ever seen next to my bedside and he's *not* my boyfriend.

A six-foot-something, blue-eyed cowboy staring at me like I'm his.

Noah's words from a moment ago repeat in my head.

Landen continued to be nice and supportive because he liked you. He

161

tried for years to get you to like him back. But I guess he finally realized
you never would and has a girlfriend now.

If that's true, this nagging feeling about the things I can't
place is going to drive me even more crazy. What would make
me *hate* anyone?

As I search my brain for answers, I realize there are a lot of
holes in my memory that won't surface.

I've never had a seizure or concussion before, so maybe this
is a completely normal side effect, but it doesn't feel normal to
me. Something is off.

Continuing to study myself, I notice a massive bruise on the
side of my forehead surrounding the bump that's covered with
gauze. I've fallen off Ranger before but never to this extent
where I've hit a barrel and caused this much damage. I wish I
could go see him right now and reassure him this isn't his fault.
We've been through so much together over the years and he
won't understand any of what happened.

Wetting my hands, I thread my fingers through the strands
around my face. I normally keep a hair tie on my wrist or in my
bag, but I don't even know where it is. Or my phone.

I'm in an unattractive hospital gown, so my clothes must be
here somewhere.

Once I've finished combing through the best I can and
washing my face, I get myself somewhat comfortable back in
bed. The pillows are too soft and the blanket is scratchy, so I'll
be happy to get out of here tomorrow and back into my
own bed.

I already know my parents are going to stress out seeing
me in here. As much as they've supported me for the past
several years, seeing me hurt is going to make them second-
guess letting me continue. It could've been worse, though.
Whatever caused the seizure could've happened while I was

driving and then I could've crashed with no one around to help me.

When Landen returns, my heart races and my chest swells with anticipation. I don't know why I'm reacting to him this way since according to Noah, I didn't even like him, but this feeling doesn't feel new. *Suppressed, maybe?*

"Hey," he says, pulling the chair out and taking a seat. "You look more awake now."

"Yeah, I scared myself when I looked in the mirror, so I tried to clean up a bit. I wish I could take a shower, but I doubt they'd let me with a concussion."

"True, you might need someone to help or at least be around to keep an eye on you."

I raise a brow. "Are you volunteering?"

"Uh…" He smiles nervously, which is adorable. "I wasn't, but if you needed my help, then sure."

I chuckle at how taken back he seems. "Sorry, that probably came off a little strong. I'm not normally this forward, but whatever pain meds they have me on are giving me loose lips."

"Trust me, I'm aware. I don't think you've said more than ten words to me at a time in the past four years. Usually, it's to tell me off, so this is a pleasant change."

Cringing, I chew my lower lip. "Yeah, Noah told me we weren't exactly friends."

"I'd say more along the lines of…*frenemies*? Though, not from a lack of tryin' on my end. You recently asked me to leave you alone because I was crossin' your boundaries and so after that, I stopped tryin'."

His words are so sincere and soft, my emotions almost take over. I tilt my head at him, wondering what in the world would've made me act like that.

Normally, I'm a quiet person who prefers to keep to myself, so for me not to like someone and be that rude wouldn't be for nothing.

But fuck, I can't remember.

Part of me wishes I could because it's going to bother me until then, but the other part...

Would it be so bad to like him? My dating history, from what I do know, consists of less than two people. One from high school and one shortly after graduation. So it's been a few years. But racing became my priority over everything else, and I didn't feel the need to date.

Landen's attractive, seems kind to have put up with me in the first place and still support my career and come to my races, and if he's Noah's brother, how bad can he be?

"How old are you?" I ask.

"Twenty-nine, soon to be the big three-oh."

"And you're not married?"

He shifts, crossing his ankle over his knee. "Nope. Not even close to marriage."

"Noah said you have a girlfriend."

I give myself a mental pat on the back for managing to squeeze in that question. Better to know for certain before I get my hopes up.

"I do not. I was seeing someone for like a week and a half. She wanted to move faster than I did, so I ended it."

My brows lift. "After less than two weeks?"

"Yeah, I guess I wasn't as ready to move on as much as I thought."

I'm tempted to ask what that means, but I think better of it. If he wanted me to know, he would've said.

Grinning, I continue, "Well, I'm nowhere near marriage

either. I'm pretty sure. Unless there's a boyfriend I've forgotten about. But if I had one, he'd be here, right?"

"I would assume so, yes." He chuckles. "Although you're close with Easton, I think."

"Oh shoot, I should call him. If I was stayin' at his uncle's ranch, he woulda been at the rodeo. Do you know where my phone is?"

"No, I haven't seen it."

"I normally keep it in my pocket. Could I borrow your phone to call mine? Maybe I'll hear it ring or vibrate somewhere in here."

"Yep, of course."

He unlocks the screen and then hands it over. I smile when I see a photo of him and his siblings on his home page.

I input my number and a contact name pops up.

Little Devil.

Where have I heard that before?

Wait…

"Is this what you call me?" I ask, turning the phone around to show him.

"Uh…yeah." His cheeks tint with embarrassment. "You weren't a fan, but it suited you well."

I burst out laughing. "I'm so confused by our relationship."

His smile widens. "You and me both, honestly."

Hitting the call button, I wait and listen for it. It's faint, but I hear it.

"I think it's in one of these closets…" Landen walks over and opens a few of the doors. "Aha. Here we go."

He brings over a white plastic bag that has my clothes and boots.

Digging around, I find my cell in my jeans.

"Whew, thank goodness. Miraculously, still in perfect condition." Once I unlock it, I check my messages and see a few from Easton. I quickly shoot him a text so he knows I'm okay.

"My hat's not in here…" I look inside the bag again.

"Oh, it's in my truck. I grabbed it off the ground from when you fell. I knew how important it was to you and didn't want you to lose it."

My heart thuds harder than before. "Wow. That was very nice of you, thank you."

An expression of amusement covers his face as if to hear me talk to him this way is shocking.

"You're welcome." He shoots me a wink and the fluttering in my chest continues.

I still can't figure out what would've made me not like him. He's definitely my type. Polite. Considerate. Willing to stay here with me after he's probably had a busy day. So why? Why did I hate this man?

"Any chance you know why I didn't like you?"

He shakes his head. "I've been askin' you for four years to tell me."

"Shit. I dunno what to say besides I'm sorry. I wanna say it's probably something silly like you tripped me, but hating you for four years over *that* would be excessive."

Landen chuckles at my frustration, but if it isn't the sexiest laugh I've ever heard.

"The day we met…" He stops himself. "Fuck. I'm not supposed to tell you."

"What, why?"

"Dr. Murray said it would confuse your mind if we told you too much. You won't know if a memory is something you're remembering or just remembering what you were told."

166

"Well, that sucks…how am I supposed to get to know you if you can't tell me these things?"

"You wanna get to know me?"

"Yeah…hasn't that been obvious?"

He removes his white ball cap and flips it backward like a habit when he's flustered.

"I'm not sure I should let you get to know me, Ellie." When he frowns, I know I'm not going to like what he says next. "When your memory of me returns, which I'm sure it will, you'll hate me even more for allowing you to get close to me."

Fuck me.

And he's selfless.

Ellie Donovan, why did you hate this man? I wish I could go back in time and smack myself for not taking the chance when it was in front of me.

Sadness consumes me, and I beg myself not to cry because I'm not a crier.

That has to be the meds making me more emotional than usual.

"But what if it doesn't?" My voice cracks. "Dr. Murray said that sometimes it never comes back."

His shoulder lifts in a weak shrug. "If it doesn't in a few weeks, then I'll tell you about the day we first met and you can decide from there if you still want to get to know me."

"Can't you break the rules a little and just tell me now? Or at least something about it? Where? When?"

He chews his bottom lip as he considers.

"Alright, but then you can't tell. I don't need Noah scoldin' me." He smirks, and I nod in agreement.

He blows out a breath as if he's preparing for the worst. "You arrived at the ranch to board Ranger. Noah asked me to help with your training so you'd be ready for the next season in just a few months. I hadn't known I was meetin' you that day and was wearin' a shirt that you found insulting. Then you caught me checkin' out your ass and accused me of sexualizing you. Granted, I made a bad first impression. You've basically hated me since then."

I furrow my brows because why would one bad introduction piss me off to this level four years later?

I would've been nineteen when we met, so him looking at my ass wouldn't have been that inappropriate. And I'm not some prude who gets upset over a shirt.

"That's wild…and it's wild that I don't remember that." I rack my brain for any sense of remembrance of that day and it's blank. Not even a blur. No memory of bringing Ranger to the ranch at all. I don't even know the last thing I do remember.

"I'm sure that'll clear. You smacked your head quite hard and havin' a concussion can fuck you up for a while."

"Can you tell me something else? Maybe during training or when we've seen each other at the ranch?"

"I shouldn't."

When I pout, he grins. "Trust me, I want to, but not yet. Maybe in a few days."

"Okay, fair enough."

"Do you wanna rest before your parents arrive?"

"I probably should. I was gonna ask for some more pain meds because my head feels like it's drowning."

Landen grabs a remote and hands it to me. "Just press the red button and the nurse will come. But feel free to close your eyes and sleep. I'm not going anywhere."

Chapter Sixteen
LANDEN

By the time Ellie's parents arrive, she's long passed out. I greet them in the hallway and their surprised expressions tell me they know I shouldn't be here either.

Still, I catch them up on what I know since the on-call doctor is with other patients.

"Thank you, Landen." Mr. Donovan claps my shoulder—a smidge too hard—but I grin in return. "And for stayin' with her. We got here as soon as we could leave."

"No problem."

I watch them go into her room, wishing I could go back in too, but they deserve some alone time with her.

This new version of Ellie is throwing me off, and I'm not quite sure if it's a good thing or not. There has to be a reason she hasn't liked me all these years. I had finally accepted I'd never change her mind about me. But now, I'm so fucking confused about what to do because this Ellie seems to like me.

She *likes* me.

But how can I just go along with it knowing she didn't before?

The moment she remembers she doesn't will destroy me after getting my hopes up for a second chance.

My heart would break worse than it did before when she asked me to keep my distance.

So maybe I should respect her wishes from before the accident.

But fuck if I don't want to do that.

When I grab my phone to order an Uber, the screen is black. After Ellie borrowed it to call hers, it must've died.

I could ask at the nurse's station to use their phone to call a cab service, but at this rate, I'll just hang out here and wait until one of my siblings can pick me up after they're awake. Plus, this way, I can still feel close to her and be here when she wakes up in the morning.

Hopefully, she doesn't remember me overnight. I'd like another few days of her not hating me.

"Landen?"

My eyes peel open to Mrs. Donovan standing above me as I lie back in an uncomfortable hospital chair.

Blinking a few times, I sit up and clear my throat. "Hello. Hi."

"You're still here?"

"Uh, yeah. Just waitin' until Noah returns. How's Ellie doing?"

"Good. They got more of her blood test results back and

said she had high-dose alpha-blockers in her system. She's not prescribed for any blood pressure meds, but of course, she doesn't remember takin' any."

"Do you think someone slipped them to her? For what exactly?" The panic in my voice is evident, but this is alarming. Ellie's one of the top pro barrel racers in the region, so she causes a threat to many who want to beat her.

"The way Dr. Murray explained it is when your blood pressure drops suddenly, it can cause drowsiness or make you pass out, but in some extreme cases, it can give you a seizure."

"Oh my God." I stand, folding my arms, not knowing what else to do.

"He also said there were other concerns with some of the blood test results. Based on how low her blood pressure got, he doesn't think the dosage of those pills would've been enough to do that on their own that quickly. He suggested she might've digested something that counteracted the meds or contributed to the side effect of low blood pressure. They're going to do more extensive testing to find out for sure. Then we'll at least know she doesn't have a seizure disorder because if she does, her career would be over for good."

Shaking my head, I blow out a breath of frustration and anger. "Someone must've drugged her. Ellie would never take prescription meds without needing 'em."

She doesn't deviate from her routine.

"I agree. But since we couldn't go with her, I don't know who she woulda been around."

I rub along my scruffy jawline, thinking. "I didn't see her before the race. She's usually at her trailer until she brings Ranger to the waitin' pen. And with the junior division also racing, it woulda been crowded with people."

"Many people who know of her, I'm sure," she says, and I nod.

"Do you think you could open an investigation into it? If someone drugged her, that'd be a crime, and an officer could question everyone who was there. Maybe someone saw her with a specific person or noticed something off beforehand."

"Maybe…it'd be worth findin' out, though." She gives me a sad grin. "Anyway, Ellie's getting assessed right now to make sure she can go home this afternoon. Did you wanna see her before she leaves?"

It's throwing me off how nice her mom is being, but whatever beef Ellie had with me, I guess it didn't extend to her parents. I'm halfway tempted to ask if she knows Ellie's reasoning, but that feels too intrusive.

Before I can respond, Noah and Magnolia enter the hospital with the babies, and I wave them down.

"There you are!" Noah scolds when she sees me. "I've been callin' you all mornin'."

"Phone died," I tell her.

"You've been here all night?" Magnolia asks, scanning around the waiting room. She's wearing one of Ellie's backpacks.

I stretch and crack my neck. "Yeah, I slept in a chair." Though I wouldn't call what I did *sleep*. More like twenty-minute interval naps in between trying to get comfortable.

Noah gives Mrs. Donovan a hug and the two speak for a few moments before she takes us down to Ellie's room. As soon as she sees us, her face lights up.

"Thank God. Have you come to bail me outta here?" she asks.

Mr. Donovan sits next to her in a chair, looking amused by Ellie's eagerness to bail.

"Not exactly, but we brought you some clean clothes and your toothbrush." Magnolia hands her the bag.

"Oh my God, thank you. I can't wait to get out of this gown and shower at some point."

When Poppy fusses, I take her from Noah's arms so they can talk. I bounce her around the small room and let her look out the window.

"Any chance you checked on Ranger?" Ellie asks Noah.

"Yep, and he's doing fine. I can tell he misses you." Noah sits on the edge of the bed. "Everyone's askin' about you."

Ellie rolls her eyes. "More like they're wonderin' if I'm out for the season so they can take my spot."

I smirk at that. Glad to see the arrogant Ellie is still in there.

"That just means you're gonna come back stronger and better than ever next year. The time off will be good for you, too," Noah says. "I'll continue trainin' with Ranger so he doesn't get out of his routine."

"I will, too," I interject, and when Noah looks at me, her brows furrow. "You have enough on your plate, and I don't mind. Plus, Ranger likes me."

"It was just his owner who didn't." Magnolia laughs at her own joke, but no one else does. "What? You can't tell me her forgettin' who you are ain't a bit ironic and hilarious?"

Of course Noah told her.

"It kinda sucks, honestly." Ellie glances at me before speaking to Magnolia. "There's so much I can't recall and it makes me feel like I'm missing a part of myself. Makes me feel a little vulnerable, too. Like y'all know a secret about me but no one's sharing it."

"I'd be happy to fill you in on the town gossip," Magnolia

teases. "You wouldn't believe what people openly share with me while I'm makin' their lattes."

Noah nudges her. "We can't, remember? The doctor said it'll confuse her."

"Even if it's not about her?" Magnolia asks.

Ellie groans. "I don't see why not. I'm confused as hell anyway."

"What if she reads something on her phone? I'm sure there are messages, emails, or something that will trigger a memory," Magnolia suggests.

"I don't use my phone much," Ellie admits. "I post on my social media pages a couple times a week, but that's about it. Otherwise, everyone I talk to is usually in person or we call."

"Damn. So no juicy tea to discover." Magnolia pouts.

"That's what happens when you stay in your lane and mind your business…" Noah directs to Magnolia, and I snort.

She's one to talk.

After another twenty minutes of the girls talking, the nurse enters and says she's been cleared to start working on her discharge papers.

Ellie goes to change out of her gown and then they discuss how they're going to get Ranger and the trailer back to the ranch. Mr. Donovan states he'll drive the truck and Mrs. Donovan will take Ellie home in their car.

"I'll let Ayden know to be ready for his arrival and he'll get him situated in his stall," Noah tells them. "Once we're back, I'll have the vet check him over just to make sure he didn't get hurt during the fall. He seemed fine, though, but I'm not takin' any chances."

"Thank you. We appreciate that," Mrs. Donovan says.

"I'll get out there as soon as I can." Ellie frowns. "Even if it's just to sit and read to him."

Magnolia rocks Willow back and forth when she gets restless. "You read to your horse?"

"Mostly when we're traveling. It can get lonely just the two of us, so I'll sit with him and read my book out loud. It calms him, too."

"Aww...that's sweet. I wish I was a horse girlie," Magnolia says. "But I'm kinda terrified of 'em."

"Willow and Poppy will be horse girlies, though, won't ya?" Noah tickles Poppy when I give her back.

"I gotta run. I'm on Cantina lounge duty tonight and need to clean up. Can you drive me to the campsite?" I ask Noah.

"Yeah, I should get back, too. Lord knows what the others are gettin' themselves into. I found Wilder halfway under the camper this morning three sheets to the wind."

Ellie's horrified look makes me laugh.

"That's Wilder on a tame weekend," I tell her.

The girls exchange hugs and Ellie promises to let Noah know when she's home. There's an awkwardness as we linger in the doorway, and I'm not sure what to say.

"I hope you feel better and maybe I'll see ya at the ranch soon?"

"Thanks. As soon as they let me, I'll be there." She smiles weakly.

I tip my hat to her parents and then walk out behind Noah and Magnolia, crossing my fingers that the next time we see each other is before she remembers me.

Chapter Seventeen
ELLIE

It's been seven days since the incident at the rodeo, and I'm so fucking bored.

Whoever said free time is amazing was a liar.

Free time sucks.

I want to be riding Ranger, going on my morning jogs, visiting Magnolia at her coffee trailer, and traveling to my next race.

But the doctor's discharge orders were bedrest for a week and then I could gradually add in more activity. But since I haven't been cleared to drive, I pace around the house, sleep, or listen to nineties sitcoms with Aunt Phoebe.

Explaining to her what happened hasn't been easy. Even though I look fine physically, minus the gash on my head, she doesn't understand the concept of me losing my memory or that she's not allowed to tell me anything.

Which also sucks for me because I can't remember what happened to her or why she lives with us. All my mom will tell me is that there was a traumatic event years ago that caused her to come live with us. Even when I dug for more answers, she was determined to stick to Dr. Murray's orders.

Between having nothing to do and not being allowed to do anything fun, I've Googled everything possible on concussions and seizures affecting your memory.

Some articles talk about how concussions can cause both short-term and long-term memory impairments, including difficulties with recalling traumatic events, but the degree of loss depends on the specific brain regions affected. Considering I also had an epileptic episode, more than one region could've been affected, but either way, it varies for everyone. It makes me wonder if whatever happened with Aunt Phoebe has a direct correlation to the stuff I can't remember because it was traumatic for me too.

The consensus is that brain injuries affect people differently and there's not always a rhyme or reason to it.

While it's somewhat helpful and reassuring that most people get their partial memories back, it's frustrating not having the answers.

Some people on Reddit wrote that forgetting their trauma was the best thing that ever happened to them. Even if it was only temporary, they lived in peace for the first time.

Part of me wonders if this is a blessing in disguise, and I should appreciate it instead of wishing for it back.

I think I'd be okay with that as long as I get to ride again someday.

Finally, after begging my dad, he agrees to take me to the ranch to see Ranger after work. If even for thirty minutes, he needs to know I haven't abandoned him.

I text Noah to let her know I'm coming and she meets us outside the stables.

"Hey, you look good!" She gives me a small hug, but I know she's just being polite. The wound on my head looks better, but I still have a small bandage to cover it. "How're you feelin'?"

"Pretty good. The headaches are mild, and I get a little bit of dizziness, but it's gotten a lot better."

"Well, that's progress at least. Are you sleepin' okay?"

"All I do is sleep." I groan. "I've slept more this week than I have my whole life."

Noah chuckles at the exaggeration, but I never sleep more than eight hours a night. Even when I don't set my alarm, my body wakes me up, but this past week I've slept for twelve hours or more each night.

"You probably needed it," she says. "Well, let's go see Ranger. He's been a little restless, but he's gonna be so excited."

I smile because she's right. The moment he comes into view, he releases a high-pitched squeal, and I almost cry at how good it is to see him.

"Hey, buddy!" I walk inside his stall and wrap my arms around him, inhaling his earthy scent. "I missed you so much."

Petting his neck, he nuzzles his nose against me.

"I'm sorry I couldn't come sooner."

Noah pets him on the other side and we talk for a few minutes while my dad walks around and checks out the other horses.

Although I can't ride, I can talk to and groom him. Though I don't have anything interesting to say, hearing my voice is enough to calm his anxiety.

When the brush slips out of my hand, I carefully bend to grab it, but when I go back up, I jump at the sight of Landen.

"Jesus Christ, you scared me," he says, a palm over his heart.

"I was about to say the same thing."

"Where'd you come from?"

I hold up the brush. "I dropped it."

"I mean, when did you get here?"

"Oh, just a bit ago. My dad's walkin' around so I could spend a few minutes with Ranger. What're you doin'?"

He holds up a thick book in his hand. "I came to read to him."

"You did? Why?"

"You said it calms him, so I figured I'd try it and it has so far. But nothing beats you being here, so he probably doesn't need me tonight."

"Wait, you've been readin' to him this whole week?"

"Yeah, we're"—he flips through the book—"about two hundred pages in."

Stepping closer, I flip the cover so I can see what it is. "Oh my God, that's my favorite book!"

He points to the title, *Project Hail Mary*. "Your favorite?"

Smiling, I nod. "One of 'em, yes."

He bursts out laughing. "You see the irony, right? He loses his memory on a spaceship?"

"Yes, it's very funny," I deadpan. "Maybe I'll solve a mission."

"You never know." He winks. "Do you wanna read it to him tonight?"

I lower my eyes and shuffle my boots in the straw. "Um...I can't read right now. My vision is still a little blurry."

He smacks his forehead with the book. "Oh shit, sorry."

"It's not your fault."

"Well, if you wanna stick around, I'll read to you both."

My heart swells at the thought of him sitting in Ranger's stall and reading to him. I know Ranger must love it.

"Sure, I can stay for a while."

As I continue brushing Ranger's coat and combing through his mane, Landen reads and it's mesmerizing. He has a great reading voice.

"Sweetheart, it's gettin' late. We should go," my dad says an hour later.

When I stick out my lower lip, he sighs. "You can't push yourself too quickly."

"I'm just standin' here," I argue.

He gives me a pointed look. "You know what I mean."

"Can you bring me back tomorrow?" I ask him.

"Maybe. We'll see how you're feelin'."

Landen flashes me a small smile, and I give him one in return. "Thanks for readin' to Ranger and me."

"Anytime, Ellie."

The smooth way he says my name sounds like he's been eagerly waiting to speak it out loud.

Dad nods at Landen, and then I say goodbye.

As we drive back into town, I get a text from a number I don't recognize.

UNKNOWN
You forgot something.

Well, that could be anything considering...but first...

ELLIE
Who is this?

UNKNOWN
Wow, seriously? You never even saved my name in your phone. Why am I not surprised?

I snort. *Previous Ellie really did hate him.*

ELLIE

Maybe I was just trying to come up with a name as clever as Little Devil.

UNKNOWN

I'm sure that was the case.

ELLIE

Well, give me an idea...what name would I have put your number under?

UNKNOWN

Probably "The Sexiest Man I've Ever Seen" or "Hottest Cowboy Ever" ...just to give you a couple ideas.

ELLIE

Wow...both great choices! However, I'm thinking of something a bit shorter. Maybe "Egomaniac?" or "Captain Ego?"

UNKNOWN

Captain? Now we're talking.

ELLIE

Glad I didn't suggest Lord High and Mighty. You'd probably require I bow at your feet.

UNKNOWN

I would never suggest that. Kneeling, maybe.

My eyes widen at the text on my screen and my cheeks heat. I glance over at my dad to make sure he's not watching me blush.

Did he seriously just say that? *Is he flirting with me?*

I'm not good at that. If anything, my resting bitch face is part of the reason I've been single for years.

ELLIE

Um…didn't you say I forgot something? Are you gonna tell me what that is or add it to the long list of other shit I don't know?

UNKNOWN

Depends. Did you change my name yet?

Smirking, I roll my eyes and edit his contact information. Then I take a screenshot and send it to him.

ELLIE

Here, I gave you a promotion.

MAJOR EGO

HAHAHA

He adds a dorky sunglasses emoji.

MAJOR EGO

Now you know this means you'll be required to salute me.

ELLIE

Of course.

And then I add the saluting emoji.

MAJOR EGO

Okay good. Well the thing you forgot was me telling you a memory. In the hospital, I mentioned I would in a few days assuming you didn't get it back by then.

ELLIE

Oh right! Better tell me something good…

MAJOR EGO

I'll let you pick. Do you wanna hear something nice or something mean?

ELLIE

Is the nice or mean in reference to me?

MAJOR EGO

Yes.

ELLIE

Uhh...nice, I guess.

MAJOR EGO

I had a horse named Sydney. Noah and I ended up rescuing her from a bad home where she was being neglected. I was the only one she'd go to while I nursed her back to health. Used to ride her all over the ranch and retreat. One day she got sick and had to have surgery to remove the blockage. She went into shock and her heart couldn't keep up. After twenty-four hours, I refused to let her suffer, so I had to say goodbye. It was one of the hardest things I've ever gone through. A few days later, you gave me a condolence card. I still have it in my truck.

Wow...I did not expect that at all. If I truly hated him, why would I go through the trouble of gifting him a card?

ELLIE

Okay, now tell me something mean.

I know I'm being greedy, but I'm dying for more.

MAJOR EGO

> I took your card as an olive branch, and a
> couple weeks later, asked you out on a date.
> You laughed in my face and walked away.

I cover my mouth, containing my laughter. It's not funny. In fact, it's really mean, but the fact that he's even talking to me after I did that is comical.

ELLIE

> I'm not sure if I should apologize or say that's
> what you get for trying to get in my pants.

MAJOR EGO

> I was only trying to take you to dinner!

ELLIE

> Sorry, I feel awful. Maybe I can make it up
> to you?

MAJOR EGO

> I'm not sure that's a good idea.

ELLIE

> Because you think I'm gonna wake up and
> remember why I hate you...

MAJOR EGO

> That would pretty much be my luck, yes.

ELLIE

> How about if I still don't remember you in a
> month, you reconsider?

MAJOR EGO

> Okay deal...one month.

Deal.

"Who's makin' you smile like that?" my dad asks when he pulls into our driveway.

"It's Landen. Apparently, I never saved his contact info and we came up with one."

"Be careful with him, okay?"

I unbuckle my belt and look at him. "What do you mean?"

"In the past four years, you've not said one thing about him. Well, nothin' nice at least."

"So?"

"You weren't interested in him for a reason, so I'm just saying…be careful. You'll get your memory back and may remember why you didn't in the first place."

"Knowing how focused on racing I was, I could see myself not being very nice to him either. It was probably for a silly reason in the first place, and I didn't like the distraction of his attention, so I tried to push him away."

He looks at me like I'm crazy. But it's feasible. Why else would I act like that and never give him a reason? Dating was never a priority because all I cared about was training.

"I just don't want you to get hurt, sweetheart."

I point to my head. "A little too late for that."

He pierces me with a scowl. "You know what I mean. Just be cautious."

"Shouldn't you be telling me to take this second chance and have fun for a bit? I coulda died if my brain injury had been worse. But I didn't, so this could be the universe giving me another opportunity to live life outside of being a pro barrel racer. As upset as I am about being out this season, this is the first time in years I've not had to worry about gettin' ready for the next race or stickin' to a routine. Granted, I hate sittin' around the house, but maybe I'll find other opportunities, too."

"I understand, sweetie. Really, I do. But I'm your dad, and I'll always wanna protect you."

I smile at his sincerity. "I love you, too."

Chapter Eighteen
LANDEN

Seeing Ellie last Saturday gave me the reassurance I needed that she hadn't remembered me or was back to hating my guts.

This version of her is fun and playful, and I almost feel guilty for enjoying it.

It's a battle I've been fighting since she woke up in the hospital, but when I found her in Ranger's stall seven days ago, I couldn't resist seeing where our conversation led. Even if it was just spending time together as friends, it'd be better than her pretending I didn't exist.

But then she came up with this one-month deal where she'd make it up to me for rejecting my offer two years ago.

I shouldn't have agreed because I know better than to get my hopes up, but how can I not when I've wanted her to give me a chance for years? Then again, how do I protect my heart from the inevitable when she realizes how close I let her get to me and she hates me even more for it?

So many what-ifs and various scenarios that I don't have

answers to. Ellie could get her memory back in a matter of weeks, months, or perhaps never.

But I knew I'd kick myself for not taking this opportunity to see what could happen. It's a risk, but I'll accept the consequences and hope we don't fall apart when it ends.

The day after, I sent her a message to see how she was feeling. That led to us texting all day long and then each night we'd FaceTime so she could watch and listen to me reading to Ranger. He loved getting to hear her voice, too. It's become our routine for the past eight days, but I'm dying to see her in person again.

Ellie had her follow-up doctor appointment for her concussion and due to some of the lingering side effects, she still can't drive or do anything too physical. I offered to pick her up and bring her to see Ranger after my shifts, but she was usually too tired by then.

Even though I always looked forward to talking to her, I woke up each morning anticipating the moment she'd tell me her memory was back and she hated my guts again. Luckily, that hasn't happened, and instead, I've been smiling at my phone nonstop like a lunatic who's falling for a girl who has the potential to destroy him.

Today's no different. We've been texting on and off all day, and she's been talking with Noah to see if she can convince her dad to drop her off for a few hours. He's been protective of letting her come after the doctor suggested she needed to continue resting. Since she hasn't had any other epileptic episodes, they're anticipating she'll be clear for casual riding in a month or two.

Even though it's Sunday, there are still chores to be done. Stalls to muck and horses to feed, but I save the breeding work for weekdays so I only have to work half a day. Unless I'm using the other half to catch up on paperwork, invoices, and returning emails.

"Incoming!"

Before I have a chance to react, a hay bale smacks into my head.

"Didn't you hear my warnin'?" Waylon asks a few moments later, towering above me as I lie flat on my ass.

I groan, giving in to the pain. "You mean the point two-second one?"

"It slipped outta my grip, sorry." He holds out his hand and helps me to my feet.

When I look up, Tripp and Wilder are in the loft, laughing.

"Fuck you, guys. Too bad I didn't get a concussion and forget we were related."

"Hey, don't include me in that!" Noah shouts behind me.

"Jesus Christ." I spin around toward her. "Where do y'all keep comin' from?"

"You'd need to remember me so I could tell you all the chicks you've already dated so you didn't try datin' them again," Waylon muses, grabbing the bale and carrying it back up.

"I was comin' to tell you Ellie's on her way out here. Her dad's droppin' her off to come hang out with Ranger, but I thought you'd like to spend some time with her, too," Noah says.

"Aren't you the one who told me not to give her false hope and now you're encouraging me?" I raise a brow.

Talk about confusing.

She doesn't know Ellie and I have been talking all week, but I still enjoy giving her shit.

"Yes, I know. But she doesn't have a lot of people she can trust, and for whatever reason, this version of Ellie seems to like you. I'm not saying start datin' her, but it wouldn't hurt to hang out as friends."

"*Riiiiight.* So you're givin' me permission to spend time with her but not to fuck her."

She playfully smacks my chest. "Landen Michael!"

"Dude, I'm already hurtin'." I rub the spot where she hit.

"Oh please. A hay bale is like forty pounds. You can lift two of 'em at a time without breakin' a sweat."

I point to my skull. "It was dropped *on my head*…"

She rolls her eyes before walking away as if this is a normal occurrence.

"Ellie will be at the stables in an hour…" she calls out over her shoulder.

Since I was done for the day anyway, I drive home and change out of my work clothes. As anxious as I am to see her, I remind myself that this is temporary.

But as I've already decided, I'll take what I can get.

Before I go to the stables, I stop by the main house to see if Mom and Gramma Grace need anything at the store for tonight's supper. I usually grocery shop on Saturdays, but I ran out of time.

"You're so sweet to ask. I'll make a list," Mom says. "I heard Ellie's comin' today. You should invite her to stay for dinner tonight."

"Okay, sure," I say.

Once she hands me the list, I scan it over and then smile. "We're havin' a feast tonight or what?"

"Don't we always?" Mom smirks, patting my cheek. "Appreciate ya goin' for me."

"No problem, Ma. I'll be back in a bit."

I drive to the stables and smile when I find Ellie at Ranger's stall. She's wearing those sexy-as-hell cut-off jean shorts.

"Hey."

Her eyes brighten when they find mine and she noticeably checks me out. "You're wearin' a cowboy hat."

"Yeah. A Cattleman. Do you like it?" I tilt my head down so she can see all of it.

"I do. How very western of you."

Chuckling, I nod. "I like wearin' it once in a while. Other times, I wear a baseball cap."

"Like at the hospital."

"Right."

"Both suit you nicely."

I narrow my eyes, and she mimics the gesture.

"What?" she asks.

"I was just waitin' for you to mock me about it or say sike and that I look dumb."

"Why? Oh, because of the whole I hate you thing?" She shrugs. "Well, I don't today. But I do have a theory."

Arching a brow, I lean against the stalls. "What's that?"

"That we're actually dating...but in secret. It's why your name wasn't in my contacts. I probably had it memorized anyway, but in case anyone saw me texting you, they wouldn't know who I was texting. It's why I would've deleted the thread. But for whatever reason, you don't want anyone to know, or maybe it was my idea not to tell anyone, but either way, we pretended we couldn't stand each other to keep anyone from findin' out."

"Have you hit your head again?" I ask.

She swats at my arm. "You can't tell me that sounds any less crazy than us being enemies for no reason?"

"I'm sorry to burst your theory bubble, but that's wrong."

She folds her arms. "Then why were you sittin' next to my bedside holdin' my hand?"

"Because I didn't want you to feel alone. Noah had just left and—"

"Why were you even there in the first place if I hated you?"

Leaning in closer, I slide my tongue along my bottom lip. "Because I never hated you."

Her breath hitches at my closeness, and I know I affect her as much as she affects me.

"We've been textin' all week like it was a normal thing for us." There's a hint of sadness in her voice like she's desperate to put the puzzle pieces together and frustrated that she can't. "It didn't feel like I was talkin' to someone I'd just met."

"It didn't feel like that for me either," I admit. "Even though I have memories from the past four years, the way we talk now is new to me, too."

"Then kiss me."

Taking a step back, I meet her serious expression. "What?"

"I wanna test my theory. If we've never dated or kissed before, then there'll be no instant chemistry or familiarity. If there is, I'll know I'm right."

I scrub my palm across my face, desperately trying to think of a way out of this. Ironic considering how long I've wanted to kiss her.

"Ellie…"

"What's the harm?"

"We agreed to wait a month," I remind her. "And I wouldn't lie to you about this."

"That agreement was for a date. This is just a kiss. One little kiss."

"You're sure about this? You're not gonna tell Noah I took advantage or something to get me in trouble?"

"Of course not!" She flinches. "Why? Is that something the old me would do?"

192

I bark out a laugh. "The old you wouldn't be standin' here beggin' me to kiss her."

"I'm not *begging*."

I smirk. "Kinda sounds like you are."

She sighs. "If you're a chickenshit, just admit it. Or maybe you're a bad kisser…"

"That's *definitely* not it…"

Her shoulders lift. "Alright, if you say so."

She moves to walk past me, and without hesitating, I grab her arm and pull her back. My palms cradle her face as I lean in and brush my lips along hers. I'm cautious at first, but when she doesn't pull away, I slide my tongue between them.

My fingers thread through her hair as I cup her head and pull her closer.

She moans against my mouth, her fists tightening around the fabric of my shirt as she takes everything I give her.

I've craved her this way for so long, and now that I've had a taste, how can I ever go without it again?

When my heart threatens to beat out of my chest, I pull away, gasping for air and seeking reassurance that she doesn't instantly regret it.

"So what's the verdict?" I finally ask, swallowing hard as I adjust myself.

"Damn, I was hopin' that'd prove we were havin' a secret affair," she breathes out, but then her fingers touch where my lips had been. "Guess I was wrong after all."

There's a hint of deviousness on her face, and then it hits me.

"You played me."

Her shoulders lift. "And you fell for it hook, line, and sinker."

"Wow…" I say slowly and dramatically. "Now that's

something the old Ellie would do. Guess she's still in there somewhere."

"It was for a good cause, I swear."

"Mm-hmm." I fold my arms over my chest and wait for her explanation.

"I read that sometimes memories can resurface from any of the five senses. So I thought maybe *touch* could be kissing you and seeing if it triggered anything."

Instead of feeling upset she used me, I do sympathize with her frustration. I'd hate having part of my memory blocked and feeling like I had no control over what I remembered.

"Okay. What's the next sense you want to try?" I ask. "I wanna help."

As much as I should dread her getting it back, it feels worse knowing she's struggling.

"Maybe smell?"

I think back to the list Mom gave me. "I have to run to the grocery store. You could come with me and maybe something there will smell familiar."

"Sure. Couldn't hurt to try."

She tells Ranger she'll be back and then follows me out to my truck. Once we're buckled in, she looks over at me.

"You don't seem that upset about the kiss."

"Should I be? I thought it was a nice kiss…"

"It was…very nice actually."

"Great. Then what's the problem?" I ask, backing out and driving us onto the main gravel driveway.

"I guess the problem is that even though I did it as an experiment, it kinda felt a little too real."

The vulnerability in her voice has me glancing toward her and struggling to keep the smirk off my face.

"That is a real problem…" I tsk. "Because now you have to

wait three more weeks for another one. Assuming I even kiss on the first date, which I'm kinda thinking I shouldn't since I'm a gentleman and all."

"Alright, I know why I kissed you, but you're the one who grabbed me and devoured my face like your life depended on it. So how are *you* gonna wait that long?"

I take one hand off the steering wheel and hold up a finger. "First, I didn't do that. It's just how I kiss. Secondly, need I remind you, I'm the one who's liked you this whole time. So kissing you, even as bait, wasn't a hardship. Third, I've waited four years for that moment. I can certainly wait a little bit longer."

There's something in the way Ellie looks at me that I've never seen in her eyes before.

Lust.

"I dunno why I'm drawn to you, and even if I'm supposed to hate you, I don't understand how. It's very confusing."

"Trust me, I get it. I felt the same way, and I couldn't explain it either. My brothers would ask why I kept tryin' to get your attention and what I liked about you."

"What'd you tell them?"

"Well, obviously, that I was attracted to you. From the moment we met, I thought you were gorgeous. But there was also a fire about you that intrigued me from the start. Most girls are eager to get my attention and just say whatever it is they think I wanna hear. They couldn't just be themselves and that made it hard to be myself in return. They'd act how they thought I wanted them to, which gets old quickly. But you never had a reason to be anything other than exactly who you were and it was a nice change to be around. I also admired your passion, dedication, and drive to succeed. Even when I pushed your limits during training and you were ready to murder me, you'd still get on Ranger and do exactly what I suggested. You exuded confidence and that was sexy as hell. Even the way we'd bicker was hot because I knew at least you weren't just feeding me bullshit lines."

"So you liked that I didn't bow down at your feet like a buckle bunny?"

I chuckle at her bluntness—another thing I like about her. "Yes. In a way, you challenged me. That wasn't *why* I wanted you. But it certainly added to it. And I was delusional enough to hope one day you'd admit you felt it, too."

"In the hospital, you said you weren't as ready to move on as you thought. Was that about me? Moving on from liking me?"

I'm surprised she remembers that. Most people with concussions struggle with short-term memory.

Nodding, I keep my eyes on the road. "I was using you as an excuse not to get serious with anyone else, so I finally decided I needed to move on from my crush and that's when I joined a dating app."

"That's where you met that one girl who wanted to move too fast."

"Yeah, Cecilia. It wasn't fair to string her along when I couldn't give her a fair chance. Even after spendin' time with her and having fun, I knew I could never fully give myself to her because there was a part of me still holding out hope for you."

I'm left with silence and when I glance toward her, she's staring at me, motionless.

"I probably sound like a psycho, right?" I ask, wondering if I've scared her.

Quietly, she shakes her head. "I can't believe I'm sayin' this, but I'm kinda hoping I never get my memory back. Whatever it is you did couldn't have been bad enough if I didn't tell anyone else."

My chest tightens at the insinuation because it's only a matter of time until she gets it back. Wishing that she doesn't is setting us up for failure.

But I can't help praying for the same thing.

"You're not curious about what you can't remember?" I ask. "Specifically the memory about why you didn't like me?"

"Oh, I am. I dream about people and situations...but I dunno what's real or not by the time I wake up. What I do know is that you are and what I feel is even if I don't understand how or why. This pull—or whatever it is—feels different than anything I've experienced. Almost as if it's always been there, but I wouldn't act on it. Like there was a shield guardin' it for some reason."

My mind spirals at what that could mean or what was stopping her in the past. If someone warned her away from me or she's connected to someone who didn't approve of me.

"Great...you think I'm crazy now like that one chick who was moving too fast," she blurts when I don't say anything. "I'll just shut—"

I jerk my truck to the side of the road, halting her words, and once we're parked, I rip off my seat belt. Then I lean across the bucket seat and unclip hers.

"No fuckin' crazier than me," I say before crashing my mouth to hers, wrapping an arm around her waist and pulling her into me.

Her tongue matches my speed as we battle in a war of wanting, *needing* more of each other.

When she climbs into my lap, I shift the steering wheel up and the seat back to give us as much room as possible. Her bare legs cage my thighs and when she moans into my mouth, her hips rock against mine, and I nearly come undone.

"Ellie…fuck, you can't do that," I plead in between her lips tasting mine.

"Why not? I can tell you like it." She smiles against my mouth when my cock hardens between us.

"That's exactly why." I squeeze her hips to stop her from continuing. "I can't go into the grocery store with a boner."

"You can't with blue balls either."

I move my lips down her jaw. "That'd be better than having a wet spot on my jeans, trust me."

Her head falls back as I suck on her neck. Shallow breaths echo between us as she continues to grind on me. "*Landen…*"

"Jesus Christ," I hiss, licking up to her ear. "You have no idea how long I've waited to hear you moan my name."

"Don't make me stop, please. I'm so close."

Sweet little whimpers follow as she uses my erection to rub against her pussy. Her hands wrap around my neck, seeking more friction.

If she continues for another second, I'm going to lose it.

And if I touch her, I'll explode.

"Lift your body," I tell her, taking off my hat.

"What? How?"

"I'm putting this between us."

I tap her hip, motioning for her to spread her legs and make room. Then I slide my hat between her thighs and over my cock.

"I'm going to crush it," she says when I move her hips down.

"No, you won't, but even so, don't care. Pick a side of the ridge and ride it till you come, baby."

When she settles on top of it, I crash her mouth back to

mine and palm her breast over her tank top. Moaning against my lips, she rotates her hips back and forth.

Her head falls back, and I lick across the softness of her neck. "Thatta girl, take what you need."

"I need you," she begs.

"Imagine it's me," I whisper in her ear as I hold the hat in place so she can feel the friction. "My fingers in your sweet cunt and my tongue flicking your needy clit as you soak my hand. Picture me touching every inch of your body."

"Oh my God…" She moans so loud, I'm grateful we're in the privacy of my old truck on the side of a country road. "Almost there…keep talkin'."

"Mm, so the dirty talk does it for ya? Duly noted." I smirk, kissing along her jawline. "I've been imagining all the ways I'd touch you for so long. I'm not sure I'll be able to stop once I do."

"Tell me…every detail."

She continues breathing heavily, and I know it's only a matter of seconds before she unravels.

"Mm…you really are a Little Devil, aren't you? Wanting to know all the ways I've fantasized about you? All the times I've jerked off in the shower imagining you in there with me…"

"Yes, just like that…"

I don't need to say another word before she's moaning through her release and shattering in my arms.

"Holy shit…did I just come on your cowboy hat?" she asks when she finally catches her breath.

I smirk, grab the hat from between us, and place it back on my head. "I can die a happy man now. In fact, bury me in this so I'm never without it."

Chapter Nineteen

ELLIE

I can't stop smiling as Landen and I walk hand in hand through the grocery store. Knowing what I do about him, putting us on public display like this is a huge deal.

Locals from Sugarland Creek love their juicy Southern gossip and this will get someone's attention to start it.

When an elderly woman greets him and he tips his hat at her, I have to conceal my laughter.

"That just feels wrong," I tease.

"Not to me." He winks as he continues to push the cart with one hand.

I can't believe what happened in his truck, and I don't know what the hell it means now, but I'm choosing not to freak out about it. My life was so structured and almost every day was predictable.

Now, I like not knowing. I want to *live* my life for once.

"Okay, here's my mom's list. Can you hold it for me?"

I grab the piece of paper from his hand and read it over as he pushes the cart.

"You shop for your mom? How sweet," I gush.

"Only once in a while. Every Sunday we have family supper and since I had to shop for myself for the week, I volunteered to grab anything for tonight she might need."

"Wow, that's sweet. So all of your siblings come?"

"Yep. Fisher, Magnolia, and their kids." He looks at me and grins. "It's a full house."

"I bet it gets crazy."

"Well, you're about to find out soon."

"Why?"

"Because you're comin' tonight. With me."

"I don't recall you askin'."

He pauses and we stop in the middle of the aisle. "Sweetheart, you just came all over my cowboy hat. That's like a dog markin' its territory, and now, you're stuck with me."

"Did you seriously just compare me to a *dog*?"

He snorts. "That's not what I said."

"I think you did. I'm startin' to remember why I didn't like you."

"Nice try." He grins. "C'mon, to the dairy section."

"Wow, best first date ever."

"Nope, our first date is in twenty-one days. Mark your calendar."

I chuckle dryly at his stubbornness to keep our deal. "At this rate, we'll be married before our first date."

He glances at me, but there's a hidden smile on his lips he doesn't want me to see. I'm surprised he's not freaking out about the word *married* like most men my age would. But again, I don't know him well enough to know if the thought of commitment would turn him away.

We start grabbing items off his mom's list and he tells me what he needs for his place. Mostly essentials like milk, eggs, and bread.

"Do you cook?" I ask when I find the bagels he likes.

"Uh…*define* cook?"

"I'll take that as a no. Well, that's not good because I don't either. We're going to starve as a married couple."

I hand him what he needs and he tosses it into the cart. "Don't worry, we'll just go to The Lodge."

"You go there every day?" I ask, walking toward the freezer section.

"At least once a day, yeah."

When he catches me giving him a judgy look, he scowls. "I work twelve-hour days. You expect me to have the energy to cook?"

"No, but doesn't that get old? Or do they serve different food each day?"

"It's on a schedule, so every Monday is broccoli cheese soup and beef tips. Tuesday is tacos. Wednesday is—"

"Wait…that sounds familiar." I pause, trying to figure out why those food items triggered a memory.

"The soup and beef tips?" he asks.

I nod. "Yeah, but I dunno why. I've never eaten at The Lodge, have I?"

Landen scratches his cheek, and I see the hesitation written on his face.

"What is it?" I ask.

"Nothing, it's just that you've been there a couple times."

"Recently?"

"Yeah, within the past few weeks."

"Did something happen when I was there?"

He sighs, and we stand to the side of an aisle. "I'm not supposed to tell you things you can't remember."

"But I remembered the broccoli cheese soup…though I wouldn't eat that. I'm not a fan of soup. Or broccoli."

He wrinkles his nose. "Who doesn't like soup?"

I push against his chest, but of course he doesn't budge. "Not the point. What happened at The Lodge?"

"You choked on a piece of beef."

"Oh my God, how embarrassing."

"Yeah, almost dying is *so* embarrassing," he drawls out.

"This is why I didn't like you, isn't it?" I scowl. "Now tell me what happened."

"I gave you the Heimlich maneuver."

"Geez. I need a prone to accidents sign on my forehead at this rate."

"We had a fight beforehand, and I was actively avoidin' you until I heard you gaspin' for air. I'd only ever panicked that hard once before in my life. I shot out of my chair and raced over to you."

My heart swells with tenderness. Knowing we weren't even friends or on good terms, and he still didn't think twice about saving me.

"What happened earlier?" I ask, but again he hesitates. "Please…I wanna know."

He exhales slowly as if he knows I'll keep asking until he tells me. "We were at the stables and you told Ranger he was a *good boy*, and I came up behind you and said *oh, thank you*. You scowled, I made a joke about it, and then you snapped. To be fair, it wasn't the first time I'd bothered you when you clearly didn't want to be, but my desperate ass was greedy for any opportunity to talk to you."

"What did I say when I snapped?" I plead, needing to hear it.

"Just…that I don't listen and you askin' me not to bother you wasn't an act because you weren't interested in havin' any conversation with me. Then I really pissed you off when I compared you to other women who would love the chance to tell a guy why they didn't like them. Then I apologized and said I'd never bother you again before walkin' away."

"Wow, I sound like a bitch."

"I pushed you a lot, if I'm being honest. I flirted with you every chance possible even after you made it clear you weren't interested. I figured negative attention was still attention from you. You had every right to get upset."

"You're just tryin' to make me feel better. It's okay. I know I wasn't the easiest person to be around. Socializing never came easy to me."

"You've been quite social with me since the accident."

"I know, but it literally feels like I knew you in another life and feel safe with you. Like we were more than friends."

"I can assure you, we were not, at least in the lifetime from three weeks ago."

"Very funny."

"See, it's about damn time you got my humor." He pulls me into his chest, and I lift my head to find his lips.

When he presses his to mine, I smile.

I've never had this before. It feels nice.

"Remember our new rule."

"No?"

He smirks, licking his lips. "You kiss the cowboy, you ride the hat."

Lowering my eyes to his groin, he quickly tries to cover himself, and I laugh. "So much for not wantin' to walk around with a boner."

"Oh, I lost that battle the moment we kissed."

My cheeks heat at how dirty it felt to rub against his cowboy hat in the front seat of his truck. Anyone could've driven by and had a free show. But it felt so good, I didn't want to stop. His mouth on me, kissing down my neck and encouraging me to shatter with him underneath me is the most erotic thing I've ever done.

And damn if I don't wanna do it again.

"Okay, what's left on the list?" I ask once we pull apart.

"Over here..." He leads us into the freezer section and pulls out a bag.

"Fish sticks?" I wrinkle my nose.

"Hey, I thought this was a judgment-free zone."

"Since when?" I muse.

"Since I learned you don't eat soup."

I roll my eyes. "Chicken tenders I could respect, but these? Very questionable tastes..."

"In the air fryer, they get nice and crispy, then I eat 'em with mayo and ketchup." He presses three fingers to his puckered lips. "Delicious little snack."

"The more I get to know you, the more past Ellie might've had a point..."

He pokes my side, making a bursting squeal come out of my mouth, and then he does it again to my other side when I twist around trying to escape him.

"You're ticklish? This is great information to have."

"I'm not! No, get away from me!" I giggle as I try to escape his stupidly long arms.

"Ellie? Hey."

A male voice halts my laughter, and I come face to face with a man I don't recognize.

He has shaggy blond hair and every two seconds whips it out of his eyes. He opens his arms as if he wants to hug me.

But I've never seen this man in my life.

At least I don't think so.

"Do I know you?" Alarm bells go off in my head as I step backward and away from him.

He ignores my hint at wanting space and comes closer, quickly eyeing Landen before focusing on me. "I'm Gage. We met a few weeks ago at one of your races. I work with your dad. We hung out at the rodeo…"

I tilt my head, studying him for any resemblance. "Sorry, I don't remember you."

"We talked about your horse, Ranger…"

Anyone who knows about my career could easily look up my horse's name, so I'm still not convinced I've actually met this man before.

"I had an accident a couple weeks ago and got a concussion." I point to my head bandage. "My memory is very hit-and-miss right now."

"I bought you a churro. You complimented my boots," he continues, then shows them off.

They literally look like any other brown cowboy boots.

"I-I'm sorry…I—"

His face reddens as his hands ball into fists. "That's bullshit! Stop actin' like you don't know who I am!"

I flinch at his raised voice and back into Landen's chest. He squeezes my shoulders before stepping in front of me and pushing me behind him. "You better watch your goddamn mouth before I put my fist inside it."

"And who the fuck are you?"

"I'm Landen, her fiancé."

My *what*?

I stand next to Landen to peek up at his face. All hard lines and a tense jaw.

He's not playing around.

"Since when?" Scowling, he crosses his arms. "Mr. Donovan said she was single when he hired me."

"Well, he's mistaken. She's not," Landen says firmly.

Gage sizes up Landen, which is a bad fucking idea considering how tall and muscular he is. Landen grew up on a ranch doing manual labor. I have no doubt he'd know how to kick someone's ass if he had to.

"I don't believe that." Gage snarls. "How does someone go from single to engaged in a matter of a month?"

Good fucking question.

But also, mind your business.

"Sorry that you got the wrong information, but even if I wasn't engaged, I wouldn't be interested," I explain, playing along with this stupid plan.

"Why not?" he asks, reaching out toward me. "Your dad thought we'd make a great couple."

"Listen...Gage, is it?" Landen wraps his arm around my shoulders, pulling me into his chest. "Last year, I shot a man in the dick for tryin' to hurt my best friend. Imagine what I'll do to a man who harasses my fiancée."

He did what? *There's no way...*

My gaze snaps to Landen again and he looks more entertained than anything by Gage's attempt to coerce me. But I'm not sure if he's telling the truth or not. If my dad thought that, I'm going to have a few questions about his taste in men for me.

"That was you?" Gage asks.

Wait, it's true?

Furrowing my brows, I whisper, "You actually did that?"

He leans above my ear. "Yep, but trust me, past Ellie wasn't impressed."

Considering the lack of context, I'm not sure if I should've been or not.

"Yep, and he lost both of his balls," Landen replies to Gage. "Now he sits in prison with a permanent reminder."

Gage finally smartens up and backs up. "Yeah…we'll see what Mr. Donovan has to say about that." He shoots him one final glare before walking out of the aisle.

As soon as he's out of view, I release a deep breath. "Why did you say we were engaged?"

He tips his hat. "You're welcome."

"For what? Now my parents are gonna hear about it and have several questions."

"For saving you from a psychopath who clearly wouldn't take no for an answer unless you were claimed. Hell, even when I said you were, he wasn't backin' off."

"*Claimed*? So now I'm a possession? First, I'm a dog, now I'm—"

Landen shoves me up against the cooler door, cups my face, and then crashes his mouth to mine. Without a second thought, I kiss him back.

Heat builds between my thighs as he holds me in place and slides his tongue between my lips. Letting him take over, I give in to the way my body reacts to him, and still, I'm desperate for more.

When he pulls away, my shoulders rise and fall with labored breaths.

Then he flattens his palm against the door, leaning close, and thumbs my chin. "There. Properly claimed." And then he fucking winks.

"Like property," I deadpan.

Shaking his head, he chuckles softly under his breath. "So goddamn feisty all the time. How is it we still bicker even after you lose your memory of me?"

"Guess you're just that insufferable or some things never change."

"Oh, trust me...plenty has changed. But I'll take it as long as it means I get to shut you up with my tongue."

My jaw drops and he smirks. "See? I know exactly what to say to rile you up so we can fight and make up all over again."

"You know it's only a matter of time before the entire town hears about our *engagement*. Then what?"

"Good, then all the other Justin Bieber lookalikes know to stay away from you."

Rolling my eyes, I push against his chest so I can move around him, but he blocks me in.

"You're being a little possessive, don't ya think?"

He cocks a brow. "You're the one who put the idea of marriage in my head, so you're partially to blame."

"How is it we haven't even gone on a first date and now we're talkin' marriage?"

"Would you like to revisit the terms of our deal?"

I cross my arms, scowling. "Depends...what would the date entail?"

"Now if I told ya that, you wouldn't be surprised."

"I'm just makin' sure your idea of a first date ain't takin' me to the jeweler to get my finger sized or to go get matchin' tattoos or something."

"Ooh, good third date idea. My fiancée needs a ring after all. Matching tats...maybe for our fourth."

"That's not funny, Landen!" I push his chest again. "My parents are gonna freak out if they hear about this."

"Why? I think your parents love me."

I scoff. "Actually, my dad told me to be careful with you."

"Did he?"

"He thinks I'm gonna get my heart broken."

He tips my chin and a tender smile spreads over his face. "I wouldn't have waited four years to try to move on if I planned to break your heart. If anything, you're going to break mine."

People needing to grab food out of the freezer we're blocking interrupt our conversation. But it's for the best since this isn't the place to continue this kind of discussion.

We finish getting everything on the list and load up Landen's truck. As we listen to music and talk, I notice Landen glancing in the rearview mirror every thirty seconds. After a couple minutes, I look out my side mirror and notice an SUV driving close behind.

"They've been following since we left the store," he explains when I ask about it. "And making every turn I do."

"Maybe they're going out this way, too."

"I dunno…" He narrows his eyes as he looks again. "I'm kinda thinkin' it's that Gage kid."

"Seriously?" Turning around, I look out the back window. Since there's not a second row, I can see behind us pretty clearly. Except whoever's driving is wearing a black hat and dark sunglasses.

"Why would he follow us?"

"Not sure, but I don't like it." Landen swerves over to the side so he can pass, but instead, the person slows down, too. "This fuckin' asshole."

Landen slams his foot down on the gas until we're speeding down the road. I watch the car get farther away in the side mirror and breathe out a sigh of relief when they don't catch up.

"That was so weird," I say, finally relaxing against the seat.

"Do you think he's tellin' the truth? Did you meet him at one of your rodeos?"

I shrug because I have no idea. "I'm gonna have to ask my dad to know for sure. It's possible, but there's no way I would've been interested in him. I was probably only nice because he's one of my dad's employees."

"I don't like the idea of him thinkin' he had a chance with you."

"Well, now no one will since I'm *engaged* and all…"

He grabs my hand, interlocks our fingers, and then brings it to his mouth for a tender kiss. "Good. I'd hate to have to threaten another man's balls. Or worse, shoot 'em."

We finally arrive at the ranch. I've never been inside the main house, but the outside is gorgeous with a white wraparound porch that has a couple swings and wooden chairs.

"I bet this was a great place to grow up," I say once we walk inside with the groceries. There's a rustic feel to it with lots of cozy vibes and family photos on the wall.

"It was hectic, that's for sure. But yeah, it was fun."

"Ellie, darlin'!" Mrs. Hollis grabs the bags out of my arms, sets them on the counter, and then engulfs me in a hug. "It's so good to see you. How're you doing?"

"I'm good. Considering, I mean." I smile and then get a hug from Gramma Grace. I've only met her a few times, but this family is full of huggers, so I accept my fate.

"I'm glad to hear it. I reached out to your parents when I heard and they were so worried, but it comes with the territory

213

of your kids ridin' horses professionally. When Noah got hurt, I banned her from ever trick ridin' again."

Landen snorts. "Yeah, that didn't last long."

"Wait, I remember that. She fractured her ankle and broke some ribs, right?"

"Oh…*that* you remember." Landen groans, putting away the groceries while Gramma Grace adds ingredients to the mixer. They've already started baking and cooking, and it smells delicious whatever it is.

Mrs. Hollis chuckles. "My kids have been givin' me heart attacks since the day they were born, so I knew the fear your parents must've been feelin'."

"Honestly, I wouldn't be surprised if they try to convince me to slow down," I admit, leaning against the island counter.

"And would you?" she asks.

I think about the past few years and how much I've enjoyed traveling, racing, and pushing myself to do better at each event. The feelings I get while riding are irreplaceable.

"No, I don't think so. I love it too much."

Chapter Twenty

LANDEN

Once we're done chatting with Mom and unloading all the bags, I take Ellie to my place so I can finally put my groceries away. She's never been here before and now I wish I would've cleaned up first.

But if she minds, she doesn't make it known. In fact, she helps herself to looking through my cabinets and drawers, snooping around as if she hopes something will trigger a memory.

"Satisfied?" I muse, watching her from my couch as she looks at my photos hanging on the wall.

"If I've been here before, nothing's clicking."

"Nope, you haven't."

She glances at me over her shoulder. "How many girls have been?"

I chuckle at the way she snuck in that question so effortlessly. "Are we havin' the body count talk?"

"Body count? Are we talkin' about murders or sexual partners?"

I blow out a tense breath. "Honestly, murders would be a more comfortable topic."

"So I'm guessing you've slept with a lot of women."

"Depends what you consider a lot."

"Well…" She paces around the living room. "Five would be a lot to me. But I'm only twenty-three."

"Right…"

"And you're twenty-nine, so…probably close to that number." The way she says it sounds like she's asking for confirmation rather than being certain.

"Twenty-nine women?"

"Yeah, I'd consider that to be a lot."

"Okay…" I scratch along my jawline, curious as to where this is leading.

"So…have you slept with a lot of women?"

"In terms of what you consider a lot, then no."

Not even close to that.

She raises a brow. "Really?"

"Why do you sound surprised?"

Her gaze roams up and down my body. "Because you're hot."

I laugh under my breath, still not used to Ellie calling me anything but how annoying I am. "As are you. Doesn't mean I'd assume you've slept with a lot of men."

"Okay, fair point. That was a little presumptuous of me. But I don't put myself out there. I didn't go out in search of a hookup. As far as I remember, anyway."

"I pretty much figured that out since all I saw you do was eat, breathe, and sleep barrel racing. What about in high school?"

"I had two boyfriends. Slept with one of them. The other guy I slept with was after high school."

"Only two?"

"Yep."

"Okay. I'd never judge you for your past anyway."

She sits on my coffee table in front of me, and I cage her legs in between my thighs. Leaning forward, I wrap my fingers around her knees and pull her closer.

"Is that what you're worried about?" I ask. "That I'm going to judge you?"

"No, I guess if you've been obsessed with me for years, you wouldn't care anyway."

Smiling at her honesty, I nod. "Accurate. So tell me what you're thinkin'."

She pinches her lips together as her cheeks flush. "That I'm not experienced enough for someone like you."

"Why would you think that?"

"I spent my first week home doing nothing but sleeping, pacing around my house, and thinkin' about the guy I met in the hospital. I couldn't do much else because it hurt my head to look at the TV screen, and I couldn't read without my vision going blurry, so you were on a constant loop in my mind. Then, this past week, I spent it texting you as much as I could and drivin' myself crazy overthinking everything about you."

Grabbing a loose strand of hair around her face, I wrap it behind her ear and then slowly slide my finger down her neck. I smirk when she shivers against my touch.

"You never have to worry about not being enough for me. I've always wanted you exactly as you are—moody and straightforward—and in case you haven't noticed, there isn't anything that'd change that."

"Do you really wanna date me? Not in like three weeks but where we're together right now?"

Grinning, I nod. "Yes. Even knowing the risks and

217

consequences, I'm all in when it comes to you. And if you accept the same terms, knowing you could one day figure out why you didn't like me, then we should make it official."

She tries concealing her overjoyed smile by biting her bottom lip.

I pluck it with my thumb and then tilt her chin until our gazes meet. "Whaddya say, Little Devil?"

"Okay."

"Okay?" I arch a brow, needing more.

"Takin' risks is something I know isn't outta the norm for me, and although this might be a different type of risk than I'm used to—especially when it's only been a couple weeks of what I remember—I'm willing to try it anyway."

Brushing my mouth against hers, I slowly kiss her, letting her take the reins and leading us to what she's comfortable doing.

She moans and seeks out my tongue, sending full-body shivers down to my toes. When I weave my fingers through her hair and deepen our kiss, she climbs into my lap and settles on top of me. I move us further into the couch until we're comfortably grinding against each other.

"You're not makin' it easy to hold out for our first date," I tease against her neck, sucking lightly beneath her ear.

"We're already engaged," she playfully reminds me.

"Mm...good point. We should already be in wedding plannin' mode."

Her neck falls back, giving me more access to her soft skin. "Hmm...what colors do you like? I'm thinkin' teal and a pretty burnt orange for a fall theme."

"Fuck, you're too good at this..." I cup her breast as my mouth makes its way back up to hers. "I'm gonna forget we're pretending."

She widens her legs and then relaxes her hips, dropping deeper in my lap.

"You're killin' me here…we have to be at my parents' house in five minutes."

She continues rotating her hips and my cock feels every painful movement.

"I guess we'll have to continue this later."

When she shifts off me and stands, I immediately take off my cowboy hat and cover up my noticeable erection.

"What're you doing?" She looks down at my lap.

"You know the rules…" I wink.

She bends down, stopping right in front of my lips. "Yeah, but I'd much rather ride the cowboy."

"Landen Michael!" Noah shouts, the front door slamming behind her. She marches into the kitchen with Poppy on her hip and Fisher behind, who looks like he's dreading this conversation. She shoots me a murderous glare and then points between me and Ellie. "You two are *engaged*?"

Everyone's head snaps toward us. Gramma Grace stands next to us with a grin.

I smirk at Ellie, who looks horrified, then wrap my arm around her and pull her closer. "Look, that only took a few hours to spread to my family. Might be a new record."

She pinches the bridge of her nose as if she's fighting the urge to smack me. "Which means my parents are next."

"One of y'all better start explainin' right now…" Noah demands. "I told you to spend time with her, not whatever the hell this is…" She waves her arms at our proximity. "You two can't be together."

"I knew it…" Gramma Grace mocks. "As soon as they walked in, I saw it."

"No freakin' way." Wilder barks out a laugh. "Y'all didn't tell her she hates his guts?"

"Of course I did." Noah whacks him in the arm when he teasingly pokes her. "But my question is how the hell did this happen? How did we go from Ellie having a concussion and forgetting Landen's existence to Ellie's now engaged to Landen?"

"I'd like to know as well…" Mrs. Hollis asks, grabs Poppy, and then kisses her cheeks.

"Storytime!" Magnolia grabs a piece of fresh bread from the middle of the table and pops it into her mouth.

"Are we gettin' a new sister-in-law?" Wilder smirks.

"Dibs on godfather this time!" Waylon shouts.

Oh my God.

I scowl at him.

"What? You called it last time," Waylon argues. "Now it's my turn to be someone's daddy."

When he waggles his brows, all stares move to Fisher, who's trying desperately to stay out of the conversation.

"That's not the same, you idiot. Magnolia was *pregnant,*" Noah reminds him, and then she nearly snaps her neck to look at Ellie. "Holy shit, are you pregnant?"

"No!" she exclaims. "And we aren't engaged."

"But we *are* together," I confirm, smiling at Ellie, who looks flustered with all the attention on her.

Noah presses a hand to her chest and exhales. "I swear to

God, one of y'all better start explainin'. But let's start with why Harlow and Delilah texted me that you two are gettin' married."

"Calm down before you pop a blood vessel..." I taunt, then tighten my grip on Ellie's waist. "Some douche was harrassin' her at the store, claiming they met a few weeks ago at one of her races and hit it off. When he got aggressive and persistent, I stepped in and told him I was her fiancé. I only said it to get him to back off."

"Aggressive how?" Wilder asks.

"Kept gettin' closer and insistin' she knew him, then once he started shouting at her, I threatened him with my fist if he didn't back off. After mentioning my dick-shootin' skills, he finally walked away."

Magnolia rolls her eyes with a smile. "You and that story."

"I'm pretty sure he followed my truck out of the store parking lot and tailed me most of the way here," I continue.

"Who is it?" Tripp asks. "Someone we know?"

"His name is Gage and he works for my dad," Ellie explains. "But I don't remember him and when I tried to explain my injury, he called me a liar."

"Where did Harlow and Delilah hear it?" I ask Noah.

"They were shoppin' downtown an hour ago and some man was talkin' loudly on his phone saying that Ellie and Landen are engaged."

"Oh my God...he coulda been talkin' to my dad." Ellie blows out a frustrated breath.

"Well, safe to say most of the town's heard it by now," Noah says, reaching for something in the fridge.

"You should tell your dad anyway," I tell her. "He needs to fire that lunatic."

"What if that pisses him off even more?" Ellie asks. "He probably knows where I live."

"Maybe you should call Sheriff Wagner and give him a heads-up," Dad suggests. He's been quiet this whole time, so I wondered if he had any opinion on this. "Better to keep a paper trail now in case he does something else."

Ellie looks at me in a panic, and I pull her closer. "Don't worry, I won't let that happen."

Once we sit to eat dinner, and I answer all of their annoying questions about Ellie and me, we move on to dessert and then scrapbooking. Tripp and Magnolia leave early to get Willow to bed and then Waylon and Wilder bail to go finish chores.

"So you do this every Sunday night?" Ellie asks when she looks at all the supplies dumped on the table.

"Yep, and we probably have an album for everything you could ever think of," I say, then find a photo of me and my dirt bike.

"You ride that?" she asks.

"Yeah, I rode it that first day we met. Again…you weren't impressed." I smirk when she rolls her eyes. "Noah yells at me when I ride it too close to the stables, so I've been ridin' it around the mountains and one of the ponds we have out there. There's a nice trail."

"That sounds fun," she says. "I've never been on one…I don't think."

Leaning in so only she can hear me, I whisper, "I'd love to be the first to give you a ride."

My fingers squeeze around her thigh and she swallows hard. Then I flash her a wink and go back to the photos.

"I should dig out my family's albums and make one. Maybe it'll spark some memories or at the very least, be a fun little project so I don't die from boredom." Ellie watches me flip through the pages of a completed one.

"Do you like to cook or bake?" Gramma Grace asks her.

"I dunno. I've never really tried. My mom cooks every night, so I've never had to learn."

Gramma Grace smiles wide, and I know what she's about to do.

"I'll teach you. I have dozens of family recipes I could share with you."

"Wait a minute…" Noah blurts. "I couldn't get my favorite peach cobbler recipe until my bridal shower because Mama said it was tradition."

"It is," Mom confirms, reaching for more stickers and floral pieces.

"Well, if they're engaged, there'll be a bridal shower soon…" Gramma Grace defends. "I can still teach her without giving her the recipes."

"Did you miss the part where they said it wasn't real?" Noah arches a brow.

"I don't wanna be a bother," Ellie says.

"You're not, darlin'. We'd love to teach you," Mom says. "Since my own daughter hardly visits anymore, it'd be nice to have you around."

"Sorry for havin' a job, a husband, and takin' care of your granddaughter."

I chuckle at Noah's annoyance. "Aww...is someone feelin' left out?"

She kicks my shin underneath the table. "With you around, I'm used to never gettin' attention anyway. You and the twins are always loud and obnoxious."

"Me? I'm just sittin' here."

Ellie giggles, and I glance over at her.

"What's funny?"

"The way y'all bicker is cute. I never knew family time could be like this. I got so serious about racin' so early in my teen years that it took over my life ever since then. We never did stuff like this. Everything revolved around my career."

"It's good to learn balance," Mom tells her. "Noah was the same way until she met Fisher and finally realized there was more to living than just workin' nonstop."

"Yep, now I work nonstop *and* manage a family." Noah smirks, turning toward Fisher, who's rocking Poppy to sleep. "I love it. Wouldn't change it for the world."

When I glance at Ellie, I see the way she looks at the three of them with admiration in her eyes. Considering earlier she said she loved racing too much to slow down once she's cleared to begin again, I wonder if she ever thinks about her future in terms of starting her own family.

Chapter Twenty-One

ELLIE

I'm covered from head to toe in flour, but I haven't stopped smiling in three hours, so I'm not even upset about it. Gramma Grace and I have been baking bread and cookies for the upcoming farmer's market. The retreat hosts a booth once a month and lures them over with fresh-smelling baked goods.

"Who runs the booth?" I ask her.

"Usually, one of the receptionists or a staff member from The Lodge."

"When it's not too hot out, I'll take her and we'll join in for a few hours," Mrs. Hollis adds.

"That sounds fun. Can I go next time?" I ask, washing my hands in the sink.

"Of course. We can go this weekend. Drag that fiancé of yours with us, too." Gramma Grace snickers and my cheeks heat at the mention of him.

Although we're not engaged, Gramma Grace enjoys teasing us about it. She offers me her old ring at least three times a week.

I've been getting cooking lessons from Gramma Grace and

Mrs. Hollis for the past two weeks. Since I'm still not cleared to drive, Landen picks me up on his morning break at nine to take me to his parents' house, and then he stops in for lunch to taste test anything we've made. Although we don't get to spend much alone time together during the week, I still love getting to see him when I can. For the past two Friday and Saturday nights, I stayed later so we could hang out at his house and mostly fooled around. Though we've not gone past making out and over the clothes touching. He's still worried I'm going to wake up one day and hate his guts again.

But the longer I go without remembering, the less likely I'll remember them at all.

And I've decided I'm okay with that. I've never felt happier.

In the afternoons, I visit him at the stud farm, and then my dad picks me up when he's done at work so I'm home for dinner by five. Aunt Phoebe asks me each night what new recipe I learned and we talk all about it until dessert.

It's a new and different routine than I'm used to, but I'm still enjoying it. It allows me to visit Ranger every day and groom him so he doesn't get sad or lonely. I watch Noah train him so he stays ready for when I can ride him. For the past few days, she's let me lunge him in the corral. She was worried I'd get too dizzy, but so far, I haven't.

After rumors spread that Landen and I were engaged, we didn't say anything publicly about it, so it was neither confirmed nor denied. It's not a huge deal since we're dating anyway.

When I explained everything to my parents about Gage, Dad fired him, and we filed a police report. I didn't think we needed to go to that extreme, but everyone else insisted.

My family knows Landen and I are dating, and even though my mom is happy I'm finally getting out of the house and having a social life, my dad warns me to be careful. He thinks because Landen's older and at a different season of his life than me that he'll be a distraction from focusing on my career when I can return.

But after reassuring him that barrel racing is still my priority, he's come around more to the idea. He thinks I'm going to get hurt, but I'm an adult, so he needs to let me make my own decisions even if I do end up with a broken heart.

Landen walks in around noon, scoops me in his arms, and plants a deep kiss on my lips.

"Oh my God, you smell so bad." I push away before my eyes start watering.

"Yeah, I fell in some horse shit."

"Landen!" Shoving at his chest, he releases me, and I step backward. "You're gonna pay for that."

He flashes me a wicked smile and goes to wash his hands.

"Oh, you're gonna have to get used to that, sweetie," Gramma Grace enters the kitchen and then refills her glass. She and Mrs. Hollis took a lunch break on the back patio to drink sweet tea and read their books.

I make a face and she laughs. "Figured you'd be immune to that smell by now."

"Not when it's injected into my nostrils." I wrinkle my nose.

Gramma Grace excuses herself and returns outside.

"How're things goin' today?" I ask Landen as he dries off his hands. "Watchin' lots of horse sex?"

"Yep, just another day of breedin' season."

Landen removes his baseball cap and then does the hottest thing I've ever witnessed. He reaches behind his neck and pulls off his T-shirt in one smooth motion. He uses it to wipe his face and over his hair before he puts his hat back on, backward.

My gaze drops to his chest and abs. Hard muscles line

every inch of him. A six-pack I want to trace with my tongue. And a thin happy trail that leads below his shorts.

Why is the first time I see my boyfriend half naked in the middle of his parents' kitchen?

That should be a crime.

A throat clearing grabs my attention, and I snap my focus back to Landen's face.

"What?"

"I saw that."

I scratch my cheek, furrowing my brows. "I have no idea what you're talkin' about."

"That was one helluva eye fuck if I've ever seen one."

With both hands on my hips, I scowl. "To be fair…you've been holdin' out on me."

He closes the gap between us, tilting up my chin. "And you've been such a good girl waitin' so patiently for our first date."

"You love to torture me, don't you?"

He knows exactly what he's doing by calling me a *good girl*. He says it every time I sit in his lap and get him hard, then he tells me to finish on his cowboy hat.

"Only five more days, Little Devil." He winks. "And then I promise to give you anything you need."

Curiously, I arch a brow. "*Anything*?"

He leans in and presses a quick kiss to my lips. "Anything."

My chest aches with the anticipation of getting to touch him. Although it's only been a month, it seems so much longer with the intense feelings I have for him.

"Are you gonna tell me what we're doing for our first date?" I wrap my arms around his neck and pull him closer.

He grasps my hips. "Nope. But wear comfortable clothes."

"That's not helpful at all."

He captures my mouth again and teases me with his tongue. "You're going to love it, I promise."

After we eat lunch together, and I'm home for the night, I help my mom with cleaning up the kitchen and catch her up on my day.

"I'll have to stop by the farmer's market and grab some bread. It sounds delicious," she says.

"It is. If you can't make it, though, I'll save you a loaf. I'm gonna work the booth this Saturday," I tell her as I organize a pile of mail.

A letter catches my eye when I see it's addressed to Aunt Phoebe. But the odd part is the return label says it's from the Nashville Women's Prison.

"Mom, what's this?" I hold it up for her and when she turns to see, her eyes widen in panic.

"Nothin', sweetie. I screen all of Aunt Phoebe's mail so she doesn't get any scammers." She reaches for it as I study the handwriting and a wave of déjà vu hits me.

"Who would be writing —"

"Just a pen pal, sweetheart."

"Oh...okay." I hand it over, wondering why a weird feeling overcame me.

I could ask Aunt Phoebe about it, but I don't think Mom gives her those letters.

Ever since my accident, Aunt Phoebe doesn't say much to

me and now that I'm spending less time at home, there aren't as many opportunities to talk to her when she's in a good mental state.

Keeping to my evening routine, I clean up after dinner, put a load of laundry in, and then wait for Landen to FaceTime me. We don't stay up too late since he gets up early for work, and I still require eight hours of sleep to keep up with my routine.

LANDEN

I'm gonna shower quickly, and then I'll call you.

After seeing him half-naked earlier, I'm feeling a little brave.

ELLIE

Or you could call me while you're in the shower…give me a preview of what you're keeping hostage.

LANDEN

I knew it, you only want me for my body.

ELLIE

Yep, you caught me. Now strip.

LANDEN

I'm more than just a piece of meat, you know?

ELLIE

Yeah, you have a fierce tongue, too.

LANDEN

You're gonna get me all worked up, and I won't be able to jerk off in the shower if you're watching.

The ache between my thighs pulses through me at the mental visual. I've touched myself every night before bed since the first time we kissed, so I'm desperate to see how he does it.

ELLIE

Why not? I want to see.

LANDEN

You're being serious?

ELLIE

Yes! And then I'll show you how I touch myself...

Two and a half seconds later, his call comes through. When I hit accept, he's already naked in the shower. My jaw drops as I take in every wet, bare inch of him.

"You're a tease," he says.

"*Me*? Look who's talkin'." I angle my screen and look down into it as if I'll be able to see more of him.

"You touch yourself thinkin' about me?" he asks, rubbing soap over his arms and chest.

"Well, duh. You've been blue-ballin' me for almost a month."

"You don't have balls, so that's scientifically inaccurate."

"Okay, smart-ass. Blue...whatever the equivalent is for a woman."

He chuckles, my frustration clearly amusing him. "I think the term is *blue bean*."

"Is it? Okay, well, then my bean is blue. Very, very blue."

"Then you should do something about that...take off your panties, and I'll talk you through it."

I slowly blink, shocked at how quickly and easily he suggested that, and also hating how red my face is when I'm the one who started this. My previous sexual experiences were mediocre and not very memorable.

But if it isn't the consequences of my own actions kicking me in the blue bean.

"Ellie…"

His deep drawl snaps me out of my trance.

"Remove your panties for me and get under the covers."

Swallowing hard, I focus on his voice and the motion of his arm that's moving below the screen.

He's already stroking his cock.

Standing, I lower my shorts and panties before sliding back into bed. I'm an expert at pleasing myself considering my embarrassing dating life, but I have no doubt that Landen Hollis talking me through it will beat every other time I've done it on my own.

"Now tell me how wet you are…"

Spreading my thighs, I ease my hand between my legs and find I'm already aroused.

"I'm soaked," I admit.

"Good, because I'm rock hard and need you to come before I do. Can you do that for me?"

Nodding, I moan at how sensitive my clit is already. I rub the pad of my fingers over it and breathe through the build-up.

"Fuck, you look so hot doing that. I bet you're throbbin' right now."

"I am," I agree. "It feels so good."

He inhales sharply as if he's trying to hold himself off, and I like the thought of him struggling for control.

"Imagine my hands and mouth on you, baby. Licking, sucking, devouring that sweet little pussy."

"Oh my God, yes…" My head falls back, and I nearly drop the phone in my hand.

"Don't lose momentum, Little Devil. I wanna hear you get yourself off."

"I'm trying…it's right there."

At the sound of his nickname for me, I moan as the pleasure increases.

"I wanna watch you come, darlin'. Turn the camera around."

Quickly pulling off the covers, I tilt the phone so he can see. Vulnerability crashes through me at how exposed I am, but his throaty groans at seeing how wet I am for him help ease some of the embarrassment.

"Spread wider, baby. Show me all of you."

I do as he says and continue rubbing myself, the build-up getting more intense and stronger.

"Look at that pretty little cunt. All mine, baby. I'm gonna devour you."

"God, yes. I'm so close." I'm breathing so hard, I sound like a panting dog, but I don't care. I've never experienced this kind of pleasure before with someone guiding me through it, but I *love* it.

"You're doing so good, sweetheart. Give that needy clit what it needs."

"It needs you," I beg, teetering on the edge.

"I'm right here." He releases short, labored breaths and I can tell he's barely hanging on. "Imagine my fingers deep inside you as I suck your clit."

That picture was already in my mind, but hearing him say it aloud has me falling apart.

"Yes, Landen…"

My body stiffens and shakes as I moan through the orgasm, unraveling at how intense the pleasure rolls through me. I've never been able to make myself come this fast before, but hearing Landen encourage me and whisper filthy sweet nothings was enough to get me there within minutes.

"Oh my God, that was—"

"Fuck, Ellie…"

When I watch his face tense, I know he's shattering through his own release, and I love seeing him come undone.

"Holy shit. I couldn't stop once I heard you," he admits, attempting to catch his breath.

Flipping the camera around, I blush when he grins at me. "I could watch you do that for hours. That was fuckin' hot."

"I didn't get to watch you, though…" I pout. "The camera wasn't pointin' down."

"I know, I'm sorry. When you moaned my name, that's all it took. I was a goner."

Giggling, my cheeks redden, and I mentally slap myself for being so damn infatuated with him. But I can't help it.

"I loved watchin' you come for me. Fuck, I think I'm addicted now."

"Adding nightly shower calls to our schedule now."

With a grin, he nods. "Deal."

Landen continues rinsing off his body and lets me stay on the call to stare at him. I admire his broad back, hoping I get to wrap my legs around his shoulders one day. I've only experienced that once and it felt more uncomfortable than pleasurable, but I have a feeling Landen wouldn't stop until he had me screaming.

After I've cleaned up myself, I dress into lounge clothes and crawl back into bed. He's long dried off and changed into boxers and a T-shirt, which he let me help pick out.

"I miss hearin' you read to me and Ranger," I say, my eyes struggling to stay awake.

"You liked that, huh?"

234

"You have a sexy reading voice."

"Do you want me to read to you now so you can sleep?"

"You'd do that?" I ask, knowing he needs to go to bed, too.

The corner of his lips lifts into the sweetest smile. "Of course. Don't you know by now, Ellie? I'd do pretty much anything for you."

Chapter Twenty-Two
LANDEN

For the past two nights, I've FaceTimed Ellie during my shower so she can watch me jerk off as she touches herself. Listening to her moaning my name as she gets herself off is the most erotic thing I've done outside of actual sex.

The intimacy of it, guiding her through her own pleasure, and letting her watch me come undone is something I've never experienced.

It's made our connection even deeper.

"No Ellie today?" Wilder asks when I walk into The Lodge for lunch.

"She had a pre-scheduled press interview with some local newspaper and then a doctor's appointment with a new neurologist. Don't worry, she'll be back to give you shit tomorrow."

Over the past couple weeks of Ellie coming here almost every day, she's really gotten close with the rest of the family. She teases and jokes with them, spends hours with my mom and grandma, and has even gotten close to a couple of the other girls who train here. Before, she was so closed off and kept to herself. She rarely talked to anyone besides Noah.

Although I've always liked Ellie for who she is, I can't deny liking this side of her, too. Whatever part of her memory that got blocked must've been traumatic enough to make her as guarded as she was. I wish I could figure it out, at least for my own curiosity, but also because I want to know and understand all of her.

"Speaking of…here comes Magnolia and Noah," Wilder says.

I grab a plate and head to the buffet since I don't have a ton of time to eat today. With how many new mares we have coming in, I have to make sure they get enough time with the stallions.

"I hear the big date is this weekend," Magnolia singsongs when she stands next to me.

"It is."

"What're y'all doing?" She starts loading up her plate, and I eye it suspiciously at how much she's taking.

"Are you eatin' for two?"

She elbows me, scowling. "You never ask a woman that, dumbass."

Chuckling, I walk down to the dessert table and grab a piece of peach pie.

"Did you just say that to get outta answerin' my question?" She appears next to me again like a shadow.

"Yes, now go away."

"What? You were all up in my business when I was datin' Tripp. It's my turn now. I earned it as bestie status."

"You forced me into your business," I remind her. "I wasn't even allowed to text his real name because you made me use his code name."

"Yeah, and you still managed to fuck it up and tell him."

Laughing, I take a seat next to Wilder and dig into my fried chicken.

"You mean, I'm the reason y'all finally got together. You're welcome."

She sits across from me and Noah catches up, sitting next to her.

"Whatever you do, don't take her for dinner and a movie," Noah says. "That's lame and boring."

"What's wrong with a nice dinner and going to the theater?" Wilder asks. "I thought chicks liked that."

Magnolia snorts. "You're so clueless, I dunno how you ever get laid."

"Got laid last weekend, thank you very much. Didn't have to take her to dinner *or* a movie…" He gloats like it's something to be proud of.

Noah grimaces. "When are you gonna grow up and settle down?"

Wilder shrugs. "I dunno."

"The only way Wilder's gettin' married is if someone handcuffs him to the bride and forces him down the aisle," Magnolia says.

"Nah, he'll just lie on the ground and play dead." I chuckle. "The only way he's gettin' hitched is if he's drunk off his ass and wakes up with a ring on his finger."

"I'll have you know I'm a very aware drunk and have never done anything that stupid." He points his fork at Noah. "Never been drunk enough to hook up with my ex's dad…" Then he points at Magnolia. "Or drunk enough to hook up with my ex and then get knocked up. So…" He lingers smugly. "Who's the grown-up 'round here?"

Laughing at the girls' scowling, I nod along with Wilder. "He's gotta point."

Wilder looks at me next. "Oh, don't even get me started on you, Mister *I'm dating the girl who's hated me since the moment we met.* I don't even know what to call what you're doing."

Shrugging, I take another bite of my food. "Hey, she doesn't hate me right now, so a win is a win."

"Just tell us where you're takin' her!" Magnolia whines.

"How about mind your business and you'll find out after it's over," I tell them.

"It's probably something cheesy like a hot air balloon ride," Noah taunts.

Wilder smacks his arm down on the table, causing his fork to go down with it. "Now why not? That sounds romantic as fuck."

"Because it's unoriginal!" Magnolia says. "Women want creativity. Put some effort into finding out what the girl is interested in instead of Googling the top five date spots."

"I don't do that…" Wilder hesitates and we all laugh at him. "Whatever."

My phone chimes with a text, and I quickly pull it out of my pocket. I've been anticipating the news all day regarding Angela's parole hearing results.

But then I smile when I see Ellie's name instead.

ELLIE

I fucked up.

LANDEN

The interview? What happened?

239

ELLIE

We were talking about barrel racing topics and before she ended the interview, she said "So I heard congratulations are in order!" and I was so taken off guard, I just said "Huh?" And then she went on to say how wonderful it is that I'm engaged to Landen Hollis, local cowboy rancher at Sugarland Creek ranch.

LANDEN

Oh shit. Then what?

ELLIE

Well, I wasn't prepared for her to bring it up and just wanted off the call, so I said "Thanks!"

I laugh because I can hear her panicked voice in my head.

ELLIE

Then she went on a little tangent about how awesome it must be to be with someone who I share so much in common with and who must be a great supporter.

LANDEN

And?

ELLIE

At that point, I just had to go along with it and said "Uh-huh."

She sends a face-palm emoji with a crying one, and I can tell she's upset with herself.

LANDEN

Well, it's not like the rumors hadn't already spread through town. It's okay, baby. Not a big deal.

ELLIE

It's one thing for our small town to hear about it, but this is for a nationwide equine website. They interview dozens of pro rodeo members. Everyone in the barrel racing community is going to read it. I'm going to look so stupid now for not correcting her and letting everyone think it's true. They're going to mention it now at every press event until there's a wedding.

Shit.

LANDEN

Soooo I guess we need to get you an engagement ring now?

I know she's panicking because it wouldn't look good if she got caught in a lie or any kind of scandal, but I love the idea of people knowing she's mine.

ELLIE

Oh don't worry, Gramma Grace said she has me covered for whenever I want hers.

She sends an eye-roll emoji, and I snort.

LANDEN

Stop freaking out. We can pretend in public if we need to. It's not like holding your hand and kissing you is a hardship.

ELLIE

Until when? We have our fake wedding?

LANDEN

You wanna get married now? I can book an officiant for our first date.

241

ELLIE

Landen!! That's not funny.

LANDEN

You're right, that's more appropriate for a third date.

ELLIE

This is why past Ellie hated you so much.

LANDEN

Past Ellie would've whacked me with a shovel by now.

ELLIE

Good thing I know where the tack room in the barn is...

LANDEN

I gotta get back to work. See you at six-thirty for our nightly shower and reading session. Clothes optional.

I look forward to our evening routine all day long.

ELLIE

Damn you and making me swoon all over again, I can't even enjoy my imaginary shovel whacking.

LANDEN

You'd miss me too much.

ELLIE

Debatable.

LANDEN

I know I'd miss you.

ELLIE

You'd be dead so how could you?

LANDEN

From the afterlife, obviously.

ELLIE

You're not allowed to haunt me. I draw the line at ghost stalking.

LANDEN

I don't remember you always being this mouthy.

ELLIE

Pretty sure you said that's exactly what made you like me.

Oh, she's not wrong about that.

ELLIE

But I have some good news. I've been cleared to drive as long as I don't feel tired or dizzy beforehand. I won't be doing any long-distance road trips but at least I can drive myself to the ranch now.

LANDEN

That's awesome! So instead of my solo showers, you can stay to enjoy them with me...

ELLIE

Before our first date? What kind of lady do you think I am...

LANDEN

One who won't stop undressing me with her eyes.

ELLIE

What can I say? I'm a sucker for a cowboy
with a backward hat and six-pack abs.

"Earth to Landen?" Noah snaps her fingers in my face.

I look up at her and Magnolia staring at me.

"What now?"

"If we promise not to say anything, then will you tell us?"

Are they still talking about our first date?

Standing, I put my phone away and grab my empty plate. "Nope."

They groan dramatically, and I smirk at their desperation to know my business.

"Bye!" I say after stacking my plate in the tub.

Every time I sit in my truck, I smile to myself at the memories Ellie and I've made in here. The way she moaned for me and came undone on my favorite cowboy hat.

Best moment ever.

When my phone rings and I see Warren's name, I know it's bad news.

Chapter Twenty-Three
ELLIE

"Thanks so much for stoppin'. Enjoy your cookies!" I say for about the hundredth time.

The farmer's market on a Saturday in downtown Sugarland Creek is prime gossip season, and I've been asked about my engagement approximately fifty million times. There's no point in denying it when there's an article coming out confirming it.

After the first hour, Gramma Grace handed me a ring.

"Wear this," she demanded.

"Are you sure?" It looked too delicate and special to just wear it around casually.

When I slid it on my finger and it fit perfectly, she winked. "It was made for you."

I nearly burst into tears right then.

I wasn't just falling hard for Landen. I was falling for his entire family.

We could set the record straight, but I don't need any more attention on me, especially the negative attention that'd come with speculations.

It's hard not to get emotional about the what-ifs when it

comes to my career and wondering how I'll make a comeback next year. I'm ready to get back on Ranger and work again. I'm grateful that Noah's continued to train him and has kept to his routine.

Twenty minutes from the market closing, a woman approaches and there's a familiarity there, but I can't place her. She listens as I explain what's left over—which isn't much—and then she holds up a recording device.

"I'm a journalist from The Creek Chronicles and—"

"Oh, sorry. I'm not doing press right now. You can email me and we can set up a time if—"

She shoves the recorder closer toward me, and I flinch. "Did you want to comment on the early release of—"

"Respectfully, ma'am…" Gramma Grace interrupts with the most stern tone I've ever heard come from her. "Miss Donovan isn't doing interviews right now, but if you'd like to purchase something, I'd love to help you."

She lowers the device and frowns. "Fine. I'll just say *no comment* then."

About what?

Before I have the chance to ask, she walks away.

"That was…weird," I mutter.

Gramma Grace pats my shoulder. "Don't worry about it, dear. Those journalists can be vultures and if you don't put your foot down, they'll continue to be relentless."

"Yeah, I've definitely experienced that, but this didn't sound like it was rodeo related."

"Maybe not, but you're still well-known enough for them to take advantage of your time and name to get a buzz on whatever piece they're workin' on," Gramma Grace says, and I nod because she's right.

"Thank you for chiming in. I always have to be careful how

I react or they'll write about how I'm a rude and ungrateful bitch or something…"

Ask me how I know.

"Of course, honey." She wraps an arm around me. "You're one of us now."

My heart swells at her overwhelming kindness. I never used to get too close to people, so I'm not sure how to respond besides with a *thank you* and a smile.

> **LANDEN**
> How's it going at the market?

My smile widens when I read his text. He's working for a few hours this morning before we meet up later this afternoon. I know he's taken our *first date* seriously since the first mention of it. I don't care what we do as long as I'm spending time with him.

> **ELLIE**
> Good! We're about to start packing up. And how're things going there?

> **LANDEN**
> Waylon and Tripp fell into a massive mudhole. Never laughed so hard in my life.

> **ELLIE**
> Are they okay?

He sends me a picture of the two of them covered from head to toe. I bring a hand over my mouth to cover the laugh that bubbles out of me. They look pissed.

> **ELLIE**
> Oh my God…

LANDEN

Wilder nearly choked to death laughing so hard.

ELLIE

How'd that even happen?

LANDEN

With the storms the past couple nights, one of the pastures flooded and the mud surfaced. Waylon slipped first and took Tripp down with him. Wilder and I were walking behind and watched the whole thing. It was like they fell in slow-mo, arms flailing, feet up in the air kinda fall. Wish I'd gotten it on video.

ELLIE

That's mean!

LANDEN

Oh trust me, they'd say the same thing if it had been me!

ELLIE

Well as long as they're okay. I'm sure that didn't feel great.

LANDEN

Waylon said he broke his butt. Pretty sure he just bruised his tailbone but he's a big baby. Tripp's more annoyed at Waylon for taking him down with him.

ELLIE

Be careful out there. I'd hate for you to have to cancel our date before we even got a chance to go on one...

LANDEN

> Oh you underestimate me, sweetheart. I'd show up in a full-body cast, every bone in my body broken with amputated limbs before I canceled our date. Nothing could get in the way of being with you tonight.

I reread his text half a dozen times, my face feeling hotter after each time, and goose bumps cover my skin in eighty-degree weather.

Jesus. This man.

ELLIE

> I don't know if this was your intention but that just got you a million bonus points.

LANDEN

> Considering I used to be negative a billion, I'll take it.

He sends a winking emoji, and I giggle like the ridiculous lovesick girl I am.

My everything shower takes a good forty-five minutes and the water's nearly gone cold by the time I finish. Every inch of body hair has been shaved off and slathered in lotion. Since he won't tell me what we're doing, I put on jean shorts and a simple gray shirt. It's too humid to wear anything more than that.

I say goodbye to my family and tell them I'm sleeping over at Landen's so they don't wait up for me. Mom kisses my cheek and tells me to have a great time.

"Thanks, I'll see y'all later. Love you!"

Landen wanted to pick me up like a proper gentleman, but I was too excited about being able to drive myself again. I wanted to meet him at his house. I felt like a burden having Landen and my dad take me everywhere and although I can't race, I'll take any amount of freedom I can get.

It also means I get to listen to my own music again.

When I turn on my playlist, a Taylor Swift song blasts through the speakers, and I get that déjà vu feeling again. I can't remember the last time I heard one of her songs, but this one from her *Reputation* album makes me think of when I used to jog every morning.

Trying not to overthink it, I blast it and sing along on my way to the ranch.

It also makes me think of Mallory because she's almost always humming one of her songs.

When I arrive, Landen's leaning against his truck, waiting patiently for my arrival.

Fuck me. He looks so good.

That white baseball cap he wears backward.

Dark gray shorts and a plain white tee.

There's no reason it should look so damn hot.

Before I can open my door, he's there, opening it for me.

"Well, hello, beautiful." He holds out his hand and then helps me out of my truck.

Muscular arms wrap around my waist and pull me in for a deep, slow kiss. When his palms cup my face and his thumbs rub tender circles over my cheek, I melt into him.

And there goes every ounce of willpower to remain in control.

He lifts me, and when my legs wrap around him, he pushes me against my door.

I tighten my hold on him, close the gap between us, and moan into his mouth.

"*Ellie…*" He parts his lips, pressing his forehead to mine.

"I thought you didn't kiss on the first date…" I remind him breathlessly.

"Guess that makes you the exception."

Once he sets me down, he takes my hand and leads me to a four-wheeler.

"We're takin' this?"

"Yep, but you gotta wear a helmet. I'm not riskin' you gettin' a concussion and forgettin' me again. Especially now that you like me."

"Very funny." I playfully shove his chest. "So where're we going?"

"I wanna show you my old dirt bike ridin' track," he explains as he secures the helmet on my head.

"So glad I spent an hour curling my hair," I deadpan.

He smirks, tilts up my chin, and tightens the latch. "Figured an adventure seeker like yourself would enjoy it." Then he presses his lips to mine. "You look gorgeous."

Once he sits on it and gets it started, I climb on behind him. He grabs my wrists and tugs me forward until my chest is pressed to his back.

"Hang on," he warns, and I squeeze tighter.

He doesn't drive too fast, just enough to feel the wind against my face. We go through a part of the ranch I've never been to before and then ride along mountain trails in between large trees before it comes into view.

"This is so cool," I say once he slows down. "Y'all just have a whole-ass racing track back here?"

He chuckles, cruising slower to the flatter part of the dirt track. "Yep. My best friend, Tucker, and I would spend hours out here during high school. We'd race all the time and just fuck around."

"Tucker? Do I know him?" I ask, not recognizing the name.

"No, he died several years ago."

My heart plummets into my stomach. "Oh my gosh. I'm so sorry to hear that."

He nods once and then revs up until we're at a steady speed, hurtling over the bumps and charging through the dirt. I keep a tight hold on him, enjoying the way it feels to experience this with him. My hair flies around my neck as we fly through the air, and I close my eyes until I feel the wheels hit the ground.

"Oh my God, that was so fun," I shout-laugh over the roar of the engine when he slows down.

"I knew you'd like it…" He brings us to a stop. "Do you wanna try drivin'?"

"Really? You'd trust me?"

Landen climbs off and faces me. "Of course. I trust you with my heart. Why wouldn't I trust you with my life?" He winks then nudges me closer and slides in behind me.

The way he effortlessly says those words has my cheeks feeling windburned and not because of the actual wind.

"I dunno how to drive this!" I panic, tightening my fingers around the handles.

"I'll teach you, don't worry."

He gives me a crash course, but most of it goes over my head because of how nervous I am.

"Ready?"

No.

"I think so…"

With his hands on top of mine, he helps me start it and guides us along the trail until I'm comfortable driving myself.

After five minutes of going at a snail's pace, he tells me to speed it up. When I finally do, he tightens his hold around me and tells me to let it fly.

It doesn't take long to get the hang of it, especially since I know he's right here in case I need him. But there's something about tearing through an off-road dusty track that feeds my adrenaline like when I'm riding Ranger.

"Okay, one more lap. Make it a good one." He squeezes my bare thighs, and I swallow back a moan.

This man teases me like it's his full-time job.

I rev the engine and fly over the last bump.

"Jesus Christ." He laughs between his words when the front two wheels bounce against the ground. "You killed it."

"I'm a champion barrel racer...are you that surprised?" I mock even though I was terrified as hell at first. He doesn't need to know that.

"Not at all. But I'm still impressed," he says with a smile in his voice. "There's a pond half a mile from here that I wanna show you. Just drive down the trail and you'll see it."

My heart continues beating rapidly as I drive us through another trail of trees. I still can't believe how large this place is.

"How much land do y'all own?"

"Hundreds of acres. Goes back here and then some."

"Did y'all ever camp out here?"

"Not really. We have family who live in Willow Branch Mountain a couple hours north of here and they own a luxury camping resort. My parents took us out there pretty much every summer growin' up."

"Why does that sound familiar?" I rack my brain for where I would've heard that name.

"It's a small town, but it's a popular place for mostly couples. We have some marketing materials posted at The Lodge. Probably saw it in there."

No, I don't think so…

"Hmm…"

"What is it?" He leans in closer to hear me.

"I'm just gettin' frustrated having these moments of something soundin' like I know them but not remembering from where or how. Happened earlier too at the farmer's market when a journalist approached me and called me by my name as if we'd spoken before. I knew she looked familiar but couldn't place any memories of her."

"Yeah, that's the brain fog associated with concussions. Wilder got sick with bacterial meningitis when he was like five or six and suffered from neurological side effects for two years. It halted his milestones because he had short-term memory issues. They wanted him to repeat kindergarten, but he and Waylon didn't want to be separated, so my parents didn't let them."

"Oh, wow…that sounds traumatic."

"He did rehab therapy to help him catch up and improve his memory and attention so he could comprehend what he was learning. Then he had speech therapy for a year and now he never shuts up, so I guess it worked."

I laugh because he's right. Wilder loves to hear his own voice.

"Okay, to the left now…you'll have to go off trail for a minute and then you'll see it."

Thirty seconds later, a truck comes into view.

"Who is that?" I ask.

"It's Fisher's truck. He's lettin' me borrow it since his has a larger bed than mine. We can park here." He reaches over and turns it off.

Once he climbs off, he helps me to my feet and removes my helmet.

"Does my hair look crazy now?"

Grinning, he smooths it down for me and then tucks it behind my ears. "It's gonna get messed up anyway, so don't worry too much about it."

"Wh—"

He winks, taking my hand and walking us toward the truck. A few seconds later, the dots finally connect in my slow-thought brain on what he was insinuating.

"You sound very confident about that."

"I am." He glances at me, squeezing my fingers. "I plan to throw you in the water."

"Wait, what?"

As we get closer to the back of the truck, I see a pond twenty feet away on the other side. It looks pretty clear, too.

"You didn't tell me to bring a suit!" I scold. "Hours and hours of preparin' and now you're going to ruin it."

"I'll carry you so you don't get wet, how's that?"

"That sounds like a trap."

He chuckles. "But first, we're gonna have dinner."

"Where?"

He opens the tailgate and reveals the cutest little surprise.

An air mattress covered in blankets, with a large wooden serving tray sitting on top of it. Two wine glasses, plates, and two sets of silverware. And then a vase of roses in the middle.

Next to it is a picnic basket.

"This is so freakin' cute and thoughtful. I can't believe you do this."

He lifts my hand and presses a kiss to my knuckles. "I

wanted it to be special. We only get to experience our first date once."

"Unless you're me and could forget in a day or two. Then you'll have to take me out on another first date."

He pokes me in the side, and I squeal. "No tickling!"

Once he helps me up into the bed and shows me what we're having, I settle comfortably between his legs, eat the little sandwiches he made, and drink the Pinot Grigio.

"This is seriously perfect," I say, staring out into the water. "It's so peaceful out here."

"I sprinkled some of his ashes out here. At the track, too."

"Whose?"

"Tucker's," he confirms. "His mom let me have some."

"How'd he die, if you don't mind me asking?"

"Um…" He scrubs a palm over his face, and I worry I've made him uncomfortable.

"You don't—"

"No, it's okay. I don't mind talkin' about him. He lost his high school girlfriend and a couple years later, he jumped off a bridge."

"Oh my God."

"His girlfriend drowned and so we speculate he wanted to go the same way she did. Even though he very much knew how to swim."

Squeezing his hand, I pull it up to my chest and hold him tighter against me.

"We had plans to meet up to spread her ashes, but he took them with him when he jumped."

"I dunno what to say besides how sorry I am that you had to go through that. Sounds like you two were close."

"He was like a brother to me. We rode our bikes almost every weekend. Went lookin' for trouble anywhere we could.

Swam in this pond all summer. During spring break in high school, we'd go up to my cousin's and spend a week in one of their luxury cabins."

"At least you have some good memories, right?" I say softly.

"Yeah, most of 'em are good." His lips press against my cheek. "You ready to go in?"

I'm somewhat surprised he'd still want to swim in the pond that reminds him so much of Tucker. But maybe it's healing for him, so I nod and let him pull me up. "Let's do it."

He yanks off his shirt, and once again, I'm drooling at the sight of him.

"My eyes are up here, ma'am."

"Yes, but your abs are down here."

"If I'd known that was all it took to get your attention, I woulda walked around half-naked years ago."

"Must be why it works on me. I never had the chance to get immune to it before I lost my memory."

He jumps down from the tailgate and then turns around so his back is facing me. "Giddy up."

I furrow my brows, laughing. "Giddy up where?"

Patting his shoulder, he says, "I'm carrying you, remember?"

"You were serious about that?"

"There's no sandy beach area, so it's all hard rocks and mud."

"Oh, shoulda told me that in the first place." I wrap my arms around his neck, and when my legs are secure, I hold on.

"Don't just drop me in there," I warn him. "I'm not the best swimmer."

"Don't worry, I'm a certified lifeguard. I won't let you outta my sight."

For some reason, that triggers something.

257

"Wait, I knew that! Have you told me that before?"

"Before your accident, yeah."

"Do you think that means I'm gettin' my memory back?"

"I dunno, maybe. Do you hate me yet?" His amused tone makes me laugh.

"Nope."

Not even close.

"Then I guess we're still in the clear."

Chapter Twenty-Four
LANDEN

I could survive on hearing Ellie's laugh for the rest of my life and never need anything else.

As I hold her in my arms in the middle of the pond, it feels like a dream come true.

And one I'm feeling guilty about more and more as I steal these moments with her I'd never get previously.

How is it after four years, I've never heard her laugh as much as she has in the past few weeks and now I'm completely addicted.

I need it to breathe.

But as more of her memories start to resurface, I'm afraid it's going to get ripped away from me at any moment.

It's why I didn't share the full story about Tucker and Talia, and my ex-girlfriend being the one responsible for their deaths. I don't want her to feel sorry or take pity on me and then later resent me for it when she remembers.

"Tell me a secret," she says as we settle into the water together. Long gone is her concern about messing up her hair as it floats around her.

"Hmm...okay. I wanna buy a few acres in this area and build my dream house for my family someday."

"That's precious. What kind of house?"

"A two-story with large windows facing the water so we can wake up every morning and watch the sunrise over the mountains. Double wraparound porches so we can watch the fireworks from the second floor. Wilder and Waylon set a ton of 'em off every Fourth of July."

"Wow...I love that. I imagine eight dogs running around, jumping into the pond, smelling like wet socks, and playing together. Kids chasing them in and out of the water, laughing, and making core memories."

"Wait...*eight*?"

She laughs again, and I soak up every second.

"I couldn't have dogs growing up, but I love 'em. My dad's allergic, so I had gerbils and goldfish."

"Oh, you poor deprived horse girly."

She splashes water in my face and then I threaten to dunk her unless she kisses me.

"You wouldn't dare..."

I push her closer toward the water and arch a brow. "Try it."

Instead of calling my bluff, she lowers her hands to my waist and curls her fingers into my shorts.

Arching a brow at how close she's getting to my dick, I say, "Gonna remove these for me?"

"Or..." The corner of her lips curves into a devious smile. "We could both go without clothes and continue in the shower?"

I scoop her up and get us out of the water as fast as I can. She giggles when I carry her over my shoulder caveman-style and put her into the passenger seat of Fisher's truck.

He's gonna be pissed we're soaking wet, but I'll deal with it later.

"Is that a yes?"

Grinning, I start the truck. "That's a *I hope you know what you just got yourself into.*"

It's only a five-minute drive back to my place and as soon as I park, I bring her inside and haul her into my arms.

"I'm afraid I'm gonna have to remove all your clothing or you'll get the carpet wet…" I taunt, pulling on the hem of her shirt and lifting it off her.

"Wouldn't wanna do that," she sasses. "Guess that means you'll have to strip, too."

"Hmm…I think you're right." I unbutton my shorts and slide them down my legs but leave my boxers. She removes her shorts next and is left in her bra and panties.

"Fuck, you are so beautiful…" Cupping her face, I bring our mouths together in a hot, desperate kiss. She snakes her arms around me, pulling me tighter against her, and my cock thickens between us.

Without breaking contact, I lift her body until it wraps around mine and then walk us to the bathroom. I turn on the water and once we remove the rest of our clothes, I pull her under the water with me.

"Mm…it's so warm." She hums as I thread my fingers through her hair.

I grab the shampoo bottle and then massage it into her scalp.

"Are you sure you're okay with this?" I ask, getting all the way down to the ends.

"With you washing my hair? I think it's pretty hot…"

Grinning, I pull down the handheld shower and rinse out the shampoo. "Being naked together."

She lowers her gaze down to my half-erect cock. "Mm-hmm. Quite okay with it."

"Even when I lower my hand down here?" I palm her breast and then pinch her nipple.

"Yes," she whispers, closing her eyes. "Very much okay with that."

"Turn around," I tell her, then finish rinsing out the shampoo.

I change the water flow to the pulsating massage speed and then lower it between her thighs. "How about when I do this?" I murmur in her ear.

She inhales a shallow breath, nearly gasping before I've even touched her.

"That's...good, too." Her eyes fall closed as her head rests on my chest.

"Spread your legs wider, baby. I'm gonna make you come hard and fast..."

With the shower spray beating on her clit, I play with her nipple again and kiss her neck.

"The pressure is so perfect," she moans in between her words. "I don't think I can stand any longer."

Her body begins to shake harder, and I tighten my free arm around her waist so she feels safe and secure to let go. "If you need to hold on to something, hold on to me."

She clasps her fingers around my arm as her moans grow louder.

"That's it...don't hold back, baby." I suck her neck, feeling her tense. "Come, Ellie."

Sweet moans release from her mouth as she does just that. She hangs onto me and shatters in my arms.

I put the nozzle back up and then give her time to catch her breath.

"That was so hot," I tell her.

She spins around, freshly flushed and satisfied. "Your turn."

"My turn to what?"

"I wanna watch you get yourself off."

Grabbing my hard cock, I give it a few casual strokes. "Okay. On one condition."

She raises her brows but continues focusing on my hand. "What's that?"

"I want you on your knees, ready to swallow it down."

I hold out my hand so she doesn't fall and then she kneels in front of me.

Cupping her jaw, I tilt her head up toward me and shove my thumb between her lips. "Such a good girl."

Instead of smarting off like I'm used to from her, she opens her mouth and sticks out her tongue.

"Jesus Christ…" I shake my head and continue fucking my fist because it's not going to take long with her looking at me like that.

She focuses all of her attention on me as I twist around the tip and then when I feel my balls draw up and my body tense, I smack my cock against her lips.

"Get ready…" I warn her, my eyes fighting to stay open, but I force them to because I'm not missing this.

Moaning through the pleasure, I give myself quick little strokes until it releases and paints her beautiful face with my cum.

"Goddamn, that was so fuckin' intense."

Grabbing her hand, I help her up and crash my mouth to hers, still messy with my release.

"That was fuckin' hot," she mutters in between kisses. "I vote joint showers from now on."

"Whatever you want. You could ask for anything right now, and I'd do it."

She giggles as she snakes her arms around my waist, rests her chin on my chest, and gazes up at me with the most precious expression on her face. "I like you, ya know?"

I chuckle under my breath, tightening my hold on her. "It's about goddamn time you caught up to me. I've been waitin' four years."

After the water gets too cold to stay in the shower, I towel dry every inch of her body, then give her one of my T-shirts while I put her clothes in the washer. I figured we'd come back here for dessert, so once we settled on the couch, I served strawberry shortcake with whipped cream.

"This is good. Who says you can't cook?" she taunts, licking the cream off her fork.

"I'd barely call it that. I mixed the strawberries with sugar, put them on top of a shortcake, and added the topping."

She smirks. "Gramma Grace has been teachin' me a lot these past two weeks. She's a gem. You're lucky. I'm not super close to my grandma."

"No? How come?"

Her shoulders lift casually. "She was a single mom, and I don't think she had great relationships with her kids, either. She comes over during holidays and for random dinners, but it's mostly centered around small talk, and I hate that."

After we finish eating, we put on a movie. But halfway through, we end up making out and Ellie straddling my lap. This time, I don't make her ride my hat and let her come grinding on my dick.

"Do you wanna stay the night?" I ask when it gets late. "If you don't wanna drive in the dark, I can take you."

"I don't mind stayin' if you don't."

"Not at all." I kiss her. "I'll be up early for chores but can come back before you have to leave."

"Have you ever had a girlfriend sleep over?"

"A one-night stand, yes. A girlfriend, no."

She gives me a disapproving face, and I chuckle. "Then why did you ask?"

She shrugs. "Because I'm a glutton for punishment, I guess. Did you burn the sheets at least?"

"Oh, they're long gone. I bought all new bedding for you. Top of the line, luxury sheets, and a new comforter."

"You did? Why?"

"Because I wanted a fresh start with you. As soon as we started dating, I wanted any trace of other women gone. None were serious anyway, so it wasn't a hardship to replace everything. I even bought new towels so you'd have high-quality ones when you needed to shower."

"I dunno if that's the sweetest thing I've ever heard or the most presumptuous that you were gonna get me in your bed…"

I scratch over my beard that's overdue for a cut. "I vote for the former."

She wraps her arms around my neck and pulls my mouth to hers. "Okay, sustained."

My phone goes off with a text, and I grab it off the coffee table before we walk to my room.

"Oh shit…"

"What is it?" she asks.

CECILIA

YOU'RE ENGAGED?!?

"I think your interview released..." I tell her, then show her my screen.

"I'm surprised she didn't hear about it sooner." She pulls the covers back and rubs a palm over the softness of the sheets. "Ooh, these are very nice."

"Good, I'm glad you approve." I flash her a wink.

I don't tell her I took Wilder and Waylon with me to buy these a month ago. It was the blind leading the blind in figuring out what kind of bedding was the best.

"Cecilia's from outta town, but yeah, it woulda only been a matter of time." I shrug, climbing in next to her.

"I dunno if I even wanna read it." She groans. "I hate doing press so damn much."

"Part of the territory, but from what I've seen and read over the years, you've always done well and been very professional."

She nods toward my phone. "Are you gonna text her back?"

"No." I pull her into my arms, interlocking our legs. "Why would I waste my time texting another woman when I have my dream girl in my bed?"

She climbs on top of me, kissing me fiercely as she straddles my waist.

"You need to tell me a secret now," I tell her as she kisses down my neck. "I told you one of mine."

She meets my gaze and furrows her brows. "Right now?"

I chuckle under my breath at how frustrated she sounds.

"Are you hell-bent on giving me blue bean?"

Barking out a laugh, I roll us over until I'm on top of her.

"As much as I want to heal your *blue bean* issues, I don't wanna take advantage of your memory."

She blows out a slow breath, looking seemingly torn on saying her next words. "Funny you say that…because my secret is that I'm terrified I'll get it back and break my own heart with the truth of why I didn't like you in the first place. I can't imagine a world in which I'm not falling hopelessly in love with you."

The walls crash around me as her words repeat in my head. *Falling. In. Love. With Me.*

I never thought Ellie Donovan would return my feelings, nevertheless admit them to me.

But even when she does remember why, I'll never forget that at least for a short moment in time, we had it all.

Chapter Twenty-Five
ELLIE

"You're doing great, Ranger…such a good boy." I lunge him in the corral after I rode him for the first time in six weeks. Noah was by my side the entire time and she made me wear a helmet, but at least I got back on him.

When I went to my last neurologist appointment, he put me on light restrictions, so it was just a matter of when I was comfortable riding again and when Noah felt safe about it.

"Talkin' about me again?" Landen says behind me, and I smile at hearing his voice.

Glancing over my shoulder, I find him leaning over the fence wearing his Cattleman hat and a cocky smirk.

"You could only dream, cowboy."

"I don't need to anymore…" He winks, and I shake my head at his relentless flirting.

I bring Ranger in and walk him toward the gate.

"I heard you rode today. How'd it go?" he asks, opening it for me.

"Good."

I tell him about it and how excited I am to get back into a

269

riding routine. It won't be for hours on end, but at least once a day to stay on top of it. I might be out for the rest of this season, but the next one starts up again right after, so I want to be ready.

"You will be. I have no doubt." He kisses my forehead and I melt into him.

A girl could get used to this.

He walks into the stables with me and helps me get Ranger into the grooming stall so I can brush him and spend a few more moments with him before he goes back in.

"So any chance I could talk you into comin' over tonight? I was gonna attempt to make some chicken pasta recipe Noah found."

I smile at how sweet he is for wanting to cook for me when neither of us seems to excel in that area, but at least he's willing to try. I've learned quite a bit from Gramma Grace, but I'm only confident when she's next to me to watch and make sure I'm not screwing up anything.

Frowning, I say, "I wish I could, but my parents want to talk to me about something tonight."

He arches a brow. "About what?"

"I'm not sure. They just said we needed a family meeting. Whatever that means."

"You don't sound too worried about it."

Shrugging, I continue brushing Ranger. "It's probably about racing or the fake engagement. They were a little skeptical that it wasn't real when they saw I was wearin' a ring, but who knows? Either way, I'd love to stay tomorrow night."

He grins and then kisses my forehead again. "It's a date."

When I walk into my house, I'm hit with the aromas of lasagna and breadsticks. One of my favorites. What's not to love about pasta and cheese?

"Hi, sweetheart." Mom greets me with a warm smile. "How was your day?"

I tell her all about it and how excited I am about getting back into regular training. The only symptom I'm still struggling with is the occasional headache and minor vision blurriness. It usually only bothers me when I'm watching TV, but the doctor was optimistic that it'll eventually go away.

"That's wonderful. I bet Ranger is excited, too."

"I'm gonna clean up and then I'll help set the table," I tell her.

I give Dad and Aunt Phoebe drive-by hellos and then go change my clothes.

When I set my phone down on my desk, I notice there are ten missed calls from an unknown number. They were sent right to voicemail, but whoever it was didn't leave any.

Probably another journalist who wants to ask me only God knows what.

After I've freshened up with more deodorant and body spray and then fixed my braids, I go back out into the living room.

Dad and Aunt Phoebe are gone.

It's close to five, which means they should still be in here watching *Seinfeld*.

I walk to the kitchen to help Mom, but she's not in here either.

What the hell is going on?

"Hello?" I call out. "Where'd everyone go?"

"You can't be here! You're only gonna confuse her!" I hear Mom yelling outside and rush to look out the window above the sink.

Who is she talking to?

Dad stands next to Mom, with Aunt Phoebe hiding behind them. But I can't see who they're talking to from this angle.

Instead of waiting, I walk outside.

"She has my money! I need it so I can start over, no thanks to her *fiancé*!"

My fiancé? Are they talking about Landen and me?

"Mom?" I shout.

The three of them spin around. Mom's clearly upset, tears welling in her eyes, and Dad looks pissed.

Aunt Phoebe looks sad and heartbroken.

I can't gauge what's happening.

"Are y'all okay? What's goin' on?"

As I walk closer, I finally see a woman leaning against a car with a man sitting in the driver's seat.

"Who are you?" I ask her.

"Very funny, Ellie," she snaps, pushing off the door and coming toward me.

"Don't!" Mom yells at her. "She lost her memory and doesn't recognize you. We're not supposed to tell her anything she doesn't remember on her own."

"Is that true or are you just fakin' it?" she asks me.

I study her features for any recognition. Light brown hair down to her shoulders that's pulled back with a pair of sunglasses on her head.

"I-I'm not. I lost part of it from a concussion," I explain. "I don't know who you are...but I feel like I should?"

My heart pounds at the realization I've forgotten another person I used to know before the accident.

She stops about ten feet away from me and crosses her arms, then studies me. "I'm your older cousin, Angela."

"My daughter," Aunt Phoebe mutters.

She has a daughter? *I should know that, right?*

"We grew up like sisters. I can't believe you forgot me." She sounds offended, and I feel awful.

"Sorry, I-I'm drawing a blank. They said it's probably temporary but could be permanent," I explain. "The brain fog sucks."

"I guess that'd explain how you're engaged to my nemesis," she scolds. "I couldn't believe it when I read it in your recent interview."

"Landen's your nemesis? You know him?"

She smirks. "Sweetheart, I dated him."

I feel a punch to my gut at those words. Landen probably dated a lot of women before me. I know he has a past, but I never thought it'd somehow weave into mine.

"Why do you hate him?"

And more importantly, why did I?

Angela opens her mouth to speak, but Mom quickly interrupts.

"Angela, wait..." Mom pleads. "She doesn't know."

"Know what?" Anxiety clamps down on my chest, and I have a feeling something's wrong. "Will someone just tell me what's goin' on? I don't care what the doctor said. I wanna know."

Dad comes next to me. "Angela was in prison for the past eleven years and has just been released on parole."

"Holy shit," I mutter although I hadn't meant to say the words aloud.

"We wrote to each other every month. You came to visit me in Nashville the day before the rodeo. We talked about how we'd be roommates and travel together when you had races."

She sounds genuine, and I'm annoyed with my brain that I can't remember any of this.

"I have no memory from after I arrived in Franklin," I tell her. "But what does any of this have to do with Landen and you being in prison?"

Angela meets my gaze, an almost sympathetic expression on her face. "He's the one who helped put me in there."

My heart all but stops at the accusation. It's racing so hard, I can hear it beating in my ears.

"That can't be right. No. *No…*" I fall to my knees before I realize they give out.

Mom and Dad are at my side before I can cry out for help.

Dizziness takes over when my chest tightens, and I clutch my throat, fighting with my lungs to let me breathe.

My mind works overtime when thoughts of Landen surface —memories of before the accident.

When we'd train together.

When he'd annoy me at the most random of times.

When I recall what he'd done to Angela.

And I hated him.

But my heart still feels everything for him.

"You're having an anxiety attack, Ellie. Try to inhale and exhale slowly, sweetheart." Mom's soothing voice is the last thing I hear before my eyes close and I lose consciousness.

Chapter Twenty-Six
LANDEN

Since I'm not cooking for Ellie tonight, I head to The Lodge to grab something to eat for dinner. Wilder and Waylon are sitting at our normal table, staring at their phones.

"Hey," I greet, but neither moves. "Y'all lookin' at porn or what the fuck?"

Finally, they look up. But there's remorse in their gazes.

"What?" I ask.

They look at each other and now I'm suspicious as hell.

"What the hell is going on?" I cross my arms, demanding one of them speak up.

"It's a news article about Angela being released from prison. She got parole," Waylon says.

"Yeah, Warren told me. So I guess she's officially out now? That's what the article says?"

Hopefully, it recaps the fact that she's a *murderer*.

"It mentions Ellie," Wilder says hesitantly.

I furrow my brows, reaching for one of their phones. "Mentions her how?"

Scanning the article, I roll my eyes at the reference to Angela's *good behavior* before I see Ellie's name at the bottom.

"The Creek Chronicles reached out to local three-time NFR qualifier barrel racer, Ellie Donovan, but she had no comment about her cousin's impending early release," I read aloud.

"What the fuck?" I look between the twins before rereading it. "Angela's not her cousin."

"We were lookin' it up," Wilder says. "There was an old article from Angela's trial and it mentions her mom, Phoebe Ryan, but her maiden name is Cotton."

"And what's that mean?" I ask.

"Ellie's mom's maiden name is Cotton, too."

"Ellie's aunt is her mom's sister. They are cousins," Waylon explains. "There's a photo of Ellie and Angela on one of her old Instagram pages from thirteen years ago."

My heart pounds as the dots connect. She's never mentioned an aunt or a cousin. In fact, she hardly talked about her family at all.

"I knew Angela most of my life. I don't remember her having a—" I pause, thinking about the six-year age difference. "Ellie would've been twelve at the time of the trial. Holy shit."

I scrub my hands over my face, trying not to panic, but I am.

"You remember she had a younger cousin?" Waylon asks.

"She'd bring her along sometimes when we'd hang out, but I just remembered that now. She was so much younger than us, I-I guess I forgot about it after all these years."

I actively tried not to think about Angela once she got sentenced.

Wilder scratches his cheek. "Ellie never mentioned her to you at all?"

"Before the accident, Ellie mentioned someone she looked

up to had been taken from her. But that they hadn't died…" I blow out a shallow breath as her statement finally makes sense. "She must've been referring to Angela going to prison."

"That could be why she hated you," Waylon suggests. "Depending on what Angela told her, she thinks you're the reason she went away."

"Because of my testimony…" I nod. "Or anything dealing with Talia's death. I was pretty vocal about it to anyone who'd listen."

"Why wouldn't she just tell you? Or any of us?" Wilder asks. "Why come train here at all?"

"Because Noah's the best in the state and Ellie probably knew Noah wouldn't have agreed to work with her if she was linked to the person responsible for my friends' deaths."

How did no one know this whole damn time?

It's not like I went digging into Ellie's past or even kept up with Angela's family. I had no reason to.

"So Ellie knew who you were or knew whatever Angela told her, and when she got a concussion, she lost all memory of it? Forgetting why she hated you because it was linked to Angela the whole time…" Waylon asks the same questions swirling around in my mind.

"I dunno…maybe…I guess." I shake my head. "Or she forgot who Angela was and everything linked to her got wiped?"

"That's wild, man. Concussions can block out trauma, so it's possible…" Waylon shakes his head as if he's just as blown away by this as I am.

I pull out the chair and collapse into it, holding my head up when all I want to do is fall apart. "How the fuck am I supposed to tell the one person I'm falling for that I finally know why she hated me?"

"I thought you can't tell her anything she doesn't remember on her own?" Wilder asks.

"But how can he keep it a secret?" Waylon says. "That'd almost be worse."

"If she found out I knew and didn't tell her, it'd be a betrayal," I confirm. "But the moment I do…she could remember everything and we'd be over."

"There's still a chance she wouldn't remember even if you tell her," Wilder says. "Best-case scenario, she won't."

"Worst-case scenario, she does." I groan.

Wilder holds up his phone again. "What if she's already read this?"

I shrug. "She's not really on social media a lot and didn't read the last article they wrote about her, so I don't think she goes lookin' for anything with her name. But that means it's only a matter of time before Angela returns and reminds her."

Who knows how much Angela's manipulated her at this point or what she'll tell her when she's back in her life? Ellie hated me based on whatever Angela told her and never asked to hear my side of the story, so there's no way she'll want it now when she realizes how close I allowed her to get to me.

"What about her career? Everyone's gonna know she's connected to a murderer…and if she supports Angela?" Waylon shrugs. "Her career's already on the line. This could break it."

"This could break everything." I close my eyes and rub my temples.

When the news broke about Talia's death and Angela's connection to it, her family got a lot of heat from the community. They weren't painted in a positive light since they stood by Angela, and if I remember correctly, her parents lost their jobs and ended up divorced.

When my head stops spinning, I stand and pull in my chair.

"Where're you going?" Waylon asks.

"I need to talk to Noah before I decide what to do."

I'm not the only one this affects. Noah and her have been friends for four years and if Ellie believes I'm the reason Angela went to prison, the ripple effect wouldn't stop at just me. It'd tarnish their working relationship, too.

"Breathe, Landen." Noah smacks my cheek when I don't exhale.

I blink a few times until my eyes focus on her standing in front of me.

"They're *cousins*..." I repeat for probably the tenth time.

"Yes, I heard you the first dozen times. Stop freakin' out or I'm gonna have to slap you."

I press a palm to my sore cheek. "You already did."

She lifts one shoulder. "Harder next time."

"Are you gonna tell me what to do or just assault me?"

"I'm thinking..." She paces up and down the aisle between the stalls of the stables. "Have you called her?"

"Not yet. She had plans with her parents tonight and we usually FaceTime before bed, but we made dinner plans tomorrow night instead."

"Okay, so assuming she has no idea about that article, you're gonna have to tell her. Let her read it and see if it sparks anything. If it doesn't, encourage her to ask her parents."

"And what if her parents take Angela's side?"

"They don't strike me as the type or they never woulda let y'all date or be fake engaged in the first place. Plus, they let her train here for four years. So either they didn't know the level of hate she had for you or they didn't agree with it."

"But she could remember hating me."

"Yes. She could..." She nods. "And you've been mentally preparing for that to happen this whole time and—"

"I can't let her go."

"No. You fight like hell for her, Landen. Whatever story Angela told her can be argued by the truth and if she's fallin' for you as hard as you're obsessed with her, she'll probably give you a chance to share your side of the story at least."

But what if she doesn't?

Nodding along, I wipe my sweaty palms down my jeans.

"Maybe I should wait until we can talk in person tomorrow night."

"As long as you understand she still might not remember, or on the flip side, not wanna hear your side if she does."

"God. How'd this get so fuckin' complicated?"

"You pursued a girl who forgot she hated you..."

"Thank you, Captain Obvious. Now give me some useful advice or—"

Noah's phone going off with a text interrupts my thoughts.

When she pulls it out of her pocket, she snaps her gaze to me. "It just got a lot more complicated."

"Whaddya mean?"

"It's Mrs. Donovan. Ellie's in the hospital. She fainted."

Chapter Twenty-Seven
ELLIE

"Hey, cousin. Glad to have you back." Angela smiles as my eyes peel open, and I realize I'm in a hospital room. *Again.*

But at least I'm not bleeding or have a headache.

"How'd I get here?"

"Your mom called an ambulance because she was worried you were having another epileptic episode."

"Did I?"

"Nah, you just fainted. Your dad caught you before you could hit your head again."

"Where're my parents?"

"They're speakin' to the doctor now. Something about tests…" She waves her hand in the air. "You're gonna be fine, though."

"I can't believe you're really here," I murmur, scanning my eyes over her. Seeing her in regular clothes and makeup for the first time in over a decade is strange.

"Before you collapsed, it seemed like you had some

memories resurface. How much do you remember?" She grabs my hand and squeezes.

"I think…right before the race when the Smith twins gave me something to drink. And some pills."

"You took pills? Why would you do that?"

"They said it was something to help my stomach…I dunno. It seemed harmless."

"Are they barrel racers, too?"

"Yeah, and I'm pretty sure they wanted me out of the competition. Whatever they gave me did the trick." I groan, thinking about it. "So damn stupid of me, but in my defense, I was gonna be sick and needed something to calm it before I threw up."

"Well, either way. You have to press charges."

"I can't prove it, Angela. It'd be my word against theirs, and mine isn't exactly trustworthy with a brain injury. They'll deny it anyway."

"Well damn. That's bullshit. Do you remember visiting me?"

"Kinda…but it's foggy. I'm still piecing other shit together too. It sucks fightin' with your brain to remember things you should know."

Frustration rolls through me as I shift to get comfortable in this damn bed.

"I know, sweetie." She rubs my arm. "As soon as you're out, we'll go over everything and fill in any gaps you still have."

"I don't think that's the problem…" I swallow and my throat burns as I try to clear it.

"Whaddya mean?"

"Landen…what you told me about him. I remember all of that."

She scoffs at the mention of his name. "I'm only lettin' it

slide that you somehow ended up engaged to him because you lost your memory. But if you want, I'll tell him myself that your relationship is over."

"No, my problem is that you lied to me."

"About what?"

I narrow my gaze, wondering how I never saw how narcissistic she was, or perhaps I didn't want to because I loved her so much.

"*Everything*. You...you told me he was the reason you went to prison and that everyone pointed their fingers at you but that you were innocent."

"I am innocent!"

Shaking my head, I feel nothing but pity. "Landen wouldn't do that unless he was certain you were guilty. I didn't think that way before because I never gave him the chance to show me who he was since I believed you without question. But once all of that bullshit got erased from my mind, I got to know him and the type of wonderful, kind, sweet man he is. I have no doubt he'd never do what you've accused him of."

"Oh my God...you're choosing a man over your own cousin?"

"Because I know him! And I know he'd never lie about what he saw that day."

"You think you do, but you don't know him like I do. He's a pathological *liar* and he ruined my life!"

"No...no, no, no." Amused by her outburst, I shake my head with a humorless laugh. "You ruined your own life when you did what you did and then didn't take accountability for it."

"Oh my God. It's gotta be the lack of oxygen not gettin' to your brain because we've discussed this at length!"

"You mean you *brainwashed* me! I was young and

vulnerable, and you took advantage! You knew I worshipped you and would've believed anything you told me."

And I did. *For years.*

She whips my hand out of her grip and flinches like I've struck her. With her arms crossed, she scowls. "I did no such thing!"

"You claimed that girl jumped and had some suicide pact with her boyfriend, but that's a lie, isn't it? Landen and his friends testified against you because they witnessed you pushing her. Not because they were covering up her depression. You shoved her off the ledge and she drowned."

"That's not true! They're all liars," she repeats the same three words I've heard for years.

"Landen would never lie about something so serious. When I started trainin' with Noah, I looked up news articles about what happened and it stated that Landen and a couple of his friends jumped into the water to search for her. But it never mentioned that you went in…" I shake my head at how obvious it is now.

"Well, I didn't need to. They were already lookin'…"

"Talia was your best friend and you don't immediately jump in to look for her?"

"Landen was a lifeguard! What good was I compared to him?"

"That's right, he is…" I say mockingly. "Which is maybe why you felt so comfortable shoving her off because you figured he'd be there to save her. But you didn't calculate her smacking her head on a boulder and drownin' before he could find her, right?"

That's what they described happened at the trial and it's insane how much of it I'm now remembering.

"It all makes sense now. Landen told me about his best

friend, Tucker, and how he jumped off a bridge after his girlfriend died. That was Talia. She drowned and he wanted to go the same way she did. If they'd made a pact, why would he have waited two years after? That doesn't add up…"

"I don't know! Tucker made that choice, not me."

"You're even more heartless than I could've imagined if you truly believe that your actions don't have consequences beyond the law."

"So I'm to blame for his decision?"

"You pushed his girlfriend off a cliff! You're the reason she died and the reason he wanted to die." I pierce her with a scowl I've only ever given Landen in the past. "You made me believe every word you said! I thought you were innocent and that they were placin' blame on you for no reason. Do you have any idea how *cruel* I was to Landen? How much resentment I held for him? And now to realize he didn't deserve it…" I sigh, giving my heart a moment to slow down. "You know what's worse, though? No matter how mean I was to him, he was never mean back. In four years, he never treated me the horrible way I treated him."

And realizing that makes me sick to my stomach.

"Sounds like he's the one who's brainwashed you…" She shrugs carelessly. "He went up in front of a judge and jury and told them I shoved Talia off purposely because I was jealous. It's laughable, Ellie! I had nothing to be jealous of."

"But you *did* shove her…"

She narrows her eyes before rolling them and scoffing. "*Fine.* But she asked me to."

I blow out a hollow laugh. "You're unreal. After eleven years, you finally confess she didn't jump and you can't even be truthful enough about it to admit you pushed her unprompted."

She holds up her hands in mock surrender. "Ya know what, believe whatever you want."

"Get out," I say, defeated.

"What? You can't be serious."

"Just…leave. Please, I can't look at you anymore. You are my biggest regret."

She overdramatically gasps, but it's all for show by the way her nostrils flare. She's only mad I'm not buying into her bullshit anymore.

"How can you say that? We spent nearly every day together as kids. Sleepovers, shopping trips, movie theater outings. I loved you like a little sister."

"You loved manipulating me. You're the reason I spiraled and became someone I wasn't."

"Don't blame me for your little depressive episodes. If it wasn't for what happened, you woulda never gotten into barrel racing and made a successful career out of it. You should be thankin' me."

I pinch the bridge of my nose because talking any sense into her is a lost cause. "You're certifiably delusional, Angela. And I don't say that as a joke, either."

"Wow, that hurts," she snaps, her jaw ticking as if she's trying to control her emotions. "What about the money, then?"

I should've expected she'd bring it up because that's probably the only reason she kept me in her life this long. She only valued me if I blindly followed her.

"Fine, you can have it. But then I never wanna see you again. I mean it, I want you out of my life forever."

"You can't be serious. We're family."

"And family doesn't do what you've done to me. If you want the money, that's what I want in return. Go start your life

286

over...far away from Sugarland Creek. Don't bother my parents or your mother. She's suffered enough from your actions, too."

"I think whatever medication they gave you is causing you not to think clearly. Maybe you should take some time to reconsider — "

I fold my hands in my lap and sit up straighter. "I'm thinking more clearly than I ever have and it's so obvious now what you did. And you're not even remorseful for it."

"Whatever." She turns and grabs a purse off the chair, then slings it over her shoulder. "I'll text you my account number so you can wire it. Once I do my six months at the re-entry center, Gage and I will find a place out of town."

"*Gage?*"

"Yeah, my boyfriend. He's been my pen pal for the past couple years. I coulda sworn I mentioned that to you?" She shrugs casually. "I've told him all about you."

Oh my God.

"Angela, no. You can't move in with him."

Even though I want nothing to do with her, doesn't mean I want to see her get hurt. Gage is bad news.

"Why not?" She crosses her arms, pouting like a defiant teenager. "You just told me to get lost and now you're tellin' me what I can and can't do? You don't even know him."

"He — "

Before I can explain, the door opens and my parents enter with Aunt Phoebe.

"You're awake," Mom cries and rushes to the side of my bed, then takes my hand. "You feelin' okay?"

Angela bails without a second glance or goodbye to her mother, and I watch as the door closes behind her.

I nod. "Great."

"They gave you something to calm your racing heart and it knocked you out for a while."

"When Angela accused Landen of being responsible for puttin' her in prison, I went into shock and started remembering things from before the accident," I tell her.

"You had an extreme anxiety attack." Mom wipes under her eyes before tears can fall. "I'm so relieved you're okay."

"I remember everything," I admit. "Why didn't you tell me when I forgot? When I was gettin' close to Landen?"

"Oh." She sucks in her lip like she's nervous. "We weren't supposed to—"

"And we didn't want to. Landen's a good man," Dad chimes in, taking me by surprise because he's the one who warned me not to get too close to him in the first place. "He treats you the way you deserve. Hard-working. Funny. I like him."

I burst out laughing and my heart swells because he's right. But all this time, I didn't think my parents thought too much about him. Turns out, they didn't want me to remember hating him either.

"We figured this was your second chance to live your own life without the weight of the trauma you went through," Dad explains. "You got to do whatever you wanted even if that didn't include riding."

"We've never seen you happier, sweetie." Mom smiles gently.

"It's true," Aunt Phoebe speaks up for the first time and squeezes in between my parents. "You went from a depressed workaholic to a vibrant, young twenty-something-year-old. Like how you should be."

"Gee…thanks?" I laugh.

"Sweetheart, Noah and Landen are in the waitin' room," Mom tells me.

"He's here?" I beam, though I'm not surprised.

"Yes, and he's a nervous wreck," Dad says.

Mom pats my hand. "Put that man out of his misery, will ya?"

I choke out a laugh, nodding. "Tell him to come in."

Chapter Twenty-Eight
LANDEN

Sitting in this waiting room brings back conflicting feelings from the last time Ellie was here. I would've camped out all night to stay close to her, but I'm glad I didn't have to because the seats were not built for bigger guys. And now, I'm not even bothering to sit. All I can do is pace and wait.

I watch as Noah talks to Ellie's parents and Aunt Phoebe. When I introduced myself to her, she looked me up and down a few times and then gave me a discreet smile.

So I think I passed whatever test she gave me.

"We're gonna check in on her and be right back," Mrs. Donovan tells me after the doctor walks away. "I'll let you know when you can go in."

Mr. Donovan claps my shoulder. "I'm rootin' for you, don't worry."

"Thank you, sir."

Fisher waits with Noah. He's not much of a talker, but sometimes I wish he were so I'd have someone else to listen to besides my own thoughts.

When Angela storms down the hallway with her arms

290

swinging and a scowl on her face, I can't tell if it's directed at me or the situation.

I had no idea what to expect coming here, but seeing my ex after eleven years wasn't it, and now I have more questions than answers.

"Let's go..." She directs to someone behind me.

When I look over my shoulder, I see...*Gage*?

What the fuck?

He takes her hand and they exit the waiting room.

Okay, well, now I have even *more* questions than answers.

"Stop fidgetin'. You're making me anxious," Noah scolds. "Sit down at least."

"I'm *fine*..." I crack my neck and each one of my knuckles, and once I'm out of things to crack, I pace the waiting room.

"Landen? Noah?"

My attention draws to Mrs. Donovan. "She's awake and ready to see y'all."

Noah jumps out of her chair. "Finally!"

I side-eye her as she runs past me.

Following behind, I blow out a tense breath and enter the hospital room.

"What have I told you about dying on me?" Noah scolds, wrapping her arms around Ellie.

"Hey, at least I'm three for three on not dying."

She's making jokes. That's a good sign.

Ellie looks at me. "Hi."

"Hi," I respond.

Noah glances between us. "Uh...I'll give y'all a moment."

When she walks past me, she pats my chest. "Good luck."

"Thanks," I murmur.

I go to Ellie's bedside and roam my eyes over her body. "You're okay?"

She nods. "Yeah."

"I—" My words are cut off by her trying to speak at the same time. "Go ahead," I tell her.

"I'm sorry, Landen."

I gulp because this is it. She's breaking it off.

"Can I at least get the opportunity to fight for you first?" I ask, pushing back the emotions threatening to surface. "Even if it's just five minutes."

Her expression shifts and she nods once. "Okay. Go."

"Oh, um…alright." I hadn't expected her to agree, but I'm going to give it my all regardless.

Inching closer, I stand taller. "I understand that someone you trusted, looked up to, and idolized told you a version of the truth, but I hope you'll give me a chance to prove how this person lied and exploited you. Angela and I dated on and off through high school and—"

"You can stop."

My mouth clamps shut.

"I don't need to hear about Angela."

"Oh. Okay…well. Then allow me to tell you about Talia and Tucker," I plead, feeling the sweat across my forehead.

She nods once again, and I spend a solid three minutes speaking as fast and eloquently as I can about how amazing my friends were and how bright of a future they had with each other.

"They sound really lovely."

"Yeah…" I lift my cap and scrub a hand through my hair. "It's why I fought so hard to get justice for Talia."

"Good. Angela got what she deserved."

"Yeah, and…wait, what?"

She smiles for the first time since I walked in and a huge weight falls off my shoulders.

"I was tryin' to tell you how sorry I am not because I got my memory back and was taking Angela's side, but because I remembered how I acted toward you before my accident. I'm embarrassed and humiliated that I treated you so horribly when you were nothing but nice to me. Hell, you even saved my life after I tore you a new one."

"You're apologizing to me?"

She reaches for my hand, and I let her take it, then sit on the bed next to her.

"Yes, and I'm not gonna make excuses for my behavior, but I wanted you to know how sorry I am and that I will never again treat you that way."

"Ellie..." I choke up because I was prepared for the worst. "You could run me over with a four-wheeler, spit in my mouth, and kick me in the nuts, and I would still love you with every fiber of my being."

Her eyes widen, and I grin. "I knew you were a masochist!"

"Only for you, though, remember?" I wink.

"Do you accept my apology? For real..."

I cup her face, lean in, and press my forehead to hers. "Yes. I accept. But I don't blame or resent you. You acted out based on what you knew at the time. It'd be different if you continued hating me after knowing the truth."

She pulls back, meeting my gaze. "Would you believe me if I said that even though I wanted to hate you, and said I did, I couldn't? I definitely hated that I was attracted to you, but I fought it hard."

"I fuckin' knew it!" I shout victoriously.

She sighs, rolling her eyes. "I shouldn't have admitted that."

"But it's nice to have the validation so I can rub it in my brother's faces."

She snorts, shaking her head at me, and I flash her a wink.

"I have to ask…what happened with Angela when she was in here?"

"I told her I never wanted to see her again. That I wanted her out of my life for good."

Tilting her chin, I meet her sad eyes. "For your sake, I'm sorry you had to do that. It hurts gettin' betrayed by someone you trusted."

"It does, but the pain is worth it to get something much better in return."

I lean in, stealing a kiss. "When I was lookin' up stuff on memory loss, I came across something interesting. After death, it's said that the human brain continues to be active for several minutes to replay its best memories before we fully die."

"Really? I never knew that. That's devastatingly beautiful to think about."

Threading my fingers through hers, I bring our joined hands to my lips and then press them to her knuckles. "When it's my time, every minute I have left will be spent replaying memories of you."

"Landen…" She squeezes her eyes as tears fall down her cheeks, but I quickly catch them before capturing her mouth.

"I do not deserve you." She wipes her face. "Are you sure you still wanna be with me after everything I've said to you?"

Amusement bubbles inside me as I fight back a laugh. "If I got offended by every snarl and snarky comment you sent my way, I would've stopped tryin' to get your attention years ago. But speakin' of, I was hopin' we could discuss this fake engagement and make it a real one."

"Whaddya mean?" She twirls the band between her fingers, and I'm not even sure she realizes when she's doing it.

"You're already wearin' my grandmother's ring, so I have

nothing to give you at this moment, but I'll happily get on one knee and beg you."

"Landen…" Her breath quickens as she lowers her voice to a whisper. "We haven't even had sex."

"Well, no…but…" I mock her soft voice even though no one else is in the room. "I've *wanted* to for the past four years. Does that count?"

She nudges me, fighting back a laugh, but failing. "No, it doesn't, but I do appreciate you makin' us wait because now I know it's going to be even more special."

"Trust me, it wasn't easy keeping your hands off *allllll* this." I slide my hand down my chest and abs.

She crosses her arms. "You are just so full of yourself, aren't you?"

"Is this where you tell me you remember why you hated me in your past life?"

She scoffs. "Oh, I'm remembering in this lifetime, too, Major Ego."

"Aye." I waggle my brows. "Previously, we discussed gettin' married for our third date and then you told the whole rodeo community that we were engaged. Aren't you the one who said they'll continue to bring it up during interviews until there's a wedding…"

"That's hardly a reason to actually go through with it," she argues.

"Says who?" I raise my brow in question and she sighs. "Now, say you'll marry me."

"Hmm. On one condition…"

"Name it."

"We can only get married *after* I win first place at the NFR."

"You only get that chance once a year…" I remind her.

"Yep, so you better make sure I win next year if you wanna make me your *wife*."

I confidently hold out my hand. "Alright, deal. As long as you're prepared for my trainin' sessions, which will include a lot of *stamina* exercises."

She holds out hers too but then pulls back. "Okay…but I'm keepin' my last name. It's part of my career now."

Lowering my brow, I counter, "Hyphenated."

She blows out a breath, contemplating. "What about our kids? That seems cruel to do to children."

"They get mine." I push my hand closer. "And I'll build us our dream house."

Her eyes light up and she beams. "With double wraparound porches and a view of the pond and sunset?"

"Yep, and I'll even throw in a few dogs."

She sucks in a breath, gasping at the idea of having dogs for the first time in her life. "You play dirty."

"We got a deal, Little Devil?" Smirking at her old nickname, I shove my hand closer.

Laughing and crying, she nods and slides her hand into mine.

Pulling her toward me, I crash our mouths together and slide my tongue between her soft lips.

"In case you haven't figured this out by now…" I whisper against her mouth. "I'm hopelessly in love with you."

"It's about damn time. Only took you four years," she deadpans.

"Sorry about that. I had to make sure I wasn't falling alone."

"You won't ever again. I promise."

I kiss the tip of her nose and smile.

"I love you," she whispers with tears in her eyes. "Thank you for waiting for me."

Chapter Twenty-Nine
ELLIE

"This ring is ridiculous…" I scowl, holding up my left hand with the massive three-carat diamond now weighing it down. "I can't wear this while riding. It'll probably fly off and get lost or I'll scratch it on a barrel."

Landen walks up naked behind me, brushes my hair to one side, and then feathers kisses along my exposed neck. "The only thing you'll be ridin' tonight is me and you *will* keep that on your finger while doing so."

"Or what, Major Ego?"

His heated stare finds mine in the full-length mirror reflection as his hand slips between my thighs. When he slides his tongue along my skin, it sends chills down my spine.

"Or I won't think twice about using that ring as a butt plug."

My gaze snaps up to his. I've never used one of those before. Is that even possible?

No, he's messing with me.

"I'm not bluffin' either…"

Goddamn him.

298

"You're so freakin' bossy…" I say, then moan when his finger circles over my clit. My head settles back against his chest. "Fuck, that feels good."

"I love watchin' you like this…" he breathes softly in my ear. "So goddamn sexy when I get to see you from every angle."

"I'm glad you enjoy it…because it's every woman's nightmare."

"You're every man's fantasy, baby. Don't you dare think anything less about yourself."

"Mm-hmm," I hum, losing myself to the sensations overcoming my body.

"Say it," he demands, moving his other hand to my breast, then rolls my nipple. "Tell me how sexy you are on display like this for me."

Ignoring him, I focus on the pleasure building between my legs. As my breathing increases, so do his movements. He slides two digits between my folds, and I gasp at how tight it feels when he thrusts them inside.

"I don't hear you, Ellie…tell me how beautiful you are with my fingers in your cunt."

"So damn good." I loop my arm behind my head and wrap it around his neck, pulling him closer. "So sexy with you finger-fucking my pussy."

He growls, twisting his wrist and then driving deeper. "That's not what I asked you to say, but fucking hell, that was hot."

His erection presses into my back, and I push against him. After two weeks of being edged nonstop by him wanting to wait until I was medically cleared from all brain injury symptoms because he planned to—in his words "throw me around like a rag doll"—and didn't want to risk causing more harm.

It's safe to say I'm ready for him to do just that.

"Landen, please...enough with the torture."

"Come on my hand first and then you can have my cock, baby." He sucks my neck harder, and I know by tomorrow morning, it'll be covered in his marks. "Keep your eyes on me through the mirror. Don't close 'em."

I do my best to keep them open, but it's hard when his fingers are so damn talented. Long, thick, and calloused—they fill me so full.

"Yes, I'm so close. Please don't stop..." I beg, breathing hard and shallow.

"Fuckin' hell, look at you. So gorgeous and aroused. *Perfection*."

His words are a soft melody, praising me in ways I've never heard before. I'd be lying if I said it didn't feel a little uncomfortable at first, but when he looks at me like I'm the only person in the world, it's impossible not to believe him.

"So perfect for *you*," I tell him, the pleasure building between my thighs, nearly ready to explode.

"Mm, that's right, sweetheart. And I'm gonna devour you. Eat that pussy until you're shaking and then hold you down until I'm properly done with you."

And that does it. One final brush over my clit and the tight invasion inside me sends me spiraling into a wave of inaudible moans. He tightens his hold on me as my legs threaten to give out.

"Hold on..." He throws me over his shoulder so my head nearly smacks into his bare ass.

"Landen!" I scold, hanging onto his thighs for support. "I don't need a second concussion!"

Laughter vibrates through his body as he carries me to the

bed and then tosses me onto the mattress. My arms flail as I try to steady myself.

"Oh my God," I breathe out.

He looms above me, caging his hands on each side of me.

"You're about to scream that a lot in a few minutes..." He winks before lowering himself down my body.

"You're supposed to fuck me now," I whine when he spreads my thighs.

"Relax for me." He drags his tongue slowly up my slit before he captures my clit and sucks on it. Then he curls two fingers so deep inside me that he presses against my cervix.

"*Holy shit.* Yes, right there." The moan that releases out of me isn't my own. I don't know where it comes from, but it vibrates from my throat and echoes through the room.

Landen's head pops up. "You were sayin'?"

"I dunno what you did, but I'm still seein' stars in my eyes."

He smiles proudly before gliding his tongue back on me.

"You said you'd let me come on your cock after your hand," I remind him, lifting my hips as he brings me closer to the edge again.

"Oh, you will..." Kisses feather the inside of my thigh. "But I wanted to taste you on my mouth first."

Groaning, I fist the blankets beneath me. "You're a tease."

"This is just the start of gettin' you back for four years' worth of blue balls."

I don't have the energy to respond before pleasure ripples through me once again. This time, I cry out his name, shattering through my pleas for him to fill me with his cock.

My body sinks into the mattress, feeling more relaxed than I have in weeks.

But Landen's mouth doesn't let up. He continues lapping up my arousal and moaning against me.

"Landen…please."

He lifts slightly. "Just because you're done doesn't mean I am…"

"*What*? I can't take any more."

"Yes, you can…" he taunts before three fingers slide into me, and I gasp at how tight it feels. My legs shake at how wet and full I am.

After more moaning and begging to give me what I need, he finally kneels between my legs and strokes his thick cock above my pussy.

"Are you ready for this?"

I agree like the sex-deprived woman I am and reach for him. "Let me get it wet for us."

Lifting on my elbows, I open wide and stick out my tongue. He slides it between my lips and I groan at how much I love tasting him.

"Relax your jaw, sweetheart." He cups my cheek, rubbing soft circles over my skin. "Good girl, just like that."

After a couple minutes of sucking him, he tells me to lie back.

"Tell me if I hurt you, got it?"

I nod, but I want it to hurt.

He eases himself inside me, so achingly slow at first, I lift my hips to speed up the process.

"Ellie…" He breathes my name out like a prayer, and I widen my thighs so he can slide in deeper. "You feel like heaven."

Wrapping my arms around his body, I pull him closer. "You're not gonna break me. I promise."

He finally stops holding back and gives me what I need, connecting us in a new way I've never felt before. My heart pounds at feeling so many things at once—how much I love him, how perfect we feel together, how deep our connection goes — I can barely take it before I'm teetering on the edge again.

"Landen, yes...I — "

"I got you, sweetheart." Snaking his arm around my waist, he lifts me and thrusts harder, vibrating pleasure against my clit.

My thighs shake around him as the climax hits me hard and fast, and I drag my nails down his back as I cry out through the intensity.

He buries his face in my neck and bites behind my ear, filling me so full, I nearly come again.

Hollow breathing echoes between us and he collapses on top of me, cradling my face in his hands.

"*I love you*," he whispers between slow, tender kisses. "But the next time I'm inside you, I'm bending you over in front of that mirror and you're gonna think I don't by the way I fuck that pussy raw."

My eyes search his face and a devious grin spreads across it.

"Then what was this?" I ask.

"This was makin' love to my future wife..."

"And what's wrong with that?"

He presses his mouth to the tip of my nose. "Absolutely nothing. But I'm not missing your face the next time I make you come."

"You're obsessed with watching me," I quip.

Licking his bottom lip, he winks. "You have no idea, Little Devil. Over four years of watchin' my dream girl from a distance. Now, I'm not gonna miss a damn thing."

I wake up sore as fuck but with a pleasurable soreness that brings a smile to my face. After a month of nonstop sex, you'd think my body would be used to this. But Landen's the first man I've been with in years and he's not let me have a day of rest in four weeks.

Even Jesus got to rest on the seventh day.

Not me.

But I'm not complaining because it's been the wildest, most fun I've ever had.

And I'm stupidly in love with him.

Even when I performed my version of self-care, it never felt like this.

Blissfully content and so damn happy.

"Excuse me, future Mrs. Donovan-Hollis? I got you some coffee..."

Groaning, I roll over and squint when the sun blinds me. "I'd like to revisit the terms of our impending marriage. No hyphen."

He sets two mugs on the nightstand. "So just Hollis?"

"Just Donovan," I confirm.

"No."

"You can't tell me no. It's my last name!"

"And you're gonna be my wife, so you should have mine."

"But my professional name is Donovan. That's how I'm known."

"That's why the hyphen."

"It's too long and wordy. By the time the emcee finishes announcing it, I'll have already crossed the finish line."

He smirks, amusement forming across his adorably boyish face. "Alright...on one condition."

"No...no more conditions!" I pout. "That's how we got here in the first place."

He climbs on the bed, caging me in between his arms. "But you didn't even hear it yet."

I shift my body, giving him room to position his legs between mine. "Fine...but it better be good or I'm voiding it."

"You marry me in a month."

My eyes twitch. "A month? We agreed on after I won the NFR. Plus, I can't find a dress and book everything that quickly!"

"That's fine. It doesn't have to be fancy."

"Landen...you can't be serious."

He dips down and slides his tongue between my lips, effortlessly shutting me up.

"Let's give the whole town...hell, the state...something worthy of talkin' about. If they're gonna whisper and make judgments, might as well get something amazing outta it. They'll be too busy gossiping about our fast-paced wedding to discuss a possible *murder scandal*."

A few days after the article published about Angela's release and connection to my name, the rumors spread rapidly through the town about me being linked to a convicted criminal. They dubbed it a *murder scandal* since Landen was involved in testifying against her and now they've made assumptions about why I'm with him. Then the equine journalists got involved and questioned my legitimacy for no other reason than to get in on the attention.

But I've learned people will make assumptions about me no

matter what I say or do and there's nothing I can do about it, so why bother fighting it? I'm not going to speak publicly about Angela's business, and I can't change who I'm related to. So they'll have to get over it.

Landen hasn't been as easygoing about it. He wants to track down every reporter who writes about me and send them a case of horse sperm to turkey baste up their asses.

After wiring Angela the hundred thousand dollars I saved for her, a huge weight lifted off my chest. I know I didn't have to give her anything and could've left her high and dry, but I'd rather give it to her knowing I'll never have to see her again. Sure, she could reappear and cause trouble, but there's no doubt I'd have Noah, Landen, and the rest of the Hollises to back me up. She'd be dumber than I thought if she returned.

Maybe she'll use the money to buy herself some integrity.

"Let 'em talk...who cares." I shrug.

"I care when it's bullshit lies about my woman." Landen presses his lips below my ear and adds, "Plus, think how hot the sex will be when I can tell my *wife* to crawl to me. I'm gettin' hard just imagining it."

"*Crawl?*" I push him back. "Now I know you've done lost your mind."

"Oh, baby, I will get you on your hands and knees. I promise."

His confident tone has me contemplating kneeing him in the balls.

"You remember I got my memory back, right? And that I can recall all the ways you tried to flirt with me or tease me to get my attention? You think *that* Ellie is crawlin' around for a man?"

"On my bed...you will crawl to me...if you want my cock inside you. You'll be begging for it. I guarantee it."

"You're next level de-lulu is what you are."

He pins my wrists above my head, feathering his lips down my neck and chest. "Say it."

"No."

"Say you'll marry me in thirty days."

"In a thousand."

His tongue swirls around my nipple, and I gasp at how sensitive it feels.

"Thirty. Days."

"In a *million*."

His teeth clamp down.

"Ow!" My back arches, forcing me closer. "That's sensitive."

"I'm gonna mark every inch of your body until you agree..."

"Pretty sure that's called coercion."

"Call it whatever you want..." He flattens his hot tongue and slides it up between my breasts. "But that's my offer. You can keep your last name as long as you say *I do* next month."

I whimper at the sensation of his body against mine, teasing and licking me. "More like *I don't*..."

His head pops up with a heated scowl. "Don't make me eat your pussy until you agree. Because we both know you will cave eventually when my face is buried between those thighs."

My pussy clenches at his words, almost feeling the sensation of his mouth down there.

Goddamn him.

"On one condition..." I re-counter.

"Wait...how many conditions are we at now?"

Grinning, I shrug because I've long lost count. "I get to sit on your face while you eat me out."

"Baby, you never have to beg for that..." He rolls to his

back, leisurely strokes himself through his boxers, and then looks at me. "Well...c'mon."

I straddle his waist and then second-guess myself. "I've never done it this way. Won't I suffocate you or something?"

"Wouldn't that be the best way to die?" He winks. "You won't. I know how to breathe in between devouring your cunt."

"Okay, but if memories of us start flashin' through your mind, tap my thigh or something. I don't wanna be a widow before we even get hitched."

He barks out an amused laugh. "Sweetheart, this memory is about to go to the top of the fuckin' list when I die."

Blushing with excitement and nerves, I wiggle up his body and over his mouth. He palms my ass and shoves me even closer.

Looking down, I only see his eyes and the narrow part of his nose. "There's no way you can breathe like this."

He responds by swiping his tongue through my slit and pulling me down more. I grab the headboard and ride his face like I did his cowboy hat.

"Yes...that's so good. Right there..." I gasp at the invasion of his tongue twisting inside me.

He palms my ass cheeks, digging his fingers into them as I continue grinding over his face.

By the time I'm ready to explode, goose bumps cover my skin, and a shiver runs down my body. The bridge of his nose rubbing against my clit has me seeing stars and then I'm floating.

"Oh my God, Landen. I'm gonna come..." I warn him, throwing my head back as I squeeze my thighs around his head.

Moaning through my release, he growls against my pussy and the vibrations make me come harder than ever before.

When he taps my thigh, I quickly sit up. "Are you okay?"

He licks his lips, tightens his grip around me, and then fucking smirks. "Thirty days, my love."

Then he smacks my bare ass.

"You're a caveman," I tell him, climbing off the bed.

Instead of denying it, he roars like a bear.

Of-fucking-course he does.

Rolling my eyes when he winks at me, I go clean up in the bathroom and then throw on my panties and one of his large white T-shirts.

As soon as I return to the bedroom, I find him on one knee.

"What're you doing? You've already proposed," I remind him.

"I'm *proposing* we get married at Willow Branch Mountain. They have a beautiful venue and you can't beat the views. Plus, I might have an *in* with the owners."

I snort, considering the owners are his aunt and uncle.

"You'd wanna have a ceremony at the same place your friend died? That wouldn't be…morbid?"

He stands, grabs my hands, and then kisses me. "What happened to Talia is devastating. I will never forget her or Tucker. But now, I'd like to try to make some new *good* memories there again so the thought of that place isn't tainted. I'd like to think of it for what it was meant for—a positive, once-in-a-lifetime experience."

"You really don't wanna wait, huh?"

"I waited a long time for you to fall in love with me. I don't see why we need to postpone starting our lives together when we've found our person. The one that'll be in our final memories."

Melting into his arms and smiling uncontrollably, I finally nod. "Okay. Thirty days."

We stay like this and kiss for a few minutes before one of our alarms goes off for the day.

"Should we tell my family over supper tonight?"

"Sure…we'll have to start plannin' right—"

After scanning down my chest, he starts belly laughing uncontrollably. Hand on his stomach, heaving forward, full-on cackling.

"What in the world is so funny?" I glance around, wondering if there's a bug or a spider on me or something.

If that's the case, I'm burning this whole house down.

"Look at your shirt."

"Jesus Christ…" I mutter when I see two black arrows— one pointing up and one pointing down. "Why do you still have this?"

"If that's not a sign, baby…" He pulls me into his arms, tilting my chin until his lips brush mine. "That you and I were always destined to be together."

Chapter Thirty

LANDEN

Ellie's been training consistently since the wedding two months ago, so it's always nice when I get her to take a little break and join me for the 4-H club.

I joined a local one as a leader and every Saturday morning, a dozen rowdy teenagers come to the ranch where I teach them various equine sports.

Today so happens to be a lesson on barrel racing.

To no one's surprise, more teens than usual showed up today. It makes me smile with pride at how much they look up to her. She's wanted more than anything to make a difference and become a mentor.

And now she is.

Once she's finished going through her tips and tricks of barrel racing, I chime in. "Her top secret is having me as her trainer," I gloat, standing behind her.

She jabs her elbow into my gut, and I grunt.

"Ignore him." Ellie stands with her hands on her hips. "We don't let men take credit for our hard work, do we?"

"No!" Mallory shouts the loudest with the other girls because of course she'd come to annoy the shit out of me. She could get lessons from Ellie anytime.

But I'm pretty sure she's here because of Antonio.

They're the same age and never stop talking during the meetings. When I mentioned it to Wilder and Waylon, they threatened to "talk to him," but Mallory begged them not to.

Then Tripp warned her that being the youngest in the family meant she had four older brothers to protect her.

Noah told her it sucked growing up with older brothers, but considering she was the first sibling to get married, and the youngest, she doesn't have much to complain about.

"Let's tack up the horses and we'll get started," Ellie says after going over some ground rules and expectations of the students.

I help the kids with their saddles and equipment, then make sure their helmets are secure.

No concussions on my watch.

Ellie works with them on posture, holding the reins, and other various skills. Though I step in to help when someone needs it, I love watching her in an element outside of riding.

She excels at teaching.

More patience than me, that's for sure.

"Well, that was fun!" She beams once the last kid gets picked up.

"I enjoyed it!" Mallory exclaims. "Maybe I'll be a barrel racer."

I fold my arms over my chest. "Last week you were gonna be a famous singer."

"So? I can't do both?" She gives me an attitude like only a fifteen-year-old teenager could.

Ellie snorts, patting my chest before she walks around me. "Good luck with that."

"Sure, go muck the stables and you can practice singing at the same time."

She shrugs. "Joke's on you. I do that anyway."

I spend the next hour cleaning the training center—putting the barrels away and sweeping the dirt to smooth it out.

"Hey, you done in here?" Tripp asks, popping through the entrance.

"Yep, just finished. Why, what's up?"

"Just caught Antonio and Mallory makin' out in one of the stalls."

My jaw drops. "Shut up. Dad's gonna flip his shit."

"Oh, I wouldn't worry about Dad…" He looks like he's fighting back a smile. "The twins were with me."

"Oh fuck."

I follow Tripp to the stables, jogging most of the way there once I hear shouting.

"Let me go!" Mallory screams.

When I walk inside, Wilder's got Antonio pinned to the wall like a corkboard and Waylon's got Mallory's arm in a firm hold.

"What're y'all doing?"

"He was feelin' her up. I saw it!" Wilder explains.

"No, he wasn't!" Mallory argues, struggling to release herself from Waylon's death grip.

"Cupping…of this area…" Wilder motions toward his chest, and I fight back a laugh at his attempt to discreetly specify where he's talking about. "And touchin' places he shouldn't be."

"Not if it's over the shirt, idiot!" Mallory retorts, and I pinch the bridge of my nose.

No way she just said that.

"There should be no touching below the neck at their age!" Wilder squeezes Antonio. "You hear me?"

"Alright, release the kid before you catch an assault charge." I get between them, helping Antonio down. He immediately darts out of the barn, and I shake my head at Wilder.

"What the fuck are you doing?"

He holds out his hand toward Mallory. "He was takin' advantage."

"No, he wasn't. I kissed him first," she admits.

"Mom and Dad are gonna kill ya," Waylon tells her. "Let's go, I'm taking you back to the house."

"Y'all are such hypocrites. As if you weren't having sex at my age."

The four of us all snap our gazes at Mallory.

"What? I'm fifteen, not stupid. I've had *the talk* half a dozen times." She rolls her eyes and then marches off toward Waylon's truck.

"Jesus Christ, I'm never havin' kids if that's what they grow up to be," Wilder says, brushing a hand through his hair. "That Antonio kid is lucky I didn't put a pitchfork through him."

I turn toward Tripp, clapping his back. "You've got a daughter at home…good luck in fourteen years."

I walk through my front door and go through the living room exploding with Christmas decorations. Even though we've not even celebrated Thanksgiving yet, she was determined to make our first holiday together extra special.

Seconds later, I find Ellie in the kitchen wearing my favorite white T-shirt.

"My wife in the kitchen in just panties and a shirt making me dinner? Am I dreaming?" I slide my hands around her waist, pulling her into my erection.

"You wish," she sasses, staying focused on the ingredients set out on the counter in front of her. "I'm workin' on a cheesecake for the open house."

"That's not for like...three or four months."

"I know, but I need to practice. Gramma Grace's recipe is complicated as hell."

Our dream house is in the process of being built. It's in the same spot where we had our first date by the lake, and I couldn't be more excited about it, especially for the day we get to move in.

I already have so many plans for us there.

Quickly scooping her up, I then set her down on the counter and step between her legs.

"Geez, give a little warnin' next time." She clings to my shoulders.

"I have a gift for you. Stay put," I demand, then go to the living room where I hid it in one of the bookshelf drawers.

When we planned our wedding, we agreed to keep things as simple as possible, which meant no extravagant gifts to each other. But I've been working on something special for her and instead of waiting for Christmas or her birthday, I want her to have it now since this month marks one year out from next year's NFR.

"Close your eyes," I tell her, walking back with the box.

She sighs, but then shuts them. "You better not be putting anything weird in my lap."

"You suck at receiving gifts, don't ya?"

She shrugs, and when I place it in her hands, she opens her eyes. They widen when she realizes what it is.

"Is this a scrapbook?" She traces over the photo on the front. "Is that the lake? *Our lake?*"

Grinning wide, I nod. "I took a photo of it and had someone make it into a pretty watercolor version. I had a large one framed for the inside of our new house. Thought it'd look good in our bedroom or living room."

"It's gorgeous, Landen! Wow..." Her gaze travels over every inch of the book. Little floral pieces surround the photo wrapped in a felt spine.

"I'm glad you love it. But now open it."

She gasps when she flips the cover and reads the first page.

"My Year to the National Finals Rodeo," she reads aloud, then glances up at me. "You made this for me?"

"I know how important this next season is as your comeback year, so I thought we should document it. I already put some pictures of you and Ranger in there, but every month leading up to finals, we'll add a page with a new photo of you two and write an update on how things are going, what you're workin' on, what your goals are, and whatever else you want. When it's NFR month next year, you'll have a whole year of your progress to look back on. So no matter how you place, you'll have a reminder to be proud of yourself. Because no matter what, I'll forever be proud of you."

Ellie will always be a winner in my mind, but I know she's much harder on herself.

"And I included a photo of us inside so you never forget I'm your number one fan."

"Goddammit, Landen," she cries out, flipping through the pages. "This is the sweetest thing anyone's ever done for me."

"I hoped you'd like it." I tilt her chin, stealing a kiss.

"I'd marry you all over if I could. I'm glad you coerced me into gettin' hitched sooner."

"Coerced or *convinced* with my tongue?"

She snorts. "What's the difference with you?"

I shrug playfully, twirling a strand of her hair between my fingers. I love when she wears it down and wavy. "I knew what I wanted, and I went for it."

"You sure did, Major Ego." She wraps her arms around my shoulders, pulling me into her for a hug. "Glad that you did, too."

I wink and she tries to wipe her cheeks before I notice she's tearing up. "We could always do a vow renewal in a few years."

"Maybe…but I love the memories we made on our wedding day. It was perfect. I wouldn't change a thing about it." She presses her warm lips to mine.

"Agreed. Best day of my life."

Saying *I do* to the girl of my dreams and then spending a week with her in their luxury treehouses just the two of us was another bonus. I showed her all around Willow Branch Mountain and everything their resort had to offer. We went shopping in their small town, tried out their restaurants, and then spent all evening in bed.

Although I hadn't made it up there over the summer when we were going to discuss a joint statement over Angela's parole, I'm satisfied with how things were resolved.

There are no more secrets between Ellie and me.

She got closure on her past and could finally move on.

And even if Angela deserved to serve more time, it wouldn't have changed anything about what already happened.

So waiting to go back until our wedding was the best choice because it gave me the chance to have a fresh start there.

The worst part was coming home and back to reality.

But I know we'll go there again soon.

Warren and Maisie made certain of that.

Epilogue

LANDEN

ONE YEAR LATER
National Finals Rodeo
Vegas, NV

"Here she comes, folks! Ellie Donovan. Fourth-year NFR qualifier in her comeback year. Look out, she and Ranger are the ones to beat!" the emcee bellows out across the packed arena.

Ten consecutive days of competitions with fifteen of the top racers in the country and today's finally the tenth and final round. We'll find out who wins the championship based on everyone's average time.

She's placed high for almost every round and has won a few of them with decent earnings and prizes. But now, she's in the running to have one of the fastest average times and win the whole championship.

I know she's exhausted after the past two weeks of traveling, press, and racing. She's running on pure adrenaline and has a thirst to win I've never seen before.

It's the most nerve-wracking thing I've ever watched.

I'm so damn proud of my wife.

As soon as the music blares through the speakers, Ellie and Ranger sprint into the arena and the crowd cheers louder than I've heard them all week. She's decked out in her signature sparkly pink hat and boots, one of her new buckles, and she put her hair back in pigtail braids today.

Everything about her is stunning.

"Let's fucking gooooooo!" Noah screams at the top of her lungs, jumping up and down while holding a large sign that reads *Finish faster than a man and you can't lose!*

A little inappropriate considering this is supposed to be a family event, but it's hilarious nonetheless. I'd expect nothing less from my sister, honestly.

Standing next to her with Magnolia on my other side, we watch as she flies around the first barrel effortlessly before charging to the second.

We continue screaming for them, but then I hold my breath as they wrap around the third.

I exhale when they clear it.

Thank God.

"Go, go, go!" I shout with Noah as they bolt to the finish line.

Everyone looks at the screen.

"Thirteen point three seven!" Noah shouts—more like screams—in my ear as she jumps.

"Holy shit..." I whistle. "That's her fastest yet."

"There's no way that doesn't bring her to number one, right?" Magnolia asks. "That was like the speed of lightning on crack!"

"She's currently at the top for this round, but it depends on how the other girls do. Once everyone races, they'll determine the tenth-round winner and then their final averages," Noah explains to her. "I'd say it's very close, though."

We continue watching the rest of the racers, mostly holding my breath and hoping none of them beat her time.

Two girls knock over barrels and won't win.

When the final racer enters, we all watch with bated breath.

This is it…

Thirteen point five six.

"Yes! That should make her the round ten winner!" Noah shouts, jumping around and making the sign smack me over and over. "Now we wait for them to calculate the averages."

Nerves and anxiety take over, and I wish I could be with Ellie right now. But I will be soon.

The final lineup for the round appears on the screen, showcasing Ellie as the winner. We cheer again, hoping she hears us. I know she'll still be happy with that. Winning the rounds pays out good earnings and prizes, too.

Ellie had an amazing year leading up to this. She's worked her ass off nonstop and deserves all her success.

The biggest scandal of the year was six months ago when Sarah and Samantha, the Smith twins, got disqualified from the PRCA for unethical behavior. Someone found proof and turned them in for drug and alcohol use, which is strictly prohibited for safety reasons.

Not sure who could've done that…

Karma's a bitch.

When the screen changes to reveal the overall average times, my breath catches in my throat, and I swear my heart stops beating for a solid ten seconds.

1. *Ellie Donovan* - 13.5

She fucking crushed it.

And won the championship.

Our section roars with cheers, jumping and screaming for her, exchanging hugs.

This is unreal.

"We need to go find her!" Noah shouts and our entire group rushes out of the arena.

Ellie's already on her way to us and when she sees us, we swarm her.

"You did it, baby. I knew you would," I say in her ear. "I'm so proud of you."

She's sobbing by the time I pull back. I know she hates crying and we're overwhelming her, but she deserves the recognition even if it's over the top.

She just won her first National Finals Rodeo championship.

"Why're you so glued to your phone lately?" I ask Waylon, nudging him to pay attention before he walks into a pole. "Especially at seven in the morning."

"None of your business."

I roll my eyes at his cocky tone. "C'mon. I tell you everything, so share with the class."

"Yeah..." Wilder adds, though he sounds utterly clueless. Though I don't blame him.

We got three hours of sleep before we had to get up for the airport. Ellie's driving the trailer back with Fisher and Noah while the rest of us fly home so we can get back to the ranch sooner.

But we spent most of last night celebrating Ellie's domination. Then we went back to our hotel and had a little naked party by ourselves.

"It's a chick, ain't it?" Wilder asks.

"Technically, it's a group chat. But there's one in here who always flirts with me."

"What kind of group chat?"

"My friend Jake added me to this horse club he's in. They mostly talk about random shit, horses, and some rodeo stuff."

"A horse *club*? Are you sure that ain't code for something else…" Wilder taunts, waggling his brows.

Give it to his twin brother to mock him. I can't remember the last time Waylon dated someone or even been interested in more than a fling.

"Sounds suspicious to me…" I join in.

"Fuck off, it's not."

"Do y'all have a code word?" Wilder asks. "Big Donkey Schlong or Monster Horse Dick."

I elbow Wilder, trying to fight back laughter because I know Waylon's not tolerating it.

"What would you know about big dicks anyway?" Waylon muses, and this time I lose my battle of not laughing. These two are about to have a verbal sparring, and I'm currently in the middle of it.

"I dunno…why don't you ask your ex-girlfriend? She's seen it…"

My eyes widen as I look between them, waiting to see if fists go flying so I can dodge them.

"Stay away from Delilah, you fucker," Waylon spits.

"What?" Wilder shrugs. "She wanted an upgrade..."

"Ooookay..." I drawl. "If I have to sit next to y'all on the plane for the next four hours, save the ass kickin' for when we get home."

When we get into our seats and buckle in, I lean over toward Waylon. "So tell me about the girl who flirts with you. What's her name?"

"I dunno. I only see her phone number."

"Y'all didn't do introductions or anything?"

"No, Jake didn't do that. I was added in after they already formed it and they were mid-conversation. When someone said something I could help with, then I chimed in. And it just went from there..."

"Well, you've got her number, don't ya? Just text her and say, Hey, I'm Waylon from the group chat. What's your name?"

He frowns. "That sounds so high school."

I arch a brow. "Asking a girl for her name?"

"I'll think about it." He shrugs noncommittedly.

"Is she local?"

"I think so."

"Well, lemme see her number. Maybe I'll recognize it."

"How? From your manwhore ways five years ago?" he asks, chuckling, but then goes to the chat and hands me his phone.

"That one..." He points to a number I absolutely do recognize.

And I recognize it because I was helping Noah file some client paperwork a few weeks ago, and I remember laughing to myself that her number had three sixes at the end of it. It reminded me of Ellie's nickname — *Little Devil*.

666.

Harlow Fanning.

Delilah's sister.

Waylon's ex-girlfriend's much younger sister.

"Well…do you know it?" Waylon asks when I continue staring at it.

I hand the phone back. "Nope. Sorry, man."

I'm not about to break his spirit when he finally seems interested in someone for the first time in years. And without even knowing what they look like.

I scratch my jawline, trying to cover up the smirk on my face. "Good luck figuring it out, though."

He frowns and lifts his shoulder. "Yeah, thanks."

Shit's about to get interesting in Sugarland Creek.

Read Landen & Ellie's bonus scene on my website:
brookewritesromance.com/bonus-scenes

Curious about Waylon and Harlow?
Find their story next in *Only With Me*

Only With Me

A forbidden age gap stand-alone from small-town romance author Brooke Montgomery about a girl who connects with a mysterious man and her sister's older ex-boyfriend who knows he should stay away...

Looking back, I shouldn't have sent a half-naked photo to the group chat.

But when someone asks about a specific horse saddle, I caution them to be careful or their ass will look like mine—covered in bruises.

While everyone makes inappropriate jokes, a guy who recently joined shows concern about my well-being. Turns out, "bruising like a peach" isn't normal.

One innocent photo turns into more and soon we're texting every day.

Only With Me

The only problem—I have no idea who he is or his age.

Even so, I find myself smiling at his messages and wanting to know more about him.

Until the time comes when we're supposed to finally meet and he stands me up.

At the advice of my best friend, I sign up for a dating app because I'm not about to let one guy ruin it for me. But one after another, they either stop responding or block me.

After stumbling across my sister's older ex-boyfriend on the same app, I ask him for advice. I beg him to teach me how to please a man and how to have more sexual confidence.

When he reluctantly agrees, things evolve between us, lines get crossed, and I find myself falling for the wrong person.

Except, I can't shake this uneasy feeling about the mystery guy from the group chat—the one who never showed up.

But people don't just vanish without a trace in a Southern small town.

About the Author

Brooke has been writing romance since 2013 under the *USA Today* Bestselling author pen names: Brooke Cumberland and Kennedy Fox, and now, **Brooke Montgomery** and **Brooke Fox**. She loves writing small town romance with big families and happily ever afters! She lives in the frozen tundra of Packer Nation with her husband, wild teenager, and four dogs. Brooke's addicted to iced coffee, leggings, and naps. She found her passion for telling stories during winter break one year in grad school—and she hasn't stopped since.

Find her on her website at
www.brookewritesromance.com
and follow her on social media:

facebook.com/brookemontgomeryauthor

instagram.com/brookewritesromance

amazon.com/author/brookemontgomery

tiktok.com/@brookewritesromance

goodreads.com/brookemontgomery

bookbub.com/authors/brooke-montgomery

threads.net/@brookewritesromance

bsky.app/profile/brookemontgomery.bsky.social

Made in the USA
Coppell, TX
14 January 2025